UNTIL WE DROWN

AVA MORWOOD

UNTIL WE DROWN

AVA MORWOOD

Harper
North

HarperNorth
Windmill Green
24 Mount Street
Manchester M2 3NX

A division of
HarperCollins*Publishers*
1 London Bridge Street
London SE1 9GF

www.harpercollins.co.uk

HarperCollins*Publishers*
Macken House,
39/40 Mayor Street Upper,
Dublin 1, D01 C9W8, Ireland

First published by HarperCollins*Publishers* Ltd 2026

1

Copyright © Ava Morwood 2026

Ava Morwood asserts the moral right to
be identified as the author of this work.

A catalogue record for this book is available from the British Library.

HB ISBN: 978-0-00-872466-5

This novel is entirely a work of fiction. The names, characters and incidents portrayed in it are the work of the author's imagination. Any resemblance to actual persons, living or dead, events or localities is entirely coincidental.

Set in (Sabon LT Std) by (Amnet)

Printed and bound in the UK using 100% Renewable Electricity by
CPI Group (UK) Ltd

All rights reserved. No part of this publication may be reproduced, stored in a retrieval system, or transmitted, in any form or by any means, electronic, mechanical, photocopying, recording or otherwise, without the prior permission of the publishers.

Without limiting the exclusive rights of any author, contributor or the publisher of this publication, any unauthorised use of this publication to train generative artificial intelligence (AI) technologies is expressly prohibited. HarperCollins also exercise their rights under Article 4(3) of the Digital Single Market Directive 2019/790 and expressly reserve this publication from the text and data mining exception.

For my mother, Ann.
Thank you for all the stories.

Prologue

When night falls, I walk down to the sea again. I leave the children in their beds and Ethan drowsing among the packed boxes, and slip out alone, towards the sound that calls like a siren from the dark. But when I arrive it isn't dark at all. The sand still clings to remnants of the tide and every pool sends back its own glimmer, while the beck flowing across the beach shines like mercury. I half expect to see a small figure standing there, staring into the water as if drawn to it, or perhaps repelled. But of course there is no one. And the moon ... the moon hangs over everything, surely bigger than it should be and too bright, casting a line of silver across the waves as if to say, *Look – this is the path you should take.*

Of course, I don't take it. Our family is leaving, moving in the opposite direction, away from the coast, and it was my decision to go. It's too late now to undo it, too late for anything. Panic writhes deep within me, trying to surface. But there is no escape, I made sure of that too, so I convince myself once more that this change is what's best for us all. I tell myself I hadn't set the plan into motion out of frustration and anger and, if I am truly honest with myself, just a little out of fear.

Still, somehow the sound of the waves turns to mockery as I make to walk away.

1

In the light of a summer's morning, Ethan guides the car away from Sandsend and along the A174. I don't think he ever knew I left him during the night to say my goodbyes; he wouldn't have suspected I had any to say. Zack is in the seat behind me, lost to his mobile phone and a teenage silence. Libby, ever the restless four-year-old, twists and turns in her booster seat, making the dog squeezed in between the children grunt in protest. Jasper, part collie and part who-knows, has been ousted from his usual place in the rear of the estate by piles of boxes that partially block the view behind us. I steal a glance in the side mirror, though for a moment I don't recognise the place we're leaving behind, no matter how long I've lived here.

The sky is striated, swathes of summer holiday blue streaked with wind-combed clouds of periwinkle, robin's egg and lavender, and it takes me a moment to realise that the bottom-most stripe is actually the sea.

It's almost as if there is no horizon; no beginning to the water and no real ending.

The sea rarely appears to be a perfect blue unless it's from a distance. Up close, it can be grey, dun, purple, khaki; colours so unexpected they take a moment to identify, the mind skipping over them like a flat stone sent skimming. Now that we're leaving, the water looks as everyone expects on holiday postcards: alluring, beautiful, a place to be desired. I suppose that summer is an odd time to be leaving the coast behind us, and for a moment, I feel the cold wash of the sea chilling my sun-warm skin. I hear laughter rising amid the crash and rattle of wave-turned pebbles.

Living by the sea was Ethan's dream, and for a long while, I had convinced myself it could also be mine. Now I'm relieved to leave it behind, reminding myself that it wasn't wrong or selfish to grab hold of something I wanted and refuse to let go. This move is the best thing for all of us. For Zack to spread his wings, for Libby to be safe, but most of all, to keep our family together.

Anyway, we're not just leaving something behind. We're not fleeing. We're heading towards something: a bigger house, not one squeezed into a little court between the seafront and a craggy outcrop of sandstone. A real garden, not one made of narrow strips of grass nestled into the base of the slope, soon lost to the prickle of gorse bushes. There will be space for Libby to play. Room for us all. We will have air to breathe without the tang of salt in it and, although we don't yet know anyone, when the kids start school in the autumn we can make new friends.

Not one of them will know the things that have passed between us. We'll leave that behind – eradicate the past like sandcastles washed away by the incoming tide.

I reach out and squeeze Ethan's hand – resting on the gearstick – as we head towards Sleights. After that, steep hills will obstruct the sea view for good. I notice we're both wearing matching friendship bracelets. Libby can't yet make them but often begs me to buy them for her, before insisting we each have one. I wonder if she's managed to prevail on fifteen-year-old Zack to join, marking us out as belonging together. The Kellaways.

Ethan glances at me and smiles. 'All right, Ellie?' He speaks as if this is a regular family outing, just popping off for the day, instead of uprooting our lives. I nod and let that smile settle over me. It holds nothing of the past, nothing we need to remember, no anger, no blame. *Gone.*

I relax into my seat as the road ascends and hear an echo of what I said to my husband when I'd first dared shape my desires into words.

'We both need to decide, Ethan. This needs to be the two of us. No – all of us, together. A family.'

Now, for the first time in what seems like an age, I know that's what we are.

Just over three hours later, the sea is so far behind it might be nothing more than a distant story. We're surrounded by shades of green, the rolling landscape of the Peak District enveloping us from every direction.

The Peaks are landlocked. I can't see a single gleam of blue from where we are, only undulating hills, soft and rounded. The word *peak* suggests to me something jagged and broken as a volcano, but I have learned that it comes from an old English word for *hill*. We've passed by the pale limestone outcrops of the White Peak region, a geology where water cannot remain but instead filters down into dark fissures and deep caverns until it is lost. As we approach Staffordshire and the Peak District's south-western fringes, the landscape becomes a gentler verdant patchwork of slopes and valleys with the occasional stand of trees dotting the hillsides. Occasionally we pass stone farmhouses that might have stood for hundreds of years, along with ruined barns that didn't stand the test of time. This is still hill country, though. The geology is that of the Dark Peak area, characterised by gritstone. Pastures are interrupted by juttings of the coarse rock and scabs of moorland; each height is capped with purpling heather and the almost colourless grasses that thrive amid the peat.

The road narrows and the surface becomes rougher. I'm so busy staring at my own thoughts I almost miss the turn. 'There,' I say, jabbing a finger towards a road that's similarly narrow: Thorncliffe Bank. Ethan swings the car into it, the lurch eliciting a giggle from Libby, a sigh from Zack and a louder sigh from the dog. Jasper does the passive-aggressive thing even better than the kids, and it makes me grin as I twist in my seat to see their reactions.

Libby pulls a face out of the window while Zack stares into his lap, refusing to see any of it. I've tried to present this place as a new adventure designed to appeal to him: cycle routes, cross-country runs, even swimming – if his dad takes him to the right places, which he probably will. Ethan loves the water too, though it's been some years since his last triathlon. There's nothing to stop either of them having everything they want. For all of us to.

'New horizons, Zack,' I say, encouraging him to look at them, but he pouts and returns to his phone, impressively unimpressed. I tell myself his lack of interest isn't altogether a bad thing – he'll need to concentrate on working towards his GCSE exams in the coming school year – but I can't help picturing him in Sandsend, treading water in his wetsuit, way beyond the shoreline where tourists paddle. My son, his dark hair plastered to his skull, a small and solitary figure, out where the sea surges with its raw power; the swells so deep and unknowable that a part of me always did want to reach out and snatch him back.

Libby squirms into life and says the inevitable words, with her own special twist. 'Are we nearly there yet, or what?'

I try not to laugh, instead giving her the raised Mummy-brows of disapproval, but she isn't looking at me. She's staring out of the window as if entranced, clutching her rainbow-haired Barbie, its braids mingling with her own honey blonde locks. I think of how far we've brought them, how different this must seem, and answer softly, 'We are, cherub. We *are* nearly there.'

Still, our new home remains tucked into a fold of the wide, sweeping hills. Out here on the crest, a stone building stands clear of the ranging views, all alone. Beyond it the slope drops away and Ethan eases off the accelerator as the road dips downward. From here it descends right into Thorncliffe village, where there is a lone pub, The Reform Inn, and a small cluster of houses. We won't be going that far. First, we reach a couple of small working farms, then another building, no longer a farm but a dwelling.

Ethan brakes to a near-halt before easing the car between narrow gate posts, one of which still bears a FOR SALE sign. It isn't for sale, not any longer. We're here; this is our home.

I've done the sensible thing by packing the kettle, coffee and juice within easy reach. Once retrieved, I fill the kettle in the kitchen, already feeling content as the others explore the rooms. Unlike the building, this kitchen is brand new with oak-fronted cupboards, and I run my fingers over the black granite worktops before standing by the sink and looking out the window. The kitchen is at the front of the house and has the best view. There's a strip of garden, a spiky hawthorn hedge punctuated by a few small trees, and a large field sloping down towards the valley, where the village remains hidden. Beyond that is half of Staffordshire: miles of gently undulating fields dotted with cattle or sheep or trees. The estate agent told us that on a clear day, we'll be able to see as far as the Wrekin in one direction and the power station at Runcorn in the other. It's overcast so I can't make them out – it's as if we've left the summer behind us along with the sea. Still, I am absorbed by the fathomless sky. There, clouds are piled upon clouds, creating new, stranger landscapes, far more vast than anything below.

'There's a mermaid, Mummy!' Libby shouts from the hallway and I tear myself from the view to go to her, wondering where Ethan and Zack are – my question answered by creaking floorboards overhead. Libby has given up on making Barbie into a mountaineer, having her climb the steps in her tiny yellow boots, and is staring intently at the little stretch of wall tucked behind the last twist of the stairs, her eyes big and round and blue. She doesn't stir when I lean over her.

'There's no mermaid, love,' I tell her. 'Not all this way—'

She puts her fingers to her lips – 'Shh!' – and points. I can't see what she's so interested in but I squeeze into the gap behind her, crouching down to rest my chin on her shoulder.

Libby is right. There is a mermaid, carved into a slab of stone built into the wall, concealed behind the wooden stairway. It isn't pretty, this mermaid. It's not an image for a child. The lines are rough, almost barbaric, as if each stroke was hacked into the stone, insistently *there*. I examine the face, torso, arms, the fishtail curling up beside her. This mermaid has one hand raised to comb her long hair, while the other is held over her heart. There's something pagan about the carving and I find myself wishing my daughter had never found it.

I reach out to touch the stone. I sense the age within its surface, as if I can feel the ripple of years beneath my fingertips. It might be as old as the house, perhaps even older. The carving, though, is sharp-edged and clear, as if refusing to be worn away. I find myself thinking of churches: the way Christians would take ancient places of worship or anything important in a landscape, and subsume them within their own structures. Perhaps I'm making the connection because the slab is little taller than a grave marker and about as wide, but it seems to me too that it possesses a certain aura. I'm perplexed as to why something that looks like a small shrine is here, in our new house, for my daughter to find.

'Where's my dolly?' Libby asks.

I know at once that she doesn't mean Barbie, the doll I bought for her, which she has let fall and forgotten. Even with that mermaidy hair, Barbie is not what my daughter wants and never will be, and deep inside, unpleasant memories shift and uncoil. I swallow down the bitterness at the back of my throat and force myself to speak brightly.

'Barbie's here, Libby. I bet she can climb these stairs really well now. Let's see her do it again, shall we?'

Libby's face crumples and she kicks the doll away. She's tired, a fuse long a-smoulder, her cheeks reddening as I watch. 'Where's mermaid dolly gone? Where is she?'

Ethan's impeccable parent radar pings. He comes stomping down the stairs. 'What's all this? Your mermaid is packed up all cosy in the boxes with the rest of your toys, Libby. She's having a good sleep, if she's got any sense.' He soothes her with the words I should have. 'The removals van is coming later, remember? You can find her then, can't you?'

Libby wails in protest – she needs her mermaid *now* – but even my daughter can see there's no helping it and her sobs fade into breathy gasps. Jasper runs to the rescue, claws clicking on the hard floor, his collie tail a-flurry. He licks salt from Libby's cheeks and she pushes his nose away, but at least she's laughing.

'Help me unpack the biscuits, Lib.' Zack appears, winking at her and holding out his hand. Impressed to have her brother's attention, Libby lets him lead her to the kitchen. Jasper trots in their wake on his little not-quite-collie legs, hopeful of a treat, and Ethan goes back to whatever he was doing. Suddenly there is silence.

I sit on the cold tiles and sigh, willing my daughter to forget the mysterious carving reminding her of her doll. Because Libby's mermaid isn't where Ethan promised. She isn't in the boxes, isn't in the van – isn't even left behind in the old house. Only I know where she really is, because I'm the one who put her there. Before we left, I took my child's favourite toy in the world and shoved her deep in the bin, hiding her golden hair and iridescent scales beneath leaking coffee grounds and bacon grease and worse. I robbed my four-year-old of her most cherished and adored toy, and I dragged my children here, away from the sea they loved against their will.

I know that makes me a bad mother. Monstrous, even. But I had my reasons. And I'd already bought Libby that bright and shiny Barbie in its place. Exchanging a fishtail for legs – isn't that what every mermaid craves? Well, I've granted her wish.

I push aside the notion that such a thing makes me the wicked sea witch of the story and stare at the carving again. It's like seeing my guilt cast into centuries-old stone. I can almost sense the expression behind those blank, half-formed eyes, watching me with silent judgment.

Now it seems somehow inevitable that this would be here waiting, something I never noticed when we looked around the property, but that my daughter found in five minutes flat. We'd been in such a hurry, I suppose: keen to find the right place for our future home – but still, I cannot fathom why there's a mermaid in my house, when we've just driven a hundred and forty miles to leave the sea behind us.

2

A postcard.

Picture it: the perfect family walking along an idyllic stretch of beach, each barefoot, where clear, shallow waves wash the shore. A mum, a dad, a growing son and a little golden-haired girl, an afterthought perhaps, but all the more precious for that. The mum had her doubts initially about living by the sea, but time has made her forget. They spend all their weekends on those sands. Evenings too. Mornings sometimes, drinking a coffee from Tides Café before heading off to work. Imagine the sunsets over that wide stretch of beach. Listen to the sounds of the coast: gulls keening at the memory of distant shores, the crash and boom of rollers meeting the cliffs, the endless chatter of wave-turned pebbles. The cries of happy children. The yapping of happy dogs.

Picture that sense of being right at the very edge of witnessing something bigger and more beautiful than anything one can hold in the hand or the mind.

Everyone is smiling, like a family in a holiday brochure. And that is how it is: one long holiday. Everyone healthy and happy, work and life in perfect balance. A life to be envied; a life to be sought.

I'd never told Ethan the reason I hadn't originally sought it. I'd smothered my reaction when he'd first suggested the idea, back when we were both teaching near Leeds. But I'd decided not to allow the past to surface once more. I'd said my *sorries*. I'd paid. There was no good reason why I shouldn't or couldn't come here and give my children this life; why I couldn't give them the sea.

I'd been guided by my head, not my heart, and Ethan's dream became reality. This is not just some picture-postcard family, a mummy and daddy and their two-point-four. This is us, six years ago.

We'd chosen Sandsend on Yorkshire's east coast, a charming little town on a pretty little beach with a beck running through it. Here, the shops are adorned with handmade bunting and the homes have charming names: Seaview, Spindrift, Spinnaker and Seaspray. This is miles away from any jangling arcades or kiss-me-quick hats or rollercoasters. We stroll along the beach hand in hand, all bright smiles and suntans, watching Zack dive into the waves without a moment's hesitation. Soon that will be Libby too. She'll be our water-baby, never anything but safe and in her element.

It's just how Ethan said it would be, never a shadow to mar the picture – only the one that occasionally flits through my mind, and I can surely banish that. It's easy to leave the past behind, after all. It began receding when Ethan first wove his dream in the air, his words erasing it little by little, and I was glad to see it go. I *will* be glad once it vanishes entirely – and I never have to think of it again.

And Ethan has made sacrifices for our family too. When I got pregnant with Zack, wanted of course, but so much sooner than we'd anticipated, he'd been set on moving to London. He'd planned on conquering the world, making a fortune in banking or brokering. I'd been so worried about the kind of life we could provide a baby raised in the city. But one night Ethan came to me and said: London wouldn't do. He'd realised he wanted something better for us all. Instead, he was thinking about post-grad teacher training with the idea of a potential bursary if he taught maths. Together, we'd give our child the best possible start in life. Plus, we'd spend all we could manage of our summer holidays forging happy memories.

I can still remember the way he'd whispered the words to the baby, his breath tickling my stomach as he'd murmured, 'Who's the best dad? *That's* the most important job in the world ... '

He was still so ambitious, still driven, but with new priorities: for the baby and for the future of his family. Even at four, Libby is no stranger to his favourite phrase, often repeating it back: *Ordinary people can do extraordinary things.*

Ethan found a job at a secondary school down in Whitby. I found one in a charming primary a couple of miles further up the coast from Sandsend. We moved into a cottage called The Anchorage, crammed into a narrow gap at the edge of the sea, and I listened to the endless call of it filling the court like water in a bucket, sloshing from wall to wall, expanding, then retreating, sometimes growing louder or fainter, but always there.

Two weeks, our neighbour told me when we first moved in. Sally lives opposite us, in The Mariners: a tall house with a tiny footprint and rooms stitched together by a perilously steep staircase. She has a wide grin and a booming laugh. Her ginger cat likes to lie in her front window and stare at us with yellow eyes. Two weeks, she'd said, until we assimilate the sea, becoming so used to its voice we won't even notice it any longer.

It turns out she was wrong about that. Other sounds quickly became familiar to me, the background to our days. Just as Ethan imagined, the court is always full of life with kids constantly coming and going to the beach, kicking off boots at the door or clattering buckets and spades. There are always new faces at the holiday lets, the *click-clack* of people adding to the piles of pebbles and fossils and sea-glass that adorn the front steps of their houses. The *fisk* of brooms brushing sand from front yards. Herring gulls shrieking and squalling as they settle on rooftops and fences. Old Mrs H – who never goes by her first name – pottering around in her slippers, always eager for a chat. It's never altogether quiet, never altogether still, and after a while I stop paying attention. Sally was wrong – I never do stop noticing the sound of the sea, not after two weeks or two months or two years. But sometimes, distracted by other things or not really thinking at all … I fail to recognise it.

One morning I get Libby ready for an outing, pulling on her yellow mac and rainhat before grabbing an umbrella and stepping outside to a clear, warm, lovely day. I rub my eyes as if I've just awoken while she tuts and pulls at her layers of stiff clothing. What I'd taken for the rushing of wind and hissing of rain were nothing more than the sound of waves filling the court. It's as if my mind, on some unconscious level, feels I'm living in the middle of a storm. Or is it that I'm waiting for one, even when the sea remains calm, whispering and murmuring my name in the distance?

I stand motionless, listening to the water's song, and feel it echoing deep inside me, as hollow and empty as a sea cave.

3

I stand by the sink and stare out into the late evening, cleaning up after a rough-and-ready meal of beans on toast. I can hardly keep my eyes open. The removals men arrived, chaos ensued, and they left a shipwreck of boxes and abandoned furniture in their wake. We've barely made a start on clearing up the aftermath. Thankfully, Libby was too overwhelmed to dwell on the thought of her doll and I found her sleeping on the sofa, abandoned like an island in the centre of the lounge. Jasper had somehow squeezed in beside her and was resting his head on her waist. Now she's tucked up in her own bed and Jasper is in his, with the occasional doggy snore rising from one corner of the kitchen behind me. Ethan is trying to make our room fit to sleep in and Zack long since retreated behind his closed door to text his best mate, Nuggie – Mike Nugent – about the injustice of it all, no doubt with plenty of acronyms: *OMG. WTF. FML.*

But we're faced with reality now, not living as if life is one continuous snapshot from a holiday postcard. For now, I am transfixed by the view. Everything has softened and faded to grey, shadows meeting and blurring, making everything uncertain. The moon hangs low over the field. Lacking the reflected glimmer of the sea to amplify its brightness, I had thought it would appear smaller here, as distant as it truly is. Instead it's swollen and yellow and glowering, leering down. I can almost see its grin.

Beneath it, something appears to move. I catch my breath and watch until it happens again. The shape is hunched, the motion awkward; I almost lose sight of it in the shadows, then two spiked ears jut from the grass as it sits up on its haunches. Not a rabbit, as I'd first thought, but a hare.

All I can think of is my grandmother and how she would have loved to see this. Gran was always one for stories. She'd told me many, from home and lands far, far away – including cultures which spoke of the rabbit or hare in the moon in place of a man, outlined in the shadows on its surface. This one has appeared by its light; it could almost have coalesced from its glow.

Gran once said if I ever saw a hare with blue eyes, it wasn't a hare at all: rather, a witch in disguise. Of course, this one is too distant to make out its eye colour – not that I'd ever believed in Gran's superstitions. I'd always loved to listen, though. She'd sit beside me after a school day filled with silence followed by a car-ride with my mother filled with silence too, running her bony fingers through my hair and murmuring her tales in my ears.

She always told me hares were born with their eyes open, which gave them special powers. They could ward off evil – or was it that they cast spells? I can't remember. I can only see Gran's eyes, staring into mine. Hers were blue too, as blue as holiday skies, and they never looked away from me.

Then I notice something else outside, another shadow out there. Another shape. This one is nearer, and taller, and the more I look at it, the clearer it becomes. I suddenly feel cold and clammy, unable to move. My heart clenches as the form seems to take on colour and life, as if the moonlight is filling it somehow, making it real.

But she is all too real. My heart stutters, as if it already knows there's something out of place here, something wrong. Or rather *someone*.

The figure is standing by the hedgerow that separates our garden from the field. I can't tell which side she's on – inside, or out? She remains perfectly still and I realise she must have been there all along, all the time I was gazing out of the window, dreaming strange dreams, allowing myself to sink into a good memory. I had simply taken her shape to be a tree planted amid the hawthorns.

I can't make out her eyes any more than I could the hare's – but I know that she's staring back at me. And I'm the prey. I'm exposed to her gaze in the brightly lit kitchen, while she remains little more than a roughly drawn outline. Her hair is the only moving thing, long and sinuous, drifting on the breeze. I am pinned, laid bare as a specimen on a dissecting table. She must see everything.

She must realise I've noticed her.

I suddenly long for all the activity of our neighbours in the court at Sandsend. A knock on my door from Sally or one of the other mums. Chatter, dogs barking, children shouting. Close proximity to other people. Now there's only a dead silence. It's a sound I haven't heard in a very long time, and I'm no longer comfortable with it. I'm conscious that we are out here alone with no one to hear us if we call for help.

I lean towards the window. *I'm* not the one who doesn't belong here so I raise my hand as if to bang on the glass, waiting for her to react. But she doesn't. I know who she is, even if her features are smudged by the distance and her hair darkened by the evening's shadow. Her gaze feels like an accusation, an unwanted hand on my skin, as indistinct yet real as moonlight.

A hand rests on my shoulder. I jump. 'I'm knackered, love,' Ethan says behind me. 'I've had enough for one day. You coming to bed?'

I don't reply. I point towards that figure, but there are only stunted trees jutting from a hedge, their twigs spindly despite the season, as if summer is passing them by. I search the shadows for her outline, expecting to see her crouching by the hawthorns or pressed against the trunk of a tree, but I see nothing. I scan the field, but now I can't even make out the hare. I know there is no one even as Ethan says, 'What are we looking at?'

There is only the moon, low and yellow.

'There was – *she* was – I thought I saw someone.'

My husband takes hold of my hand and lays kisses on my knuckles. 'There's nothing there, Ellie.' He turns me to face him, resting his forehead against mine. 'Listen,' he says. 'If anyone comes, Jasper will bark his head off. You know that we're *home*, right? You're happy now, aren't you?'

I can't bring myself to say anything, so just nod.

'You're spooking at shadows. They're unfamiliar, that's all. You'll get used to them.'

I reply that of course I will, though my words don't entirely ring true. In the back of my mind I see my grandmother's smile, even though she's long gone.

I shake the image away. What Ethan is saying makes sense. I'm tired and stressed from the move and my imagination is running wild, that's all. As wild as Gran's ever did; as wild as my four-year-old daughter's ever could. I will enter this new chapter with a sense of adventure, new possibilities and with hope. It's the new start I wanted, far removed from everything and everyone we've ever known. There is only us and this place: the endless hills, all the miles of green between us and the sea.

You're happy now, aren't you?

I smile at Ethan and tell him of course I am.

4

A postcard. This stretch of beach is all flat smooth sand. The sun is bright and high and the sea is quiet, rippling around our toes. Shallow wavelets play with glimmers of light, pulling them down deeper, until they are lost. There are none of the rocks here that stud the shoreline further along the coast near Whitby, and no wash-ups of tiny sharp stones that feel like pinpricks on the soles of tender feet. There are only a few scattered pebbles, rounded and sea-polished, set into the sand like buttons on a waistcoat.

Ethan, Libby and I are in our swimwear, despite the season having turned to autumn. The brightness of the sun is deceptive and the air is cool, but Ethan has assured me the sea's memory is longer; that it still carries the summer's warmth within its depths.

Ethan's muscles ripple under the skin, every movement neat and contained, a line of dark hair trailing his belly before disappearing beneath the waistband of his shorts. I'm in a black one-piece, while Libby's costume is lavishly adorned with fish and bubbles and a little ruffle skirt. Bright orange armbands make her arms jut out unnaturally from her body, something Ethan objects to as he claims it'll teach her to rely on them, but I insisted. She's only just turned four.

Despite Ethan's assurances about the sea, she shrieks at the cold sting of the water as she dances in the shallows, her movement turning the brine to froth.

'Libby, just for today, you have to be sensible.' Ethan grins at her. 'We're swimming out past the bigger waves, see? Into the smooth bit. Then we go left' – he points – 'just a little way. We come back in to shore there, where the steps start.'

Ethan and I have already discussed at length what *just a little way* means, and I make sure Libby sees the steps. They're really a sea break designed to protect Sandsend from powerful waves, but they resemble seating in an auditorium, as if a crowd might show up at any moment to watch the endless spectacle of the sea. She tilts her head, listening to the strange sound of the breeze cutting across the surface of the concrete steps, deeper and stronger than that of air blowing across the top of a bottle.

The sea break isn't the only measure designed to protect the town. Plenty of its homes hug the shoreline, coming as close to the sea as they dare, but they also fend it off with floodgates. The coast road runs along the top of a sea wall, with waves crashing over the top and washing the tarmac on stormy days. Sandsend seems to flirt with the sea yet simultaneously keeps it at bay, attracted and repelled, stepping forward, dancing back.

Now that we're standing at the sea's edge, this swim doesn't seem like such a great idea. Libby is so small and still only learning. My picturing her as a water-baby seems stupid. She's just a baby, to me anyway, and the water is so very vast.

I remember what Ethan had said to me. 'This is our home, and Libby's. A pool isn't the same. She has to be able to handle what's on her own doorstep. To know what to do.' He'd been so sure, so keen to break down my reservations. 'The earlier she learns, the better. Even babies take naturally to the water. It's adults, and their fears, that stop them reaching their full potential.'

He'd looked at me pointedly then, until I'd relented. I'd often turned down Ethan's suggestions that the two of us go swimming together, but I couldn't bear the thought that I'd be holding Libby back.

I close my eyes, still haunted by what happened when I took Libby to her first pre-school swimming class. The way she had stopped dead as we passed the leisure centre's main pool on our way to the learner's zone, her hand slipping from mine.

A girl was gliding beneath the water alongside us, wearing a monofin. Libby was enchanted as she flicked her tail and swept upward, surfacing with water streaming from her hair. Then she wriggled free of the fin, transforming into a girl again, swapping her mermaid's tail for her usual legs.

Libby had jiggled with excitement. 'I want one!' she yelled, her voice bouncing across the water, and

I shushed her, already picturing Libby trying to swim with her legs bound together. Moving away from me. Sinking deeper.

'Shh, love. We have to learn to swim first, don't we? Then we'll see.'

'I can use my blanket.'

Libby's eyes lit with joy at the idea, and I knew at once what she meant: her aquamarine blanket, quilted into fish scales, one she liked to wrap around her legs while she watched *The Little Mermaid*. It was all very well for pretending on dry land, but in the water it would quickly become waterlogged and drag her down. 'No, Libby. Swimming first. Paddle and kick, remember?'

Ethan was right: she needed to know what to do.

Today she grins at the sea and says to Ethan, 'Are we going to swim like fish, Daddy?'

'Yes! Just like a fish.'

The two of them laugh and Ethan flashes me an *okay* sign. I smile back, even if the expression feels fake. So what if it is? This is the best thing for Libby, and I won't teach her to be afraid. Ethan's ease, his natural confidence, is contagious. He's showing our child how to dive right in, to throw herself into life headlong even when the water is deep and cold enough to steal her breath, and to laugh while doing it.

Still, as I turn to the sea my heart flutters in protest, something Ethan doesn't notice, but why should he? He doesn't doubt me. He doesn't *know*. Nor will he – because I'm determined to finally move on. In fact, I tell myself I'm already over it. To an outside observer, we're a typical family enjoying their day on the beach. In fact, that's exactly what we are.

Zack is out here too, with his friends and his new surfboard, which he's proclaimed is *sick*. He adores every minute he spends in the waves. This is what we moved here for, and I *will* be part of it. I don't want my life – Libby's life too – to be tainted by something that happened when I was a teenager. Once upon a time I was a girl who loved the water, too.

And so I smile at the sea. I listen to its voice, nothing but a gentle *shush*, and Libby's laughter pealing above the sound. Each wavelet glints in the midday sun. The breeze ripples across my bare arms. Libby jumps up and down, flinging up clods of claggy sand with her toes.

Ethan leads the way into the water, his legs strong and lean, barely making a splash. Soon it's over his knees and the sea closes around his limbs, embracing him. I hold Libby's hand and we follow her dad, out to where the sea feels cooler. As the foam adorns the water, forming camouflage patterns of bubbles that hiss all around us, I feel a jolt of adrenaline. Out towards the horizon, the sea looks as if it really could be on a summer holiday brochure: a flat, perfect blue.

Libby catches her breath as the water swells and I lift her hand high, a reflex response as if to say, *She's mine*. The words are fierce in my mind but Libby laughs, snatching at the waves with her free hand, as if to drag herself into it. She doesn't seem to feel the cold any longer. She's floating, taking to this just as I once did, *Like a duck to the obvious*, as my dad had put it all those years ago. Ethan's right: I was stupid to worry about her. She's doing well in her lessons, already a water-baby. I tilt my head to the sun and feel its faint warmth on my eyelids. Water lifts and surges around me, eager to carry me too. Libby squeals in delight and I squeeze her hand. 'Ready, Flipper?'

She doesn't need to answer. Of course she's ready, she always was. I lift my feet from the floor and the sea bears me up, the cold quickly fading to something that feels welcoming. It laps against my lips and I taste the salty mineral tang, strong and harsh. Libby doesn't seem bothered by the taste. She's all long honey-coloured hair, wet smooth limbs and bright smiles.

I look around for Ethan but can't see him. That's fine; we all know where we're going. I stretch downwards with my toes to push myself higher, but there's nothing beneath me and without thought I gulp in a breath and get a mouthful of brackish water.

I cough, but keep hold of Libby's hand, not wanting to let go yet. Her fingers are slippery in mine, but she's okay. Her lips are at water level too and she blows against it, making bubbles. *Like a fish*. Everything is fine. We're just swimming. *Wild* swimming, in the sea and under the sky, natural and free. I gesture with my chin to signal the right direction and Libby nods, her eyes big and serious.

I force myself to release my grip. She slips away, salt water filling the space between us, viscous as amniotic fluid. My girl is swimming. I see flashes of damp hair, bright orange armbands. I tread water, watching, then follow after her into the surge and swell. I catch sight of Ethan in the distance, well ahead of us. Surely he's gone farther out than we agreed? Waves by turn reveal and steal him from view. *Just a little way.* At the rate he's going, he'll soon have done with our swim.

A swift surge carries me towards the beach. When I look back, I realise I'm a long way from Libby. I'd planned to stay by her side every moment – but she's moving in the wrong direction. Libby isn't heading parallel to the shore but swimming straight out, towards the horizon.

I go to call her name but water rushes into my open mouth. It's harsh against my throat, causing me to cough, and my stomach roils. The sea shifts beneath me, as if its movements are purposeful and now it is gathering itself, preparing to strike again.

This is how it happens, I think. The sea is all around and beneath me. It is powerful and fathomless and unknowable, just like it always was. My heart races and my breathing becomes faster and shallower. I try to call Libby but her name is an empty gasp of air that tastes of salt. I feel the shape of it on my lips, *Lib, Lib,* but she's too far away to hear. My girl, my baby, who came from inside me, who came from water and is going back to water …

My eyes sting and I swipe at them, filling them with brine. A wave wraps around my limbs, dragging me down. I try to take a deep breath but an iron band squeezes my lungs. There is air all around me yet I can't take it in. I stretch downward with my toes again, seeking something solid to anchor me. Suddenly I'm under.

I'm in that place I never wanted to see or even think of again. A place that part of me never truly left.

Once upon a time, there was a girl who loved the water.

I'm a good swimmer, a strong swimmer, everyone says so. They say it with a pride in their voices that makes me smile. My body is lithe, I'm fourteen years old and my hair is long, my belly taut. I'm wearing a bikini – I wouldn't be caught dead in a one-piece – and the sun is shining as I swim in the sea. I can swim like an eel. Like a *fish*. I'm free.

We're staying in a little boarding house on the north coast of Wales, my parents and their friends' family for the summer holidays. They've asked me to watch the younger kids while they fetch ice creams and bottles of water but more likely sneak a cheeky pint at the pub.

One of their sons is eight. His name is Ben. He's not a strong swimmer, but he doesn't like armbands, doesn't think they're cool. Still, he can doggy-paddle across the pool at home, and besides, he's with me.

I can see Ben as clear as day, a small boy like so many others in the water: curling white-blond hair, tanned skin pink on the shoulders, eyebrows bleached white by the sun. I'm careful not to lose sight of him as he races in and out of the shallows, splashing and shouting *Aaaarrr* like a pirate. I've told him it's stupid, but he just smiles and does it again. With that pale hair, he can't pass for a pirate. He's more like a storybook prince, a golden boy whose ship has sunk. Perhaps he's trying to find it.

I watch as he wades deeper, out where the water is smooth, and he isn't laughing or grinning any longer, but he's still okay. He's not crying or shouting. He does his rough doggy paddle, face reddening with quiet concentration. I lie on my back, elbows planted in the sand, feeling the sun baking my legs. Ben is floating. He's out in the sea but not far from shore, bobbing on the surface with his arms outstretched. His lips are right at sea level. I watch as they dip and lift, now in, now out of the water. He's watching me too. He watches me steadily, his expression unchanged, as if unsure what he sees. Only his hands move, fingers clenching and releasing, like sea creatures sifting for food. Or perhaps he's patting the surface, like the water is his pet. I wonder what he's thinking about. He never takes his eyes off me for a second, but somehow it isn't uncomfortable. He's simply watching me as I watch him drown.

The boy vanishes in a froth of water and a fresh wave carries me sideways.

Lib—

I gasp, panicking now. I can't see her. She's been taken. This is the price I had to pay for what happened years ago. I try to shriek her name and choke – but I catch a glimpse of the top of her head, flanked by those bright orange armbands I made her wear. *Thank you thank you thank you.* She's still on the surface. But that doesn't mean she's safe. I should know that more than anyone.

I'm her mother and I have to protect her. I'm all she has out here in this moment, and I force myself to pull air into my lungs, flatten my body and arrow towards her. The memory of this lives in my muscles and bones. That girl who loved the water is somewhere inside me, and she shifts into a powerful front crawl. Pull, kick, breathe. Again. The technique flows through my limbs but still Libby is moving away, sliding down the far side of a wave.

I try to move faster, finding the rhythm, pulling up each rising wave and using the downward glide to close the gap to my daughter. With the next stroke I almost touch the sleek plastic of an armband. Still there's water between us so I push through it, moving in like a shark closing on its prey, so close that the sea surely can't snatch her from me again. I have her; my hand is in her hair. I pull her close and hear her breathy gasps and my heart skips at the knowledge that she's all right, she's here. I drag her half onto my chest, rolling onto my back before striking out for the shore.

When we're almost there, she begins to flail. Her little fist strikes out but I grab her around the chin, continuing to move until the back of my heel strikes sand. I stagger out of the water and onto the beach, dragging her with me. Libby is crying. If she can cry then she can breathe. I reach out to comfort her but she slaps my hands away. 'Let me *go* … '

Ethan jogs towards us, all concern. He drops to his knees so he's at Libby's height and takes her in his arms, calming her. 'What the hell were you doing?'

He doesn't mean Libby. He means me. And that's when I know that my daughter was all right, that she was always going to be all right. She was happy, and I ruined it. I spoiled her fun, spoiled everything, but I don't care. I pull her from him and wrap myself around her, burying my hands in sea-knotted hair.

From the corner of my eye, I see people milling around, concerned but uncertain whether to intervene. I don't suppose we're such a pretty picture now. The postcard of the perfect family at the beach is ripped in two.

Ethan glances around, his expression closed off, and I know how much he must hate those eyes on him, the way we've been turned into a spectacle. Well, let him hate it. Is that all he cares about? 'You left us,' I say, turning on him. 'What happened? We were hardly in the water and you were *gone*.'

He has the temerity to look hurt. When he speaks, it's loud, as if to exonerate himself in front of anyone who can hear. 'Of course I didn't leave you, Ellie. We agreed I'd lead the way, didn't we? I'd never leave you.' His tone changes, as he lowers his voice. 'What went wrong? It was a simple enough swim. Wasn't it, Libby? You're okay, aren't you?'

He lifts her up and Libby wraps herself around him, limpet-like, all sandy feet and straggly hair. She nods and rests her tear-stained cheek against his chest. At least the onlookers are merely embarrassed for us now, turning aside and wandering away.

'You never should have left.' My voice fades; I have no air and can't speak any longer. I bend and rest my hands on my knees, allowing my lungs to work. It's odd, but it's only now I'm on dry land that I feel as if I'm truly drowning.

Ethan doesn't see it. He doesn't know I panicked because he wasn't there. Suddenly, I don't want him to. He sees weakness as an obstacle to be defeated.

And why not? There's no reason why he should understand. He doesn't know what happened when I was fourteen years old, what I did or didn't do that day. He doesn't know that I watched a child drown because I had no idea what drowning looked like. I had thought it would be loud, marked by screams and flailing arms and gasping, like in movies. I had thought that Death's arrival would be dramatic. It surely couldn't be mistaken for anything else; not a pair of lips hovering at the level of the water, not that quiet watching.

He doesn't know because I never told him and now I don't get to make this all his fault.

'She's fine,' Ethan repeats, his voice softer. 'Look, Ellie, I know you had this. You didn't need me out there for anything – you're strong. I trust you, yeah?'

His words sink into me and my anger starts to dissolve like foam on the ocean. Why shouldn't he trust me? I *did* have this. There's no way I'd have let Libby go, no way I ever would.

She shifts her gaze between the two of us, uncertainty haunting her expression. What must she be thinking? *You left us,* I'd said, when the whole point of this swim was to teach her not to be afraid. Ethan smiles and holds out his hand, which Libby eagerly grabs. He puts his other arm around my shoulders and kisses my cheek. I hug them both tight.

We pull on the clothes we'd left in a pile on the sand and walk away together. It looks as if the sky has been broken into little pieces and scattered across the beach; clouds reflect back from every patch of wet sand. Ethan talks as we go, gesturing at the sea, the cliffs, all of it. 'This is what I wanted to show you. You'd love wild swimming if you got into it, Ellie. It's just you and the elements. You and the water, in the moment, and nothing else. It makes you feel what it's like to be completely alone.'

But I don't want to feel alone. We stand together on the shore, watching the waves coming in. Pebbles are snatched and tumbled by the backwash, sandcastles are swept away and our footprints vanish as soon as we make them. I've seen this place in so many weathers; the beach and the sea lit gold and blue, or else both darkened to the same mud colour. I've seen the sand pockmarked with rain or washed to a mirror by the outgoing tide or strewn with disturbed and shifted rocks. I've seen it surly and moody and louring and bright. Everywhere, there are reminders that nothing lasts: not the sand or the shore, not even the cliffs. All of it seems to whisper, *Forget the past.*

I tell myself I can. I *have*. Even if it surfaces, it has no power unless I let it in.

After that day, Ethan gives up on trying to get me to swim in the sea. He announces he's joined a wild swimming club and I feel nothing but relief at not having to accompany him, as if a great pressure has been lifted from my chest. It doesn't strike me until afterwards that it contradicts everything he's told me about the sea: about how it's just him and the water and the sky, being in the moment; that, and nothing else. *Completely alone.*

5

I let Jasper out early on our first morning in the new house – he's gone in a flurry of black and white tail, his mouth open in a doggy grin. He heads off to explore his new kingdom, and I step out after him, crossing the lawn in my slippers and leaving a trail of silvery footprints in the dew.

I walk right up to the hedge. In daylight, I can see that it has tiny leaves clinging to it after all, though they do little to cover its thorns, and I can see clean through it. The trees are spindly too, growing on a slant, leaning away from the prevailing wind that sweeps up and across the field. I remember what Ethan said when we first saw this place – *It must be bleak in winter*. The way I'd brushed aside his concerns: *Nothing we can't handle*. It's not like the coast couldn't be grim at that time of year too, with icy winds coming off the sea, cutting through however many layers of clothing we wore. Still, I find myself hoping what I'd said was true.

The house here feels exposed, separate from the gentle, rolling fields spread out below us, as if it lies just beyond the edge of civilisation.

I stoop to examine the ground beneath the hedgerow. There's nothing but grey, tight-packed earth, which wouldn't even retain a footprint. Besides, I'm no longer certain where the figure last night stood – where I *thought* she stood. Now, what I mainly remember from yesterday is filling my head with my grandmother's stories: magical, strange, impossible stories. We were all tired and under strain, and there was no one standing out here at all. Let alone *her*.

I turn back to the house and see Ethan standing at the kitchen window, just as I had the night before. He's watching me.

Judging me. My stomach plunges and I catch my breath. Of course, he isn't – and in the next moment he grins and waves. I wave back before heading inside, leaving Jasper to come in when he's ready.

Ethan hands me a mug of coffee as soon as I walk into the kitchen. He's been busy: eggs rattle and tap in a pan of boiling water and he's sliced some bread. He says nothing about me poking around in the hedge. Hopefully he didn't see what I was doing. I move in close and he puts one arm around me, careful of the hot mug. Zack comes in and grunts and Libby trails after her brother, shouting her excitement at waking up in a new house, as if she's forgotten that yesterday happened at all. I set the coffee down and sweep her up, releasing a burst of giggles into the air.

'This is our first day!' I say. 'Hurry up, then we'll all get out there and explore, shall we? A family walk!'

Zack wrinkles his nose but doesn't protest and Ethan ruffles his hair. Zack dodges out from under his hand and goes to answer the scratching at the front door and then Jasper is everywhere, pawing at everyone's legs in turn to remind us that he needs his breakfast too.

We easily find a path to follow. There's a stile built into the fieldstone wall on the other side of the lane, pretty much opposite the house, and we climb over to find ourselves in the midst of purple heather. A narrow gap winds across the side of the hill. To our left, we can see for miles and miles and the clouds look like they go on forever. Rays of sunlight caress the land with a golden hue and a cool breeze ruffles Jasper's fur as he runs off ahead. He soon doubles back to herd us along with him, true to the collie part of his nature, even if he's so short that his tail only just plumes above the heather. I've always suspected a fair degree of lapdog in his makeup, though Ethan always protests otherwise. As Jasper was a rescue pup, there's no way of telling.

Libby soon starts to complain. 'How far is it?' she whines, and when we say we don't know where we're going she screws up her face as if she doesn't believe that's true. I half expect Ethan to tell her off, a familiar routine – *You can try harder than that, Libby* – but instead, he swings her onto his shoulders. We'll meet the road before long, anyway. The path slopes gently upwards, towards the top of Thorncliffe Bank, and there's the occasional murmur of a passing car, though I can't see any. Before we reach it, the path opens out and the ground flattens into a natural shelf cut into the hillside. Within it is a pool.

It's like a segment of the sky, cut out by some giant hand. Or it's a mirror, though the reflection isn't quite perfect; its surface glimmers a little more brightly than the sky above us, as if the pool holds magical secrets simmering within its depths. As I step towards it, the surface only reveals reflected clouds. I can't sense what lies beneath. The water might be an inch deep or entirely bottomless, and for a moment I simply stare.

Then a little shape rushes by me. Acting on instinct, I snap out a hand and grab Libby's arm, pulling her back. I'm not sure why. Did I really think she'd jump right in? I hear her gasp, but she isn't thinking about my actions. She's focused on her feet which are sinking anyway, even here on land. A silvery rim of water has appeared around her wellies, lapping at the yellow plastic, and I watch as it creeps over her boots, stealing them from sight. She pulls one free with a *gloop*, finding it coated in black smeary mud. She wobbles like she's balancing on a sponge, and I tug her towards me, to the safety of firmer ground.

I glance at the water and notice that she isn't reflected there. Nor is Jasper, who's leaning over it, cautiously sniffing the air, his whole body rigid.

To show Libby there's nothing to be afraid of I take a bold step closer, onto a clump of wiry grass. I'm strangely drawn towards the pool. I'd like to peer beneath its depths.

My efforts reveal nothing. Even from the very edge I can see a few tufts of dead grass just below the surface, but any deeper than that the water appears black. When I look out over it there is only silver light, the brilliant shine of the sky. The pool must be saturated with peat washed off the hillside; perhaps that's why it makes such a fine mirror.

Jasper releases a flurry of barks that startle me before I hear it too: the flickering whirr of wheels. A cyclist appears over the top of the rise, from where the road must intersect the path. There's a steep drop between him and the pool but he skirts around the lip of the ridge, finding a track among the heather and marsh grass before bumping down the slope towards us. When he's a few metres away he stops and puts his foot down. He takes off his helmet and asks, 'Are you looking for the mermaid?'

Libby squeals in delight so vigorously she almost overbalances. Ethan moves to grab Jasper's collar, but the stranger crouches and holds out his hands and within seconds, the dog has a new best friend.

'Where's the mermaid? Where is she?' Libby demands. 'Is she here? Can I see her?'

'She's in the pool, of course! There are loads of mermaids in the Peak District. Didn't you know?' The cyclist tells her.

I push away the thought of the rough carving in our house. He must be joking, though I wish he'd picked a different subject. Still, Libby is rapt, and I won't spoil her fun. Like any child, it's fairy tales she loves best. Perhaps my grandmother's legacy flows in her blood.

'A sailor found this one in the sea and he fell in love,' the man explains. 'So he brought her all the way out here when he came home again, only – well, mermaids live longer than people do, you understand.'

Libby nods seriously, as if to say *Yes, everyone knows that.* Mermaids and magic are her fields of expertise. She should have magic, she deserves magic, and I tell myself it's fine. She can have her mermaid story, her happy ending, all she desires. It can't do her any harm, not now.

'So the sailor, he eventually died. After a long, long time, of course.' The man looks concerned at this mention of death, but Libby isn't troubled by the man's fate in the slightest. It's the mermaid she cares about. 'And so his mermaid was left here,' he continues. 'She couldn't find her way back to the sea on her own, so she was sad and wept till the pool turned salty. They say that animals won't drink from it; birds won't fly over the water.'

It's not such a happy ending – but what mermaid ever had one of those? His story has the ring of folklore about it, something rooted in this particular place or perhaps a particular person, as if there might be a grain of truth at its heart rather than make-believe to entertain an inquisitive child. It gives me that same prickle of unease I felt when I saw the carving in the house, as if this was waiting for me here, mocking me for believing I could ever leave the past behind.

I wonder if Ethan feels it too as my husband stares into the pool, unsure if he's fixated or just keen to avoid meeting my eye.

'There's a whole other version of the story,' the cyclist says. 'Though that one's not so nice.' He flashes me a glance, waiting to see if it's okay for Libby to hear this version, as if the story he's already shared of a mermaid bereft of love and trapped here forever was the happy one after all. I don't change my expression. Libby fidgets as her feet sink into the mud again. The peat clings as if greedy for her before releasing its grip, resuming its shape as though she was never there, resisting even her footprints.

The cyclist shifts his gaze from me to Ethan and back again, perhaps sensing something *beneath*. I try to soften my expression. He seems like a nice man, someone who enjoys meeting people and sharing things he considers amusing and interesting. He has a kind smile.

'Blake Mere Pool's a pretty nice place for a dip, on a hot day,' he says, changing the subject. 'I ride down from Buxton and cool off in the water before heading back. I sit on those rocks and dry out after, if it's sunny.' He points towards the far side of the pool, under the shadow of the berm, where grey rocks are planted in the grass like toadstools.

'Course, the water's cold. The bottom's all slimy. Oh, and sometimes you have to dodge the tadpoles.' He winks at Libby and mimes breaststroke, or perhaps pushing aside an imaginary mass of wiggling, gelatinous creatures. 'Course, they've all turned into frogs, now it's summer. You might spot dragonflies, and swallows swooping around. I've never spotted any fish – the water's dark with peat, though, so the shower's pretty mucky afterwards, I'll tell you. I try not to stir anything up. It's best just to float on the surface.'

Libby is excited all over again, bouncing on the spot. 'I want to swim!' she cries. 'I want to swim with the mermaid, Mummy!'

'You mustn't, Lib. It's not safe for little girls,' I say sternly.

'Ew,' Zack says, for his sister's benefit. 'Not nice, Libby. Slimy, remember? It's not like the sea.'

'I want to swim!' Her cheeks flush and I cast a glance at Ethan in demand for parental back-up, but he isn't looking at me. He's still staring down into the water, his head tilted, as if considering what he sees.

The stranger, now an apparent mind-reader, comes to my rescue. 'Oh, you don't want to do that. The water can be dangerous. It's quite deep, you see, especially on this side. And there are *things* down there.' He gestures towards something I hadn't noticed before: a little sign on a foot-high post, at the other side of the pool. It says: SUBMERGED OBJECTS. DO NOT ENTER WATER.

I wonder why the cyclist hadn't mentioned that before, particularly with all his talk about taking a lovely dip. Libby glares, her lip trembling, her demands blown away on the breeze.

'I did hear there's old farm equipment dumped in there. It could cut your feet if you're not careful.' The cyclist appears thoughtful for a moment and then adds, 'Besides, she's not a very nice mermaid. If you come up here at midnight, she'll—'

'Daddy has a mermaid,' Libby announces. 'And *she* said I can swim anywhere I want.'

My throat tightens and I feel Ethan's eyes on me. I zone out when he speaks, not caring to hear what he says. Then sound returns and I hear something about cycling routes, catching Zack's interest at last, and the three of them turn their backs to the pool and survey the surrounding land.

I place my hands on Libby's shoulders and guide her away from the water.

'Over there, that's the Roaches, see? It's a fair walk, though not as far as it seems. Certainly not so bad on a bike.' The stranger is telling the boys. 'The Roaches sounds an odd name, but it just comes from a French word that means *rocks*. That smaller outcrop is Hen Cloud. It's supposed to look like a roosting hen, but I don't see it myself.'

The land beneath our feet is almost as vast as the sky above us, but not altogether soft and rolling after all. Off in the distance, where the stranger points, the gentleness of the scenery is interrupted by a long, craggy ridge: an escarpment, followed by another, shorter outcrop, resembling tidal waves rising from a calm sea. This could almost *be* the sea. Everything has taken on a misty cast, shading into soft greys and blues, and despite the season, the air feels as damp as sea-spray.

I ignore Libby, who's pulling on my hand, trying to get my attention. I try to focus on the cyclist, but he's putting on his helmet and saying goodbye. As we wave, Ethan moves to my side and puts his arm round my shoulders. He kisses the edge of my lips.

He's reminding me what he can't put into words: that he's here with me. That we're a family. That it's me he loves.

Not *Daddy's mermaid*. Not a lovely, slender figure stepping from the sea, one with shapely limbs and long golden hair, though once she reaches land, walking with a noticeable limp.

I remain silent too. All the words I could say cascade in my mind, scrambled in a storm with no way to correctly assemble them. Then Libby's fingers twist into mine like the questing tendrils of a sea anemone. I have a vivid memory of the weight of her when she was born: at once so light and so heavy, her skin damp, the tiny pads of her fingers wrinkled from the fluid inside me. I was her ocean, then. Her whole world. My daughter, and Ethan's. She'll always be ours, and he's still my husband, and Zack's my son, and no one is taking them from me. No one ever will. Not even *her*.

We shouldn't be shaken by a stranger's story or the careless words of a four-year-old. Children *are* careless, it's in their nature. Libby doesn't understand, and why should she? She's forgotten already, glancing over her shoulder, hypnotised by that gleaming surface. She still yearns for the water. She wants to swim with a real live mermaid, so I summon a new story, the kind she needs to hear: a story to keep her safe.

'Don't forget, Libby,' I say, 'the mermaid in this pool isn't a good mermaid. This one's more like the sea witch. You know all about the sea witch, don't you?'

She gives a nod of understanding. I hope she'll remember my words, and yet I know that my daughter is four. She likes me to brush blue eyeshadow across her cheeks and paint them with silver scales. She likes to wrap an aquamarine blanket around her legs and wish they would morph into a fishtail. Sometimes she refuses to speak, relinquishing her voice like the little mermaid in Hans Christian Andersen's story, all for the love of a man who didn't love her back. I've often tried to coax Libby out of it. I don't want my daughter to wish herself mute, or to place a man's happiness above her own. Fairy tales can hold such beautiful and terrible dreams for children to wish upon, and yet I'd adored that story once too. I'd found it as lovely and compelling as the sea.

'Come on, boy. You ready? Good boy!' Ethan calls out and Jasper answers with a gruff rumble in his throat. I laugh; we all do. Ethan spreads his arms wide like a tightrope walker and steps towards the pool, balancing on tufts of grass. He reaches down and dabbles at the surface. 'Come on, Jasp. Need some? You must be thirsty.'

Jasper is reluctant. He follows, but when he starts to sink, hops back and casts a quizzical glance at Ethan.

The stranger's words echo in my mind. *They say that animals won't drink from it.*

Ethan isn't the type to give up once an idea is in his head. He scoops some water into his hand and offers it to the dog. Jasper sniffs, uncertain, but he trusts his master. He lowers his head and drinks.

'Done!' Ethan says. 'Come on, then. We can walk back along the road.' He puts Jasper on the lead and heads towards it. The road isn't busy, but the occasional cars zip by fast and close. We'd gone this way ourselves only yesterday on the drive to the new house, passing right by the pool, without even suspecting it was here.

Ethan keeps the dog on his inside and I do the same with Libby, holding her hand tightly in mine. Before long we reach something else that we'd passed: the building standing alone on the crest of the hill. It seems even larger and more formidable than it had from the car. Its stone is darkened by the passing of years, but this time we can make out the printed signs telling us it was once a pub and is now a holiday let. It comes as no surprise to see that its name is the Mermaid Inn. After everything we learned this morning, I could hardly expect anything else.

6

A memory.
My grandmother's house. It isn't very far away, separated from mine only by a field. I ignore the path around the perimeter and cut straight across the long, neglected grass, skirting around the stagnant green pool at its centre, and pass through her gate. Gran is what's known by our neighbours as an eccentric. When Mum speaks of her mother, she purses her lips with disapproval. She forms the word carefully on her tongue: *ecc-en-tric*, as if it isn't particularly far away from *mad*.

Gran's garden can be spotted a mile off. It has a Buddha statue on a plinth, musical chimes over the door, and what I consider *twirlers* – colourful, sparkly wind-catchers hanging in the branches of an old oak tree. There's a tiny fairy door set into the base of that tree. Gran swears that it simply appeared there one day, that she hadn't cut it from wood, painted it purple and nailed it to the trunk.

That door won't open, not for me. I tried pulling on the little handle when I was five, then six, then seven – before eventually giving up. Sometime after that, I stopped listening to Gran's stories, even though I'd once loved them. They'd begun to seem too wild, too odd, too strange. Too *eccentric*. Even years ago, I had thought they were too young for me.

Now, I have found them again. They are a comfort to me. A salve. Listening to stories, I have learned, is far better than being in them.

Look! There goes that girl, who ...
That girl who didn't ...

Ben, the boy who drowned, used to live quite close to us too. We can see his house through our dining room window from our position at the table when we eat our tea. It doesn't look as if it has any stories to tell, that house. It's just a house. There's nothing to show it's special, or to suggest it's not. Just a bluish slate roof, a chimney, and red brick walls, the same as all the rest – except for the absence inside where a boy once lived. A boy whose parents used to be friends with mine. But they're now absent too. They don't visit and my parents never speak of them.

It's the same at school, or when Mum sends me to the corner shop. The owner, Mrs Bentley, has a son in my year, and I know she understands what happened that day. It's there in her eyes when she looks at me. It's in the eyes of the other customers, and their kids too. They all know, everybody does. It's even worse when they touch me, or try to avoid doing so. I hear the words whispering in my mind when Mrs Bentley gives me my change and her hand brushes mine, before she snatches it back again. *That girl who ...*

I don't like to visit the shop anymore, though Mum sometimes insists. My brother Nick offers to go instead, but she won't let him. It's not far, it's safe, but he's only eight, like Ben, and it's as if she thinks his death is a disease that will come for her son if she lets him out of her sight. She's happier if Nick doesn't go anywhere.

I don't go anywhere I don't have to either, except to Gran's. It's easier if I remain invisible. Not seen and sometimes not even heard. I've stopped going to my friends' houses. Occasionally, I wish I no longer have to be in mine. A memory drifts to the forefront of my mind: Mum seizing my arm too tight, shortly after we'd got home, leaving Wales behind us for good – we all knew, without speaking it aloud, that we'd never return. And I remember her asking:

Didn't you see him? Didn't you see?

Gran is easier to be around. Gran tells stories, she doesn't ask for them. She doesn't look at me with eyes brimming with the knowledge of something I can't bear to think of yet cannot forget. Something I must keep pushed down, deep beneath the surface.

'Bless you, angel,' Gran says. She is like something out of a fairy tale herself, greeting me with her comforting crinkled smile, furrowed cheeks, and a wiry, bird-boned hug. Amid the wrinkles, her eyes shine the brightest, clearest blue. Her clothes are bright too. Today she wears a tie-dyed top in shades of pink and green and yellow. Her skinny wrists clack with bracelets made of painted wooden beads. There is reddish brown cake fresh from the oven, cracking and cooling on a rack. She's made parkin, even though she says it's from Yorkshire, not her beloved Lancashire. Whatever its shortcomings, it permeates the air with warm scents of sugar, ginger, syrup. She cuts blocky slices, arranges them onto mismatched plates with flowery patterns, chipped gold peeling from the rims. She hands me one. Smiles with her eyes, their colour the clear blue of a holiday sky. She leads me through the kitchen, past her alcove. She must have had a sitting today, since the little round table is adorned with a velvet cloth and a candle burned down to a stub.

Gran claims she sees ghosts. She speaks with dead people, as if they were still alive. She says she *channels* them. I never know how to feel about this. It makes me think of Mum rolling the word *eccentric* around on her tongue, and how it's only one step away from *mad*. But lately, I don't know how to feel about a lot of things. Sometimes I lie in bed at night and think it would be comforting to know he's still out there somewhere: Ben laughing, Ben splashing around in shallow waters, shouting *Aaaarrr* like a pirate, his eyebrows bleached white by the sun. To believe he just carried on, somewhere impossibly distant yet close by; a little boy who went on holiday and never came home again.

But I don't believe in ghosts. I can't allow myself that comfort, can't countenance the possibility of it, even though it feels like Ben is there all of the time. Even though I see him whenever I close my eyes; sometimes even when I don't.

I wonder who came to see my gran today, and who they were trying to reach. I wonder whether their ghost wanted to be found, or if they were happy enough wherever they were. Whatever took place, Gran doesn't tell me. Right now it's as if there are only the two of us in the world, and I'm content with that. She settles us on wrought iron seats in the garden, and we eat warm gingery parkin and for a while we stare out at the field.

When Gran has pressed her long index finger, adorned with silver rings, to each crumb on her plate and put it to her mouth, she sits back and begins.

She tells me of Cinderella, consigned to the kitchen, unseen and unnoticed beneath layers of cinders from her labours. Of how her fairy godmother comes to her rescue and helps prepare her for a ball – and while Gran murmurs, she plucks the bracelets from her arm one by one, then threads them onto mine. She tells me how one day, a prince will sweep Cinderella away. She tells me how her life will open into sweet new vistas, and she'll never, ever have to think of the past again.

I drift a little as she speaks, having heard this story before. What I'm thinking of is another: one that she told me, not about lands far, far away, but this one. The one just outside Gran's garden.

Be careful of that pond, my love. That's where Jenny Greenteeth lives.

Gran had told me that story often in the years before we went to Wales. But never since. Never after.

She doesn't just have horrid sharp green teeth. She has long straggly hair and green wrinkly skin and green eyes and long green arms tipped with cruel green claws. You've seen the pond when the duckweed grows so thick it resembles the finest lawn. You've seen how lovely and tempting it looks, just begging you to step onto it.

Well, that's where Jenny lurks, down in the murky waters, waiting for silly little girls who venture too near. And if they do, if they wander too close, she will POUNCE ...

Here Gran would jump from her seat, grabbing me with her skinny fingers. Making me shriek. Making me laugh.

If Gran sometimes thinks of that story too, she doesn't tell me. Instead she speaks of maidens who are beautiful and good and misunderstood, their long hair as black as ebony or red as a fox or bright as gold. Maidens who will one day meet their prince; maidens with a happily-ever-after. And I know that the stories are too young for me, more so now than ever, but they're also the ones she told me as a little girl and somehow that makes them all the more magical.

Because there's always a happy ending, isn't there?

After everything, there has to be.

7

There's something wrong with Jasper. Ethan says it's nothing, that the dog's just upset by the move. But I don't like the way he's taken to standing in one corner of the kitchen with his head bowed down. He doesn't move when I make lunch or follow us to the table when we eat. Normally he lurks by our legs, trying to rest his head on someone's knee – whoever he thinks is his best chance for a cheeky snack. Often that's Libby, sometimes Zack or me, never Ethan – but today there's no sign of him. When I take the plates through he's spark out on his bed, facing the wall. His breathing is loud, as if he's panting in his dreams, and I pause, watching the knobbly curve of his spine flexing with each rapid breath.

I fill his dish with kibble and add some leftover chicken to entice him. Usually he'd be all over that, trying to put his paws up on the counter, his eyes lighting up like Christmas. Today, he doesn't even raise his head. Perhaps he has bellyache from that peaty water, but he often drinks from filthy puddles on our walks and it never slows him down.

They say that animals won't drink from it; birds won't fly over the water.

But hadn't the cyclist also described swallows swooping over the pool, practically in the same breath? So what did he know?

'He's fine, love,' Ethan assures me when he brings some glasses through and sees me staring. 'Let him sleep.'

I'm no longer sure that Jasper's sleeping. There's something about him: a sense of watchful listening. I've never heard him breathe quite like this before. I lean over him and make soothing noises, placing my hand on his ribcage.

In a split second Jasper is on his feet, leaping at me, all growls and snapping teeth. I lunge back so fast my feet slip on the tiles. But I still have to keep moving as Jasper scratches at me, eyes dark, drool-coated teeth exposed. Something shatters. Ethan has dropped a glass in the sink.

In the next moment Jasper has forgotten my presence. He crawls back to his bed, circles and flops down with a grunt, his back turned once more. That sound starts up again, the breath huffing in and out of him.

I lean against the worktop and stare. Jasper has never growled at me. He's never once tried to bite me. I've never been afraid of him. I look down at the pale claw marks scored into the denim of my jeans. What if I'd been wearing something thinner? What if he'd reached my arms – my face?

I remember bringing Jasper home when he was a wriggly slip of a puppy. Even when teething, the worst thing he bit holes through was an old wooden coffee table. We got him soon after we moved to Sandsend. Our doggy daycare lady, Mel, who fed and walked him while we were at work, always said he was good as gold. Zack was nine then. He was an excitable, energetic boy fond of playing excitable, energetic games, but Jasper never once got carried away and nipped him. A couple of years after that, Libby was born. I'd watched so carefully to make sure they'd be okay, but Jasper adopted her at once. She took her first steps with one chubby fist clutching his back. For a tense moment I wondered: had I stupidly endangered my children?

Did I not *see*?

No: Jasper had always been so gentle, this must be something else. There's something wrong with our dog.

'Bad dog, Jasper. But I told you, Ellie, leave him be for a while, yeah?' Ethan is standing between us.

'Thanks a lot,' I say. 'I think he might be ill. Don't *you* see—'

'He's not ill.' Ethan sounds exasperated. 'There's nothing wrong with him. He's just been uprooted from his home and everything he knows, he's tired, he's *knackered*, Ellie, he's had a lot of disruption and a long drive and now he barely knows where he is. And all he wants to do is sleep it off, and he's not even allowed to do that, is he? What did you expect? Why can't you just leave it alone?'

I stare at him, shock fizzing through my body. I try to blink back the tears that are forming. I suppose I must have known this resentment hid inside Ethan. It's not really about the dog at all – but what could *he* expect? It's nothing he hasn't agreed to. Our previous conversation replays in my mind.

We both need to decide, Ethan. This needs to be the two of us. No – all of us, together. A family.

'I'm sorry, El,' he says softly, stepping towards me and drawing me close. 'I didn't mean it. I'm tired, that's all. A bit grumpy. We all are. Not just the dog, eh?' He pulls back, gives me a wry smile.

I sniff back my tears. He's right, we are. *I* am. I rarely cry, and I won't, not over this. As Ethan says, it's just tiredness. There's no resentment, nothing hanging between us, not now. We're together. A family.

'He went for me,' I say, my voice barely a whisper.

Ethan lets out a sigh. 'Not really, love, did he? If he'd actually wanted to bite you, he could have. You know our Jasp. He wouldn't do that. It was just a little show of temper.'

Just a little show of temper – and he's not the only one. But Ethan's sorry, and no doubt Jasper's sorry too, in his own doggy way.

'He probably dreamed that a rottweiler was stealing his dinner or something,' Ethan suggests, giving me a playful nudge. 'That's what he meant to go for. Not you, love.'

I gaze down at my dog, who's never once hurt me and surely never would, and nod. I know Jasper though. And I can't help imagining that murky water he drank finding its way inside him, swelling his belly and filling his mind with strange, dark thoughts.

I shake my head to try and come to my senses. The pool, in my mind, seems almost to be made of stories: the one the cyclist told us. Fairy tales, like my grandmother's. And another, perhaps; the one I'd always loved most of all. I wonder what, if anything, could really live in its depths. A mermaid, or a sea witch? Would she be weeping or cursing? Or simply combing her long, long hair?

I remember the carving in its stone slab at the heart of my new home and shiver as the words of warning echo.

She's not a very nice mermaid. If you come up here at midnight, she'll—

But what would she do? I hadn't asked, and the stranger we'd met on the moor never had said.

8

A story.
 The one I would come to love deepest and best. The first time, perhaps, that I fall in love, not with a person, but with words. With the power of them; the way they can tug at your heart, stronger and deeper than any ocean current. And this one is told not by my gran, but by my mother.

I'm tucked up in bed. But I'm not seeing my pink-painted walls, the gauzy hangings over my window or my mushroom-shaped nightlight. I'm not in my room at all. I'm looking upon an underwater garden, and at its heart, there is a marble statue of a human boy. A mermaid, the youngest and most beautiful of them all, gazes into his eyes and imagines the world above, a world made of stories she can only dream of.

The story is Hans Christian Andersen's *The Little Mermaid*, and this is what my mother tells me, or something like:

When the mermaid princess turned fifteen years old, and only then, she was permitted to swim to the surface of the sea and look upon the human world. There, she saw a ship that belonged to a handsome prince, festooned with lights for his birthday. Soon, a storm blew up. The ship broke apart and the prince would have drowned, but the little mermaid took him in her arms and swam to shore. She left him there, unconscious and pale as death, before returning to the deep.

But she could not forget the prince. She longed to win his heart, and along with it, a human soul – for mermaids have none, and when they die, they become nothing but foam on the ocean. She decided to journey to the sea witch's lair, across a barren seabed where nothing grows, only polyps with grasping, snake-like limbs that entangle and snatch at whatever life comes within their reach.

There, the mermaid made her bargain. The sea witch agreed to give her a potion to turn the mermaid's fishtail into human legs, so that she may seek her prince, but there was a price – for there is always a price, is there not?

'You will have your wish, for it will bring you sorrow, little princess,' said the witch. And she told the mermaid that every step she took on land would feel as if her feet were being stabbed with knives. Not only that: she must first give the sea witch her most precious possession – her lovely voice. She would have only her eloquent eyes and graceful body with which to speak to her prince, and if she failed to win his love, her heart would break and she would die.

The mermaid allowed the sea witch to cut out her tongue and took the potion. She walked on the ground on her own two legs, and felt invisible knives piercing her feet, all for the love of the prince. When the prince saw her, he took her into his palace and gave her fine clothes, allowing her to sleep on a velvet pillow outside his room, but he did not love her as she wished. He cared for her as one might love a child, and soon his wedding was arranged to another. He wed a neighbouring princess, the girl who had found him on the shore after his near drowning. Imagining she was the one who had saved him, he vowed to love her as he would a wife.

The little mermaid danced at their wedding. With each step she felt unseen blades stabbing her feet, though it was her heart that hurt most of all.

That night, her sisters swam up through the waves. They had sold their hair to the sea witch in exchange for a bewitched knife. They told the little mermaid she must stab the prince to his heart. When his hot blood spilled upon her feet, her legs would become a fishtail once more. She could return to her home in the ocean, to her family in the deep.

So the little mermaid went to the man she longed to marry. She saw him caress his wife's hair in his sleep. She heard him sigh her name. And she did not harm him, but flung the knife into the waves. She felt the heart in her body break in two and she became nothing but foam on the ocean.

But the little mermaid was given a second chance. Because of her love, her sacrifice in placing the prince's happiness above her own, she was transformed instead into a spirit of the air. By doing good deeds for three hundred years, she could still win a soul and a place in Heaven. And if she happened to see a good child ...

I don't hear what will happen if the mermaid sees a good child. I don't even care. I'm too busy crying, because I'm not fooled; little girls know heartbreak when they see it. I know what a happy ending should look like, and this isn't it, not by a long way. Becoming a spirit of the air? The mermaid should have the prince. She loved him; he should love her too.

Mum gives a wry smile and brushes the tears from my cheek, but it isn't enough. None of this is enough. I yearn to hear different words from the ones she's told me, but it's too late now and I can't unhear them. I can't stop the image of them, the prince and *her*, the wrong bride, not the heroine. It's all wrong. The little mermaid was the youngest and most beautiful of them all, wasn't she? The story said so. She had the loveliest voice in the ocean, eyes that were as blue as a lake, grace in her limbs and in every step she took, even if each one pained her.

I'd had no idea there could be such a story. I hadn't known words could cut so deeply. And yet I was still in love with fairy tales, could hear them turning around and around in my head. I craved their beauty and strangeness and everything they conjured, even while not knowing or understanding what it was I loved, not really.

My mother closes the book, putting it back on the shelf, as if that was an end to it, as if there ever could be.

But I don't want that to be all, and I find my voice. 'Didn't he ever love her?'

She rubs my head. 'Well,' she says, shrugging as if it doesn't even matter. 'You can't just make them, sweetie.'

I frown. He was the *prince*. She was the *mermaid*. I feel as if I'm grasping after something I cannot reach. Something that is already sinking into dark waters too deep for me to follow. I can barely do a doggy paddle, so I don't even have that. I could never save the prince from drowning, not if he was right in front of me. I couldn't save anyone. So how could I ever be the heroine in a story?

Mum turns off the light. She moves to the door. Before she leaves, I call after her.

'Can I learn to swim?'

The mermaid couldn't win her prince. But the girl already knows she could love the water.

Mum smiles.

The end of a beautiful story. The beginning of the real one.

9

I close the kitchen door, trapping Jasper with the nightmares that might be running through his head. I tell the kids he needs some quiet time, to give him some space to sleep it off. Zack is in his room anyway, setting up his Xbox. Ethan and I still have plenty to unpack, a home to build. Books need to be put in their places on the shelves in the lounge, so I tell Libby she can watch a DVD while I sort through them. I can keep an eye on her that way, ensure she doesn't go poking around in the kitchen. She squeals, pelts towards a labelled box, and in two seconds flat she's found what she wants.

To Libby, watching a DVD only means one thing, and Disney's version of *The Little Mermaid* is soon on the screen. It's the original, animated film, with its perky, irrepressible tunes – the newer live-action movie is too old for Lib, a PG instead of a U certificate, and by the sound of it, the sight of the sea witch alone would terrify

Libby into fits. Anyway, this is the one my daughter loves. Soon she's rapt as the youngest and loveliest princess in the sea runs off to make her bargain, so eager to do anything she must for a man she's barely met. At Libby's age, she can believe that's how love works: at first sight, without the need to actually talk to one another.

By chance, the next box I open isn't full of books. It's Libby's dressing-up things: blue and green hair paints, iridescent eyeshadow, a necklace of shells, and her aquamarine fish scale blanket. She squeals in delight at what I've unearthed, and I can't resist indulging her. I brush streaks of colour into her hair and over her cheeks. She snatches her blanket, drags it to the sofa, pats it around her legs.

'I'm Flipper!' she announces.

'Lippy, more like.' Zack walks in, detangling a bundle of cables we've dumped together in the corner to retrieve a phone charger before vanishing again. 'Flibbertigibbet.'

'It's *Flipper*!' Libby screams after him, and I can't help but laugh. There are times when she remembers that the little mermaid can't speak, so she'll turn puce with fury even while keeping her lips pressed tight over her words. But Libby makes herself heard when she wants to. She starts bellowing along with the next song, jiggling and kicking her legs in the air. *Flibbertigibbet*. That means mouthy too; well, good for her. I rub the top of her head and sing along.

On the screen, we've reached the stage in the story where the sea witch – a dark, velvety creature resembling a squid or an octopus – tells the mermaid she must give up her voice. She'll still have her lovely body, her graceful movement and her pretty eyes with which to speak and win his love. Isn't that enough?

I sigh, but Libby is leaning forward on the sofa, rapt at what's unfolding. She wants to see the mermaid get her wish. This is the story I loved, yet it's not my version of the story at all. I've never read that to Libby. In her imagination, it wouldn't occur to her that any fairy tale heroine could fail to win the love of the prince. Suddenly I'm glad that this is the version Libby loves, the one she chose for herself.

I hear Jasper scratching at the kitchen door, just as Ethan walks into the room. He glances at the screen then pulls me to my feet. In mimicry of any perfect fairy tale ending – the wedding – he solemnly takes my hand, then pulls me into a kiss.

'Ew! *Daddeeee* ...' Libby groans, slapping at our legs with her blanket, but Ethan ignores her. He continues to gaze, and I return it in earnest. And I know that we'll be all right. I've still got my prince, my happily-ever-after. After everything, he chose me. I may not be the mermaid, but I'm still the bride in this story.

I'm his wife, and he is promising me again, silently, that he will never love anybody else.

10

A memory.

I sit down by the stagnant pool in the field at the bottom of Gran's garden. There's no duckweed, not now, but the water is so green and murky there might as well be. I'm waiting for Jenny Greenteeth to see me with her gleaming green eyes, to rise through the water with her wrinkled green face and reach out to me with long green arms, before dragging me under.

I'm hungry. We'd been having our tea. The four of us, sitting around the table. Mum and Dad. My little brother, Nick, who will one day escape the cotton-wool wrappings of his over-protective parents, the constant *be carefuls* and *don'ts* and *nevers*, and flee all the way to Australia. And me. It was a perfectly normal meal, as far as anything feels quite normal any longer, fish and mash with peas from the freezer, except that Dad happened to ask what I fancied doing once I leave school and I'd said at once that I want to be a teacher.

It's not like Mum said anything, not at first. She didn't even look at me, though she rarely does these days. Her gaze drifts a little behind and past me, as if someone's standing at my shoulder, and sometimes I wonder who or what it is she's seeing; then I remember, and quickly try to forget.

I don't know why Gran would ever want to see ghosts. Why would anyone? And yet she welcomes them in with her candles and velvet, her cards and crystals, all her talk of energies and vibrations and auras.

Mum stared silently out of the window, and I knew at once what she was looking at: a perfectly ordinary house just beyond the rooftops of our immediate neighbours.

Dad started talking, 'That's lovely, love, lovely,' as if he couldn't think of anything else, and my brother stuck his fork into his fish, and Mum and I went on staring at that house.

'If you're – sure,' she said at last. It sounded like she was speaking through a clump of claggy potato. 'You know you'll – be responsible, don't you? Will you be all—'

'*Viv.*' Dad's voice had almost dried up too.

Suddenly, I was right back there in that moment with Mum grabbing my arm. *Didn't you see him? Didn't you see?*

I had a mouthful of grainy mash and globular peas that I wanted to spit back onto my plate. Outside the window, the house sat there, as it always had. On the surface: a perfect calm. There was no flailing or screaming or thrashing, like you might expect. Nothing to *see*. It revealed nothing and everything at once.

I pushed back my seat. 'May I be excused? I'd like to go to Grandma's.'

That's how we talk now, a lot of the time. Polite, perfunctory phrases to help us get through the day. *We need to go. Time for school. Be ready in ten.*

Now I'm sitting by the pond and shiver as I stare into the murky green surface. I suppose it will hurt, when Jenny Greenteeth comes. She'll dig her claws deep into my arm. *Don't you see? Do you see now?* She'll grin a grin full of sharp, green teeth before pulling me into the slimy water. How long will it take before I draw one last desperate breath and open my lips to let it in?

How long did it take *him*?

I had learned to swim, learned to love the sea, but it hadn't helped in the end. It had bewitched me and called to me and yet eluded me. I could slip through the waves like an arrow. Like a mermaid. But I hadn't saved the prince. I hadn't saved anyone at all. Not even myself.

I sit and stare into the water and I wait, but Jenny Greenteeth doesn't come. The light starts to fade, and still there is no sign of her. The vivid green begins to turn a murky grey; the breeze shushes in the long grass. And I know that she was never going to come, that she never will, because Jenny Greenteeth is simply a story, one designed to keep children away from the water in which they might *drown*, and I find that I am crying.

I feel, rather than see, the figure that creeps up behind me. They stand at my shoulder for what seems like a long time, before sitting down beside me. Eventually, I turn. I see wrinkled cheeks, skinny limbs, bright eyes gleaming through straggly hair. The look in them is one of kindness.

'Bless you, angel,' Gran says, and she wraps a crocheted blanket around my shoulders: it captures every colour under the sun. And then, seeing my expression, her voice low and soft as the breeze playing in the long grass, she begins.

Once upon a time, she says, and her comforting words seep into me, so familiar, so safe, and I smile, because I know the next part, and it's the best thing of all.

In a land far, far away ...

11

Jasper is scrabbling at the kitchen door, over and over, *scratch, scratch*. When I open it, he won't emerge. Instead, he hangs his head low, eyes rimmed with pink. He's gouging the paintwork, but I'm too exhausted to care about that. I'll paint over it later. I'm more concerned with the way my dog is regarding me as if I might be a stranger. I try the usual bribe to get his attention, dangling a dog biscuit in front of his nose, but he doesn't even sniff. He sinks to his belly on the cold tiles so I drop the biscuit into the bin and close the door on him again. If he's no better tomorrow, I'll call the nearest vet. I'd noted their number before we moved, as well as a doctor and dentist, in case of emergencies.

Eventually, Ethan and I grow tired of trying to arrange the house. We've finished in the office, Ethan's stuff on one side, mine on the other: essential papers, notebooks, lesson plans, endless stuff about phonics for me, maths textbooks for him, all prepared for when the new term starts in a few weeks. We talk Zack into joining us downstairs for a bit. He's pale from being cooped up inside; I brush his dark fringe off his face and Zack jerks away. I ask him to choose another film for us and he rolls his eyes but picks out *Finding Nemo* for his sister, and I smile my gratitude. He's a good lad for trying, considering this is hard for him, leaving his friends behind – but wouldn't it have been harder on us all if we'd stayed?

It isn't dusk quite yet, but despite the season the world outside is dull. We might almost have moved to a different climate; every dark cloud that ever haunted a summer seems to be gathering over the Peaks. In the distance, layers of rain hang in the air like tulle. The clouds are massy and louring, transforming all the colours of the hills and fields to grey. The quiet rain falls stealthily. All I can hear is the television, its burbling punctuated by the rustle of hands digging into a bowl of microwaved popcorn. Beneath that there's nothing. I close my eyes and feel the weight of the silence from everywhere and all around us.

When I look out again, she has appeared.

This time it is plain to see the colour of her hair. It is pale gold and drifting in the breeze, despite the rain. Amid all the grey-green she looks more than ever like a mermaid, and in the soft light she is younger and lovelier – more *innocent* – than ever.

I can't move or speak. My voice has been stolen. I am turned to marble, a chill creeping into me, intensified by her gaze.

I try to reason with myself. I'm simply seeing the image so often burned in my mind. She's a passer-by taking a walk. Or a neighbour come to call on us, brandishing a bottle or a cake, intent on friendship. I want to laugh. I can see that this woman would not wander or ramble. Anyway, she has no umbrella, no coat, no hat. She doesn't try to shield herself from the rain. She just stands in that same spot, silence hanging between us, until something intrudes.

Scratch. Scratch. Scratch. In the kitchen, Jasper is going frantic.

I hear Ethan yell 'Cut it out!'

The woman continues to stand by the thorny hedgerow, unseen currents catching in her golden hair. Watching my home, my family. Watching me.

A graze of a finger on my neck makes me catch my breath.

'What's up, love?' Ethan says. 'It's beautiful out there, isn't it?' He leans in, pressing his chin into my shoulder. He must have seen her too and I wait for him to say something. When he doesn't, I point towards her.

'What is it?' He nuzzles against my neck, and briefly he is reflected in the glass: a milky form swimming in layers of deep water, there and then gone.

'Don't you see?' I keep my voice low, to avoid worrying the kids. 'There. By the field.'

Ethan leans closer to the window. Behind us, the television rumbles on. I hope the kids are too occupied by the film to hear us.

'What? There's nothing out there, love.' He turns my face towards him, places his hand on my forehead, as if testing for a fever. Then he lets out a spurt of a laugh. 'Maybe we should have an early night tonight. Reckon we could all do with one.'

I jab my finger towards her again, to make him *see* – but there's nothing. Only the hedge and trees and an empty field. I tell myself she's just ducked out of sight or headed for the road, but wouldn't I have seen her? Wouldn't we both? It feels as if she's dissolved into the rain, becoming one with the water and the hills and this whole forsaken place.

Ellie, pull yourself together.

Ethan's gaze turns thoughtful. 'El, we're fine, aren't we?' I feel his whisper on my cheek, his words weighing on me. 'We're here, like you wanted. You can relax now, can't you? Don't stress. Enjoy this.'

I reach out, untwisting the cord to lower the blind until it covers the glass, and think, *Damn right*. Of course no one was out there, in the miserable rain-drenched evening, staring at me. She was *nothing*. Just lack of sleep and anxiety of the move and everything that went before it.

I hear scuffling in the kitchen, claws ripping through woodwork, and Ethan rolls his eyes and shouts, 'Jasper, would you just shut *up*!'

Libby, on the sofa next to Zack, jumps. Her elbow knocks the bowl of popcorn and upturns it in Zack's lap. Corn and unpopped kernels and crumbs spill across his shorts, the sofa, the floor.

'For God's sake, Lib!' Zack snaps, tired and out of patience – *He's bound to be grumpy, we all are* – and after a shocked silence, Libby starts to cry. That only makes Zack more annoyed as he scrapes popcorn back into the bowl.

'It's not my fault!' Libby wails, and then everyone's bickering, all as tired as Ethan predicted, as tiresome as each other. Meanwhile the scratching intensifies, interminable, desperate. It strikes me that I can't remember the last time we let Jasper out. I throw up my hands in a *Can no one else ever* gesture and stride towards the kitchen.

This time, when I open the door, Jasper doesn't back away. There's the brush of rough fur, then his legs almost slip from under him as he scurries to the hall. He starts scratching at the front door, just as frantic.

'All right, all right, Jasp,' I say, fiddling with the latch to swing the door wide. The rain doesn't give Jasper pause. He's gone in a second without a backward glance, as he rushes onto the lawn. He heads straight for the gate. He can't slip through it or under, we've made sure of that, but I see a flash of white, the tip of his tail, as he leaps at the wall that divides our garden from the road.

There's a scrambling, the scraping of claws on stone, and just like that, my dog is gone.

12

A memory.

I'm running across the grass, stretching out a hand towards a shape that eludes my grip, remaining just out of reach. I leap into the air and land hard but I'm laughing as my friend Priya scoops up the frisbee, shaking her head at me. She tosses it back and this time, I catch it.

I'm in a good place. I'm miles and miles from home, at university in Leeds. I'm no longer *That girl who*. I'm no one, and I love that. A few of us have come out to Woodhouse Moor, a park that sits between the campus and Headingley. We're going to bathe in the sun, drink illicit vodka from our bags and goof around for the afternoon. There are plenty of other students milling around, seeking out a moment's peace between lectures. I can hear the buzz of traffic on nearby Clarendon Road. Even so, it feels as if we're miles from that too, as we slump down on a blanket to catch our breath. I feel a little light-headed from the day's exercise and the bright outdoors. From the freedom of it. From the absences – not that of a child who used to live beneath the slate roof of a neighbouring house, but other things I left behind: the strange looks. The whispers. The things people know and the things they think they do. All of that is gone and I remind myself that I need never, ever think of it again. My life has opened before me. Not just endings, but beginnings: sweet, wide vistas of possibility.

Jess taps my foot with hers and I rouse myself, grabbing the vodka from my bag. Beam at my new friends. Cate is from our halls, a couple of doors down. Jess is training as a teacher, like me, and Priya – well, Priya's so outgoing, she knows everyone.

I no longer feel like I'm wading through deep water or floundering as I try not to drown. Inside, I'm still chasing across the grass, launching myself into the air. I'm practically flying. I take a swig of vodka before passing it over to Jess. She reaches out.

My smile fades.

I close my eyes and a sudden wave of nausea comes from nowhere, twisting a knife in my gut. Someone stands before me – an impossibly tall figure. I don't want to look at their face, yet I sense their anger anyway, can feel it emanating from them in waves even before their hand snaps out, hard and fast, as if they too are trying to catch something. Except this isn't a game and that's not what they're doing.

The sharp sting of the slap spreads across my cheek. A word comes to me: *Daddy,* and I open my eyes. It comes as a surprise to see that my fingers are wrapped around a bottle, that I'm *here*. There's only Jess standing in front of me, her fingers still touching mine. I snatch back my hand. When the contact is broken all sense of her father's presence is gone, and so is the pain. The drink slips from our hands and spills across the blanket.

We fuss around, bemoaning the loss of good vodka, the state of the blanket. I keep apologising while my friends laugh, poking fun at my clumsiness. I try to convince myself that the moment is already forgotten, consigned to the past. A daydream. A figment of my tipsy imagination. Something I'd sensed about Jess, or something she'd once said, coming back to mind in the most careless of moments. I tell myself it was any or all of those things even while the loudest part of my brain insists, *That did not even happen. It did not.*

It *could* not.

I don't sense auras or vibrations or other people's memories. I don't feel the things they feel. I'm not eccentric. I'm not *mad*.

I am not my grandmother.

Gran died a year ago. She would have been happy to see my life here. She'd have loved that I'm forgetting the past, allowing the future to open up. That I'm concentrating on all the stories with happy endings, striving to make them a reality. She might even have laughed to see that I'd crossed the border into Yorkshire in order to do it.

I spring to my feet. I need fresh air. I tell the others I need to clear my head and walk away. I don't look back, though I can imagine the expression that must be in all their eyes at the sight of me heading off with barely a word. I've seen it before, so many times.

That girl who ...

That girl who took change from Mrs Bentley and knew exactly, in the second she touched her, what she was thinking. That girl who'd brushed Jess's hand and felt in intimate detail one of the worst days of her life. That girl who'd heard all the whispers, just as loudly as if they were inside her own head. That girl who sometimes saw a young boy standing across a room or in a crowd, never speaking, only gazing steadily back at her ...

I'm too lost in my thoughts to notice where I'm going. Afterwards, it seems funny. Almost inevitable. A romantic meet-cute, though I'll never tell him what drove me to blunder straight into him.

He reaches out a hand and I flinch – but this isn't the figure I'd seen in my mind. *That I hadn't seen, couldn't have seen, never saw at all.* He catches my arm, steadying me so that I don't fall. Still, I can't yet bring myself to raise my eyes and look at him. I can still feel his fingers on my arm, his skin touching mine, and I wait for something to pop into my head: a memory or feeling. What he had for breakfast perhaps, or what he's thinking of me right now, this clumsy girl who just walked into him. A moment passes but nothing materialises that might be hiding beneath. Relief blossoms inside me even as I lift my gaze.

There is only his smile.

There is only Ethan.

13

I step outside, not caring that I'm only wearing my socks and the wet earth is cold and unpleasantly soft. I call my dog's name, then louder, starting to panic.

There's nothing. No sound, no movement, no Jasper. I forget the rain and stride to the wall, leaning over the slippery stone to peer along the road. Towards Thorncliffe, a few sparse lights cut through the mist gathered into the crease in the landscape. In the other direction, there is only the moor. Nothing else. I peer across the road, trying to spot a white-tipped tail pluming from the heather.

I shout Jasper's name again, half expecting him to come crashing from the bushes as water soaks my hair and drips down my neck. There's no scrape of claws, no bark, no rustle of leaves. The sound of rain is all around me, a soft hiss of mockery. I *will* Jasper to hear me and come back, but there's no sign of him. I stare into the sky, where legions of clouds have gathered. Jasper can't have vanished into thin air. He wouldn't run away, would he? Strange behaviour aside, he's still our dog.

A voice from behind prompts me to turn back to the house. Ethan stands in the doorway. 'Ellie, are you out there?'

It's when I open my mouth to tell him that the shock seizes me and my throat constricts. 'He – Jasper's gone. He jumped.' I point at the wall.

Ethan fetches his trainers then comes to my side, pulling on a waterproof. The rain on his hood is a sharp crackle. 'He can't have, love. What do you mean, jumped? He wouldn't. He couldn't. Why didn't you stop him?'

I don't bother to point out his contradiction. Finding Jasper is more important. He doesn't know this place; he'll get lost. I hurry past Ethan and into the hall, putting on my own trainers and coat.

'What's up?' Zack emerges from the lounge rubbing his eyes.

'Stay inside, Zack. Watch your sister.'

He pulls a face but knows my tone is serious, so he does what I ask. Outside, Ethan is leaning over the gate, just as I had a moment ago. It's useless; there's nothing to see, only sheets of downpour. I unlatch the gate, cross the road and go to the stile. It's the one place we've been for a walk which Jasper might recognise. The stile's easy enough to cross, one wide stone step and a flat slab over the top. Had he smelled sheep on the moor and decided to explore? I hope not. He may be part collie but he isn't trained to herd sheep. If he worries them, a farmer would have the right to shoot him. It wouldn't be Jasper's fault, but he would be killed on the spot.

I call his name and my voice vanishes into the vastness of the moor. All I can see is twiggy heather and grass and damp earth. For a moment I picture him crouching under those bushes, his body pressed low, an odd gleam in his eyes. Jasper, but not himself; possessed by something different and strange.

'Why'd you let him out, Ellie? Couldn't you tell something was bothering him?'

'Jesus, Ethan. Couldn't I *tell*? Of course I could tell. I'm the one who said he was ill. You're the one who insisted he was fi—'

'I'm going out to find him.'

The voice isn't Ethan's. Zack is behind us, zipping up his coat.

'No,' I say, as Ethan adds, 'Go back inside.' At least we're united in this.

Ethan gives Zack a gentle shove. '*I'm* going to look. Both of you, go back in. We can't all be wandering about the hills in this. It won't help.'

'The pool,' I blurt out. I hadn't known I would say it, but once the words are uttered they make sense.

'What? Why?' Ethan pauses. 'There's nothing up there.'

I picture the water, softly glimmering. Secrets hidden under the surface. *There's everything*, I think, though I don't know why. I picture the woman I'd seen, all long, flowing hair. And the thought comes to me: why hadn't Jasper barked at her?

Instead, he'd run away – and seemingly vanished.

Unless the reason he hadn't barked was that she was never there at all.

I usher Zack in front of me towards the house, making sure he goes inside. Libby is on the sofa, picking fluff off popcorn, the sound of it on her teeth like crumpling paper. She rubs her cheek with the back of one hand, a sure sign she's tired and ready for bed. I wonder if she napped through the whole ordeal, when she pipes up, 'Is Jasper gone?'

Suddenly, I'm swallowing back tears. I won't let her see them. I take a deep breath and say, 'No, sweetheart, of course not. I'll take you up to bed and he'll be there when you wake up. He'll give you a big doggy kiss.'

Jasper isn't allowed to lick her face, but he does it anyway. He loves her—

I carry my daughter upstairs. I smile as I tuck her in and kiss her forehead, as I always do. For once she doesn't ask for a story and I don't offer one. I'm too busy telling myself that Jasper will be home soon. Ethan will find him and bring him back, then we'll go to bed and catch up on that sleep we desperately need.

Downstairs, I slump down on the sofa next to Zack. The television's on but we stare through it and don't take in a word. I put my phone on my lap in case Ethan calls, the ringtone turned up to maximum. At least the rain seems to be abating, though it's growing dark. When I open the blind once more I see little more than droplets gliding down the glass, glimmering in the flickering light from inside the house.

I think of our little dog. The lapdog in him will be cold by now. He isn't built to spend time out in the wilds, no more than he's trained for herding. He'll be lost. Scared. I keep picturing Ethan wandering the hillside as night draws in, approaching Blake Mere Pool. *Black* Mere, silent and still, showing nothing in its depths but a reflection of the rising moon. Perhaps he'll find Jasper standing at its edge, not drinking, not touching it, simply staring out across the water. It might be midnight by then. Perhaps he'll see something rise from the depths.

I shake my head and go to the window, to watch for Ethan – for them both. All I can see is my own face, swimming palely in dark water.

It's still the best part of an hour before I hear the metallic clang of the gate latch followed by the crunch of footsteps on gravel. I listen for the patter of claws too, but Ethan is alone.

'No sign of him,' he says, before we can ask. His voice is strained, clamping his emotion down tight. 'I can't see a thing out there now. We'll have to search again in the morning.'

Zack and I turn to each other in dismay, then back to Ethan, as if that will change anything. I feel the emptiness in the house: no Jasper jumping up to us on the sofa, nestling into our sides, demanding fusses. No Jasper sticking his nose in the popcorn bowl when no one's looking, or circling in the kitchen before flumping down with a sigh. The whole downstairs is too still and I feel empty too. I have no words left, it's Zack who protests, but Ethan shuts him down as soon as he gets out a 'But—'

'But nothing, Zack. It's getting too dark to do anything else. You're not going out there, before you say it. We'll go up to bed, get some sleep, then go out early and find him. 'K?'

It's a command framed as a question. So that's what we do, and soon I'm lying in the dark, Ethan's back turned to me like a wall. I'm pretty sure I can still hear the *tickety-tick* of Zack's headphones coming from his room, but I don't have the energy to go and tell him to turn his music off. I could do with listening to something myself, to take my mind off what happened; that, and Ethan's words.

Couldn't you tell *something was bothering him?*
Of course I could. I *knew*.

Now Jasper is out there on the hillside somewhere. He's never been out alone at night before, certainly not in the dark, cold expanse of these hills. He likes the comfiest seat on the sofa. He loves to snuggle into his family's warmth.

Not long afterwards, the rain starts up again. It patters sharply on the roof then spits at the windows. I lie flat on my back unable to sleep, listening to the sound and aching for my dog. I imagine finding him, Jasper going mad with joy, licking the tears off my cheeks without a protest from me. Still, there's nothing but the sound of the rain. After a while, I almost convince myself it's the noise the sea makes as it echoes around a narrow court of tall thin houses, and I half believe we are there again, all five of us, in our home by the shore. For once, that rushing, hushing sound is a comfort, nothing unsettling about it, so much better than silence, than *nothing*.

The rain gathers itself and redoubles, pounding the walls and the roof, knuckling against the windows, hissing through gutters, bouncing from leaves and lawn. It ticks from the eaves and trickles down the road. This storm is insistent, as though furious with us, with *me*, and I cannot blame it for that. At last, I find I can sleep.

14

A memory.

I'm in my room in a tiny shared student flat, still in bed although it's almost midday. Ethan and I are wrapped around each other. I feel sated, warm, lazy. Each time he shifts his hand to stroke a different part of my body, it makes me shiver, like sending ripples across a pond. I stare deep into his blue eyes. Clear as water. Nothing hidden beneath the surface, only their bright shine. When I'm with Ethan I don't mind being looked at. I no longer want to be invisible. When he gazes at me like this, it's like I'm the only thing that exists in his world. I can read his whole heart in those eyes. More than that, I know how he feels. I know it on a simple, basic level, that has no need for anything *eccentric* or *mad*.

Those things in me have stilled now I've found contentment.

There have been no whispers. No visions. No sense of revulsion – Mrs Bentley giving me change in the corner shop. No impressions of a father who wasn't mine striking my cheek. No echoes of my grandmother's *auras* and *vibrations*.

Nothing.

There's nothing else between us, and I'm very much okay with that. Ethan gives a smile as lazy as I feel and lifts his head to kiss me again. My lips are still tingling from the last. I kiss him back and there's only him, nothing to intrude or rattle what I believe – want – normality to be. No secrets, no surprises.

That's how I know this is my home now. *Ethan* is my home.

He makes me feel like I'm standing in the sunlight. A light bright enough, powerful enough, to chase away the ghosts.

With Ethan, they never stood a chance.

Of course, it's quite possible that Gran was always wrong. Perhaps she was blinded by her desire to help and misled in her ability to do it. Such powers might never have been there in the first place, and their echo in me was nothing but a manifestation of the sorrow and guilt I've carried too long. Maybe it's just that I'm happy, and I don't need such things any longer. Maybe Gran can see that, wherever she is, and if she's at peace, whatever strange qualities she may have possessed can rest with her.

I'm happy for them to stay as memories and nothing more.

This is who I want to be. It's who I can be, now I'm with him.

'We should talk about what we're going to do after Uni,' Ethan starts, propping himself up on one elbow, and the words thrill through me. *We.* What *we're* going to do. Together. So matter-of-fact and just-like-that. I laugh, playfully slapping him on the shoulder, but his expression doesn't change. He looks at me like everything is obvious, and perhaps it is.

There's nothing mystical about Ethan. He's straightforward and easy to read, in the best of ways. Being with him seems at once impossible – because I'm not sure why he's picked me – yet entirely simple. He's always whisking me off to dinner, or a picnic, or some outing he's dreamed up. Those are the words that come to me when he's around: whisked. Whirled. Whooshed.

What are you doing, hiding away in the library? You're the most beautiful girl on campus, Ellie.

He's always saying things like that too. Paying me compliments. Saying I'm the loveliest of them all, the greatest, the best. It feels like reaching the shore after an exhausting swim with leaden limbs and cold waters. He sends me huge bunches of flowers, tasteful sprays of roses and baby's breath. The other girls envy me. *How can he afford it, and him a student?* They ask. But Ethan's an orphan. His parents had left enough to support him for a while, though he's only ever told me. It's not like this has been easy for him. And I've said that I really don't need flowers, or all the whisking and whooshing, but he just smiled and rested his forehead against mine and said, *I know what I want, Ellie.*

And he does.

He's telling me about his plans to go to London. I could find a school to teach at there. He'll secure an internship. Brokering, probably. A job with career growth. There are limited places and it's competitive, but he talks as if he'll coast through it and that makes me sure that he will. I see our lives stretching out ahead of us, a single path. I'd never thought of London, but why not?

    I smile at myself, remembering Gran's stories of Cinderella, preparing for a ball. I know life won't be like that. There'll be work and struggle and arguments. We'll have to find somewhere to live and it'll be expensive and no doubt poky and grey, at least to begin with. But there will also be Ethan. I watch his strong jawline, peppered with stubble, forming the words to paint our future, making it feel like something within reach.

    He's so confident I cannot doubt him.

    He's strong. Handsome.

    He's a prince.

    He spins words in the air, showing me that reality is the greatest fairy tale of all.

15

It's before seven a.m. but Ethan and the kids are already in the kitchen when I go downstairs, Libby tousle-haired and frowning in her pyjamas, Zack in his jeans and hoodie. He insists that he wants to start searching for Jasper, but Ethan tosses boxes of cereal onto the counter. 'Breakfast first, then we'll come up with a proper plan. It's no good all whooshing off in different directions.'

I'm busying myself putting the kettle on and getting out bowls when Libby pipes up. 'Mummy, you said Jasper would be back by now. Where's my kiss?' She hugs her Barbie tight to her chest and pouts.

Suddenly, everyone's looking at me. Ethan raises his hands in a *What the hell* gesture. Zack rolls his eyes at the hopelessness of his mother, and this time I have to concede he has a point. As Libby waits, guilt creeps over me, colouring my cheeks. Why on Earth had I said that? I suppose I was trying to convince us both, trying to *will* it true somehow. Now I realise I've only delayed the moment when I'll have to explain the situation.

'We all hope he will be soon, sweetie,' I mutter, but it's no use, tears glisten in her eyes, so I do what I can: I give her a hug.

'I thought I'd head out in the car,' Ethan says through a mouthful of Weetabix. 'I'll coast around a bit, see if I can spot anything. Zack, I know you want to be out searching too. I don't want you on the roads, but you could check the moors again, okay?'

Zack nods before Ethan can change his mind. 'I'll go to the pool first. Jasp knows that place, right?'

I'm glad someone is heading up there, just to see. Ethan never did say if he'd been to the pool last night, and I don't want to ask now.

'All right,' Ethan agrees. 'But all of us – yes, you too, Zack – meet back here at midday and touch base, okay? No messing. Ellie, if you can stay with Lib?'

'Course. We'll make some phone calls.' I keep my tone bright for Libby's sake. 'The nearest vets, shelters, anywhere he might be handed in if someone finds him. And we could create a poster with his picture on, just in case we need one.' We won't, though, surely. We'll have found him long before that.

Ethan loads bowls into the dishwasher. I fetch some snack bars and orange juice cartons from the fridge and pass them along to Zack and Ethan.

Ethan grabs his coat and keys before driving out of the gate, then my son tops the stile and he too is gone.

I settle Libby in front of *Peppa Pig* and return to the kitchen, sitting at the breakfast bar and staring at my phone, willing it to ring with news. It's too early to call anyone so instead I fire up the laptop to work on a poster. I type the word MISSING and stare at the letters in disbelief, then scroll through our photos. There are many: plenty of the two of us, and hundreds of the kids. There's one from the quad at Uni, taken over fifteen years ago. I can't remember who took it, but Ethan and I are laughing fit to bust, our arms wrapped around one another as if clinging on for dear life. Another is from my flat, hand cradling my belly, as if I *knew*, though I don't think I did, not then. The next photo fills my mouth with the taste of brine. It's of Ethan standing on a beach in a dripping wetsuit, yellow bands prominent on his shoulders. He'd been training in the sea for a triathlon, and when he'd kissed me salt was encrusted on his lips.

I flick to the pictures of Jasper. There are plenty of those too. It's like he's always been part of our lives: running alongside Zack's bike or lying on top of Libby, her face crumpled in outrage or hilarity. I find one where he isn't a blur – sitting, waiting for a biscuit – and add that to the poster, then type our details at the bottom. I save the file to OneDrive. I don't think there's enough ink in our printer to manage more than a few low-resolution copies. These will be better done at a copy shop if there's one in Leek, our nearest town.

Then I start making phone calls. I try the local vet, an animal shelter, the RSPCA, the dog warden at the council and the registration company for Jasper's microchip. I ensure they have our new address and phone number, so they can contact us if Jasper turns up. Still, I sense my dog getting further away from me each time I hear *No, we don't have him.*

Lost for anything else to try, I call Mel, our dog walker who took care of Jasper in Sandsend when we were at work. Lost dogs sometimes head back to familiar places that feel like home, don't they? Some travel hundreds of miles to show up scrawny and footsore on their old doorsteps. Mel's upset by the news that Jasper's missing – of course she is. She loves all the dogs she's cared for, keeping pictures of every single one on her fridge. We agree he couldn't have got to Sandsend so fast, but she'll be on the lookout, just in case.

Then I remember that the tag on Jasper's collar is inscribed with our old address. My mobile number is on there too, and it's unlikely anyone would drive him halfway across the country without calling first, but who knows? So I try our old house. Kath, the new owner, sounds happy when I call her. She thanks me for the lovely champagne I left for them, and her cheeriness brings tears to my eyes before I explain the reason for my call.

'Oh my God,' she gasps, 'I'm so sorry.' Her sympathy makes everything worse. She promises to watch out for him and ring me the second they hear anything, if they do. I put down the phone and realise that's it; there's no one else to call.

Libby is standing in the doorway watching me, her eyes big and round, her hair resembling something she's scribbled with a crayon. I scoop her up and carry her upstairs, making her brush her teeth and get dressed, combing the knots from her locks. She keeps waving her Barbie as if to show me what hair is supposed to be like, and I smile and nod, as if I can conjure rainbow braids up for her right now.

I kiss her head. 'Come on, Lib. How about we go and look around outside?'

'Can we can we?' is her response, so we head out. We cross the road and I help her over the stile, pausing to take in the view. The moor looks almost friendly now, the purple heather aglow where sunlight spears through the clouds.

I try not to think of my dog lying injured somewhere under that heather or trapped in a fissure in the rocks. Or incapacitated, poisoned by the water he drank. But there's no point dwelling on my worst fears. I lead Libby downhill towards the village, but she pulls on my hand and points the other way. 'Let's go swimming, Mummy, like on the beach. We could take mermaid dolly.'

The pool, so clear in my mind's eye, ripples and stirs.

'We can't swim there, Lib, I told you. It's dangerous, remember? And Zack's gone there already. Why don't we go somewhere else?'

She pulls a face, as if it's occurred to her she has every right to cry and she's giving it some thought. I squeeze her fingers as we go, pointing out some sheep in the distance, and beyond those, Hen Cloud and the Roaches. I don't know why the sight of them makes me feel uneasy. Perhaps because amid the soft, rolling green around them, so gentle and somehow so very English, they seem to disturb the landscape.

Libby tugs on my arm. 'What would Jasper want down here, Mummy? He wants the water. He wants to swim with the mermaid.'

I know she's using our dog as leverage in the hopes I'll grant her wishes, but a prickle runs through me.

She scowls. 'If we were still at home, we'd still have Jasper.'

I take a deep breath, smoothing down her hair against the breeze to soothe her. 'We *are* home, Lib,' I say, but she won't or can't hear me. I remember Kath's happiness on the phone in our old house. She might be chatting to Sally this moment, the two of them thick as thieves already. Or she'll be standing in the court with Mrs H, trying not to stare at the old lady's slippers. Libby starts sniffling, telling me 'Dolly's hungry,' so I decide it's time we headed back.

I make enough sandwiches for everyone and cut the crusts off Libby's before sitting her in front of the television again. I can't think of anything else to do. I suppose for now, there's nothing. I close my eyes to try and rest but somehow it is there: the pool, softly glimmering in its hidden hollow, a secret within a secret.

The cyclist's words drift back to me. *There's another version ... that one's not so nice.*

I need to discover the story behind this other version. My mobile is on the table, among piles of books I still haven't put in any kind of order. I wake the screen and google, wondering if there'll be anything at all on the internet to support the stranger's tale.

For such a tiny stretch of water, one that should surely be inconsequential other than as a watering hole for sheep, there are a surprising number of hits. I even learn that the place has several names. Blake Mere Pool. Blakemere Pond. Or simply – as I'd once found myself thinking of it – Black Mere. There are plenty of photographs, too. Even on such a small screen it appears almost magical, a shimmer of light amid the dull grass.

I find the story of the sailor from Thorncliffe, and realise the cyclist never finished his first tale.

A man in love will do terrible things, even when he's trying to do right. That was true hundreds of years ago, as it is today. Long years since, a man from Thorncliffe went away to sea, as no Peaklander should. There, he saw a mermaid. He listened to her song, and never wanted to hear anything but her voice from that moment on.

The voice of a mermaid can be a powerful thing. It can raise a storm or calm it, and as anyone knows, it can bewitch a man. It can lure him to his death or offer his heart's delight.

This man was lucky, or perhaps unlucky; he fell in love. But the mermaid didn't lure him to his death. She decided she loved him too.

So he fulfilled his greatest wish: he took her away with him and gave her the only home he could, a lonely pool on a lonely stretch of moor. Still, the mermaid was happy, and so was he, for he could visit her there to sing their lovers' songs beneath the moon.

But as any child will tell you, mermaids are strange creatures. Their lives cannot be counted as may a man's, and so it was that he grew older, sickened and died, and yet she lived on, just as young and beautiful as she ever was.

She wept at his death. And as her tears turned the pool to salt, so her loneliness and grief turned her love to bitterness.

She lives there still, though not quietly. For if any lone traveller should trespass near the pool, especially a single man, she will use her voice against him and lure him to his death.

Stare at the surface of the pool as midnight strikes and she will rise from the water, combing her hair. She will draw you towards her with her siren voice. And there, in her arms, you will surely drown.

I stare at that last word. No: it seems the cyclist hadn't told my daughter the full story at all. Was this why Andersen's mermaid had to give up her voice before she could win a man – because with it, she'd have been far too dangerous?

Then I find the other version, the one the cyclist must have meant, and it is darker still and yet somehow more real, as if it were based on true events.

Once, there was a young woman of the Peak, shapely and beautiful, who was offered the love of a local man, Joshua Linnet. However, she spurned his advances and rejected him. Driven almost to madness, Linnet accused her of witchcraft. He convinced the townsfolk of her wickedness and together they dragged the girl to Black Mere Pond, beat her and bound her and threw her into the water.

She began to sink beneath the surface, but still, she fought; with her very last breath, before the water took her, she cast a curse upon him.

Three days later Linnet was found dead by the pool, his face disfigured with claw marks.

As for his witch? She haunts the water still, as a demon mermaid, or perhaps the ghost of the unfortunate girl – now forever nameless.

To this day, livestock will refuse to drink from the pool, and birds won't fly across the dark waters.

Since so many in these parts claimed to have seen her, the local men gathered once more, this time to drain the pool and find out if it is truly bottomless. They began digging at the southern end, keen to discover its secrets, and perhaps they did, for the mere-maid appeared to them. She threatened to flood the nearby town of Leek if they did not grant her peace, so they headed home, defeated.

But peace was not to be hers, for over the centuries, Black Mere has been the scene of numerous drownings ...

Drownings. My stomach churns at the word. I think of that glimmering pool on the hillside, the clouds reflected in its surface, so motionless, so peaceful. Still, it had been so small; scarcely worth the tiniest dot of blue on a map. We used to live near the *sea*. I feel a stab of gratitude for Ethan, always diving right in, so comfortable around the water. We've done the best thing for our kids. We've made sure they can both swim. *Like a fish.*

The pool isn't anything to be afraid of. There's nothing there but stories.

16

A postcard.
A scene anyone would want to remember. Zack is in the pool. He's way out in front, his arms a blur, barely rippling the surface. Shouts echo from the ceiling, from the water, as his classmates cheer him on. I can make out his name and ours: *Kell-a-way, Kell-a-way.*

He's going to win the race. He's only in his first year at secondary, travelling into Whitby with Ethan every day, but his time is going to put the older boys to shame. We're lined up with the other mums and dads to watch, gathered here for a special aquatic sports day, and we lean forward in our seats.

Ethan always said he would win. I reach for his arm now just as he pulls it away to applaud the sight of Zack touching the white tiles edging the far side of the pool. He's so happy whenever Zack does something first: crawling. Getting to his feet. Taking a few tottering steps. Riding his bike without stabilisers. Always so competitive. He lets out a loud whistle and faces turn towards us as people smile at him: not just a proud teacher, but a proud dad.

One or two of the mothers' gazes linger. *Look all you want*, I think, and wrap my hand around Ethan's arm. I run my fingers over his watch, the one I'd bought for him when we moved here. Since he loved swimming so much, I'd wanted him to have one that was waterproof, so he could wear it anywhere. I'd had it engraved on the back: *For the years to come. All my love, Ellie.*

I wave at a couple of mums I know from Sandsend, Jinny and Rae, who have kids Zack's age. We'd greeted each other with big hugs and grins. Ethan knows more people here than I do, since the event is for his school – Whitby has become more Ethan's territory, the little villages up the coast mine – but he stuck to nods and smiles and handshakes, ever the professional. Now he whistles again, team *Kell-a-way*, and I poke him in the ribs and laugh at how into this he is.

The boys are still in the pool, swapping *Well dones* and *Hard lucks*. Zack spins around, floating, and he scans the crowd; then his eyes meet mine.

Everything stops. There's only an echoing all around, distorted voices circling back to my ears, but different:

Didn't you see him? Didn't you see?

His lips are under the water. I jump to my feet, suddenly panicked he's drowning. They all are: the boys clinging on the surface, arms outspread. All of them staring at me.

I shake my head. *Not real.*

It's not even something I've imagined, more like the distant echo of a memory. It's been a long time since I thought of Ben – or of Gran and her ghosts, all the odd, eccentric things she told me. Anyway, it was an *accident*. It's nothing that need concern me any longer. It's not like I'm haunted; there are no ghosts. I hadn't known what drowning looks like, but now I do, and we have taught our son to swim.

I put my hand on my belly to feel the bump swelling there. From within, the little form swimming inside me gives an answering kick. Zack pulls himself out of the pool, neat and water-slick. He isn't drowning, he's winning. Jinny waves again then points towards him, mouths the word *awesome*. Ethan hasn't noticed my wobble, too busy basking in the glow of our son's victory.

And he should. This is everything he wanted when we first made plans to come here. Proof, if any were needed, that we're doing okay. Better. *Best*. I run my hand over my bump, smooth down my maternity dress, and know that we are.

17

It's fifteen minutes past twelve when I hear a car pull up outside. I hurry to open the gate, peering through the windscreen to check for a white-tipped tail wagging from the back. Still no sign of the dog.

'No Zack?' is all Ethan says when he gets out of the car, and I shake my head. It's not like he didn't know Zack might lose track of time. Like father, like son.

We eat our sandwiches on our knees, exchanging partial sentences between bites.

'No news?' he asks me.

'Not a sign.'

'No one's seen him?'

'No.'

We watch the clock as it creeps towards one, then quarter past and slowly, twenty past, and still there's no sign of Zack. I clear the plates away and stand at the window. The hedge is outlined against the field and the idea that someone could have been standing there seems more absurd than ever. Once more, I am startled by a touch on my neck; Ethan, creeping up on me as softly as a ghost. He doesn't say anything, just stares down at the floor, and I sense he's completely drained of energy.

The front door opens and he rallies. At last – Zack is home. We don't hear anything else, so we enter the hall to find our son standing inside the door, looking around as if he doesn't quite know where he is.

'Well?' Ethan says, expecting an apology, but Zack doesn't respond. Something about his expression unsettles me. He seems dazed, hypnotised even. He looks straight through us both as if we're the ghosts, before walking past us, towards the stairs.

Ethan grabs his arm. 'What do you think you're doing?' He gestures to the trail of black muddy footprints Zack's trainers have imprinted on the tiles. Zack appears confused, as if he doesn't know how they appeared.

I put a tentative hand on Ethan's arm. 'He's worn out, love. Let him have some lunch, then we'll talk.'

I guide Zack to the sofa, sitting him down, then bring him sandwiches. I don't complain when he wolfs them down teen-style, two bites each, as if he's been starving for years.

'So you went to the pool. Then what?' Ethan's annoyance is still simmering.

Zack frowns. 'Wha— Hmm. I suppose so. Yeah – yeah, I did.' He takes another bite and mumbles through a mouthful of bread and cheese. 'There's nothing to see.'

'So why've you been so long? Oh, never mind.' Ethan sighs, too tired or fed up to start a fight. 'Look, we can go into Leek this afternoon. We'll leave the mess in the hall for now – you'll clean it up later, Zack. Your mum's made a poster we can get printed, and we can pick up some supplies, have a break, clear our heads.'

Zack begins to protest but Ethan cuts him off. 'Yes, you too, Zack. You're coming with us. All of us are – as a family. That's what we came here for, isn't it?' He pauses before he adds, 'We're just wandering, here.'

He murmurs this last as if he's touching on some deeper truth, and my face stiffens. Does he mean today, the past, or the future – our whole lives? But Ethan isn't saying. And there's something else that no one needs to say: we haven't found Jasper, *won't* find Jasper, not like this. Somehow, it feels as if our beloved dog has vanished off the face of the Earth.

An hour later, we're in the middle of a supermarket in Leek, surrounded by shelves of all the staple items. We're buying the mundane necessities: bread, milk, juice, veg, chicken nuggets, oven chips. I'm carrying a cardboard folder full of posters of our missing dog. Outside the shop are tall buildings, paved streets and roads. We're outside the boundaries of the National Park here, and it feels firmly back in reality. I'm just considering that this is where Ethan and I will be teaching once everyday life resumes in the autumn, when I hear the word that seems to be haunting us: *mermaid*.

Libby peers up at a display stand of beer. At first, it seems to have nothing to do with her precious mermaids, but then I spot the name printed on them:

Mermeg. An older man wearing an apron is standing nearby, saying goodbye to the lady he's been chatting to. Seeing Libby's interest, he waves at her. 'That's brewed in Flash,' he tells her, and I think he means *in a flash*, but he explains: 'Flash is the highest village in England. Mermeg's named for one of their helpers, plus a special story from these parts.'

I sigh. Not so firmly in reality, then – I suppose Leek isn't known as the Gateway to the Peaks for nothing. Now here's another stranger filling my daughter's head with a fantasy about mermaids. Which version will it be – the ageing sailor, or the man called Linnet who had the woman he loved drowned as a witch?

'Blake Mere Pool,' Zack murmurs, as if he's just awoken.

'No, not that one,' the man replies. 'There are others. Plenty of mermaids in the Peak District, if you know where to look.'

I think of that carving in the heart of our home and feel unease stirring inside me. Once again, I have the sense that they were waiting for me, these mermaids, or perhaps for Libby. But then, she adores them and eagerly seeks them out. She'd summon them if she could, casting a spell with her own dearest wishes.

'Where?' she wants to know.

'Well, there's one on Kinder Scout,' the man says, 'in Mermaid Pool. If you see her on Easter Eve at midnight, she might grant you immortality. There was an old feller from Hayfield used to visit her, and he lived ever such a long time, so it must be true.' He taps the side of his nose and Libby's eyes widen.

'Or maybe she won't. Maybe she'll just pull you in.' He winks. 'It depends what mood she's in.'

Libby isn't worried a bit. She gives an earnest nod. 'When can we go, Dad? Can we swim there – Dad? We can take my mermaid dolly. Can't we, Dad?'

'Kinder Scout's a long way from here, love,' Ethan tells her. 'The highest village in England and now the highest peak. Is there nowhere your mermaids can't get?' He ruffles her hair. Glances at me and then quickly away again.

Libby's face falls. She sticks out her bottom lip.

'Oh, well, there's a mermaid nearer than that,' the man adds. 'Maybe you could find her, if your dad says it's allowed, of course. There's one that lives right on top of the Roaches. Mind you, some say all three of the mermaid pools in the Peaks are connected. They say they're bottomless, with watery tunnels running between them and all the way to the sea. They also say the mermaids are related. Sisters, you know.'

Libby is all excitement once more. Before she can ask, Ethan says, 'Maybe later.'

I know Libby will take that as a promise and cling onto it. Sure enough, she announces, 'I'll need to get my mermaid doll first,' as if it's already a guarantee. She slips her hand into mine, her mood lifted by the anticipation of the day when she can hunt for this new mermaid. She hardly needs to search at all; it seems that, no matter how far we travel, the mermaids will follow in our wake.

18

That night, I dream of mermaids. Scales gleam like mother-of-pearl, water slides from smooth skin, the remnants of the sea drips from long, golden hair. Something is thrashing next to me, squirming and sinuous, and it takes me a moment to realise it's Libby. She's clambered into our bed and is sleeping between us, lost in her own dreams. I clutch her to me, holding her close, but she won't settle.

Ethan promised her before she went to bed that we would go and find her mermaid. We can even search for Jasper at the same time. We'll be able to see for miles from the top of the crag.

Once we've finished breakfast, I pack a rucksack with snacks and drinks, tape one of the MISSING posters to the outside of the gate and place a bowl of water by the front door, in case Jasper returns while we're gone. We clamber into the car and drive down the hill, through Thorncliffe, then follow a tiny road leading between some pretty houses before turning upwards once more. A little further and we reach the laybys at Roaches Gate, the nearest point to the escarpment accessible by car. There's no way-post, but there scarcely needs to be one, since we could hardly miss the crags rising above us. The laybys are crammed with summer visitors. Some walkers are just setting out up the hill, armed with hiking boots and walking poles. The climb looks steeper than I'd thought it would be, but Ethan has already offered to carry Libby on his shoulders if needed.

We squeeze the car into a small space left behind a Land Rover and follow the hikers, ascending a field dotted with sheep, the grass covered in scat and scraps of wool. Hen Cloud looms on our right, and I can't help agreeing with the cyclist that it doesn't much resemble a hen. It appears more like a fortress, or perhaps a line of jagged teeth. The Roaches are much larger and further off, away to the left, looking wilder and lonelier, broken giants turned to stone.

I spot something I'd read about online yesterday. There's a large boulder by the path to Hen Cloud, balanced on three smaller rocks. It's called the Bawdstone, and people used to believe it had healing powers. They'd crawl underneath it to scrape the Devil off their backs, but the church didn't approve. They gathered together and painted the stone white, though judging by old photographs, all they accomplished was making it visible for miles, a beacon to anyone who'd wanted to find it. Now the paint has worn off and it's just another part of this place.

As we start up a steeper slope towards the Roaches, they seem to grow higher still. Massive slabs of gritstone slice the air, telling of brutal geological processes and untold centuries of upheaval and struggle and cold, entirely unlike the soft, rolling green landscape spread below. *Barbarous* is the word that comes to mind, and I wonder whether the good Christians could have tolerated them. Is that why they're merely named *rocks* – in an attempt to convince themselves they were harmless? Perhaps they couldn't find a name to encompass them.

Even when I focus on the dry, almost sandy track in front of me, I sense them waiting, colossal and dark. When I look up, strange forms seem to half emerge before hiding again in their notches and folds. If the rolling fields of this region are gentle, safe, *ours*, this place feels ancient: *un*gentle.

Libby puffs out her cheeks and blows hair off her forehead. To keep her mind off how much further we still have to go, I embrace Gran's spirit: I tell her stories. I'd found several of those too, reading into the night on my phone while Ethan slept beside me.

'So,' I begin – it's not quite *Once upon a time,* but it will have to do – 'we're going to find Doxey Pool, Libby.'

She wrinkles her nose. 'What's Doxey mean?'

'A – a naughty lady.' The spelling is different from *doxy*, an old word for prostitute, but I imagine the meaning is much the same. Still, I'm not going to explain that to my four-year-old.

'Like bawd,' Zack chimes in helpfully.

'Yes. *Thank you*, Zack. A bawd is a naughty lady too. Anyway, Doxey Pool is where the stories say the mermaid lives. Only this isn't a nice mermaid either, Libby. This one is wicked.'

I don't know why I'm telling her this. It's as if I've caught some mermaid-story-telling disease from the people we've met, or perhaps these tales really are seeping up from the land where they've nestled for hundreds of years. Here, surrounded by these implacable rocks, the idea doesn't seem so very strange.

Libby doesn't care where the story came from. She only wants to know, *What next?*

'This mermaid's got a name. Not many of them do. She's called Jenny Greenteeth.'

I pull a scary face and open my eyes wide. After a moment Libby bares her teeth at me and brandishes her little fists into claws. I snarl back and we giggle together.

I don't tell her that I've heard of Jenny Greenteeth before, miles away and years ago. That once upon a time, she used to live at the bottom of my grandmother's garden, in Lancashire, not the Peak District. I wonder to myself how she came to be here. Perhaps people had moved to the Peaks from my old home and brought their stories with them, depositing her in this pool, just as a sailor once brought a mermaid back from the sea. She must have been useful, a cautionary tale to teach children to stay away from the water, and so her legend lived on.

I remember sitting by the slimy pool near my grandmother's house, the water so green I might have walked on it as easily as grass. Waiting for Jenny to drag me in. All because of a terrible accident I could never forget. Now I have found Jenny again; another water spirit displaced from her home and cast up here, on a huge rock in the middle of a wide green sea.

Libby is more eager than afraid. She's waiting for me to continue the story, as obsessed with mermaids and unicorns and fairies as any other girl her age.

'Some people call this mermaid other things,' I say. 'Some call her the Blue Nymph. Some say she's simply a spirit of the water. A bad one.'

My daughter looks puzzled, as well she might. The old tales have run together like droplets of rain into a stream, flowing into a river, then the sea. But perhaps there were reasons for that.

They also say the mermaids are related. Sisters, you know.

From what I'd read online, they might be more than sisters. Some said they were manifestations of one creature, a single spirit of the water who could travel between the mermaid pools – perhaps using the watery tunnels described by the man in the supermarket – adopting different guises as the desire took her. Perhaps she could look like Joshua Linnet's maid or the love of the old man of Hayfield, maybe even Jenny Greenteeth herself; anyone who joined her in her watery home.

'What happened next, Mummy?' Libby pulls on my sleeve.

'Well, legend has it that Jenny Greenteeth came up here and fell into the pool at the top of these rocks. It was foggy, you see, and it would be very dangerous up here in that weather. Can you imagine it? You could fall *right* off the edge.' The story of this Jenny differs from the one I knew, which makes it better somehow. I grab Libby and make her squeal. 'So now Jenny's turned ugly and mean.'

'*Mummy*,' Libby says, as if I've crossed a line, or worse, broken the rules of storytelling. 'Why would anyone want her if she's ugly? She's a *mermaid*.' She puts her hands on her hips and pulls a face. Now it's my turn to laugh.

'Well, she can wear whatever face she chooses,' I explain. 'So she makes herself appear like a beautiful girl and lures young men towards her. She acts as if she needs their help, as if she's afraid of drowning. It's only when she has them in her grasp that they see what she truly looks like. By then it's too late – she pulls them down and down, into the pool.' I mime them being grabbed.

Libby wrinkles her nose at the thought of any mermaid being so wicked. Of being a monster. Or is it only her ugliness she's not happy with? I wonder how anyone could claim to know what Jenny looked like anyway, if she dragged them all to her doom and there were no survivors. She's become as malleable as the stories, all these aquatic creatures blending into one. A *spirit of the water*.

'There's a chance that one person did encounter Jenny and live to tell the tale,' I remember. 'A little girl came up here for her morning bathe, in the mid nineteen hundreds. She saw a weird creature emerging from the water, but she was lucky and managed to run away. She said it was all slimy and weedy and she never did see its face.'

'Mummy,' Libby says, 'Why would she climb all the way up here for a *bath*?'

I remind her that the word was *bathe*, but I can't deny it's a good question. Libby scowls at the sight of the path still rising ahead of us, and so I tell her a different tale, a real one this time.

'When it was wartime, there wasn't quite enough food for everyone and their animals,' I tell her. 'There was a man here who had his own private zoo, which they said he had to close. So he released a whole colony of wallabies onto the moorland. You'd think they'd struggle, but they didn't. They ate heather and lived here quite happily for a time. What do you think of that, Libby? Do you think that little girl might have seen a wallaby taking a dip?'

'Don't be silly, Mummy,' she protests. 'It wasn't a *wallaby*. She saw a mermaid.'

I laugh, tousling her hair. 'Maybe, love.' Of course, Libby would never stand for a prosaic explanation. I remember the way she'd loved to peer at the sea, imagining fabulous creatures swimming there. Or how she'd come back from the beach with Ethan, blurting about seeing her precious mermaid before she'd even been able to catch her breath, glancing at her dad and miming zipping her lip. Mermaids didn't speak, after all; they never told their secrets.

I reach out to help her clamber over a rougher section, holding out my hands to catch her if she falls.

Libby climbs on regardless, eager to reach the top, even though I can tell she's getting tired. I think of yet another story I'd found last night, a *not so nice* one that tried to explain why a mermaid would live all the way up here. That one didn't begin with a mermaid, though. It began with a witch.

A woman known in these parts as Old Bess Bowyer once lived in a cave at the foot of The Roaches. Her rough home was full of her handiwork: jars and pouches filled with her hedge-cures, and bundles of dried herbs hanging from the ceiling. Her room was lit by nothing but firelight, and a stream ran through it, providing all she required to meet her needs – and those of her lovely young daughter.

The cavern also provided something else of particular use. For there was a tunnel that led right under the craggy heights of the Roaches and out onto the moors on the other side. For a fee, Bess would give refuge to poachers and other rough men who found themselves here, allowing them to wriggle through its dark and secret path to escape the reach of the law. She was said to be no stranger to such ways herself, since she was descended from Bowyer of the Rocks: a leader of outlaws.

Her daughter was a bonny lass with dark eyes. She had a voice as pretty as her face and could be heard singing on many a fine evening with songs that echoed from rock and water until they struck upon a man's ears in a peculiar way. On a clear night, it reached them long before they laid eyes on her, and could be heard even from the pool on top of the crag.

That pool was already thought of as strange, since it remained full to the brim even in the height of summer, though it lay hundreds of feet higher than any known spring. Song-haunted, the rumours about it spread, and some began to wonder if a mermaid dwelled there.

Those with uglier thoughts would scoff. Doxey Pool, they called it. In fact, doxy – a woman of easy virtue – was one of the more polite names they gave the girl, whom they claimed wasn't quite so fine as she ought to be.

One day, the singing stopped. Old Bess Bowyer was found wandering amid the rocks, half out of her senses, weeping bitter tears. She said that her daughter – doxy or no – had been carried off by villainous men. The girl was never seen again, and her heartbroken mother lay down and died in the cavern that was once her home.

But it is claimed the maiden's voice haunts the pool to this day; for it remains there, full to the brim, dark and lonely on its peak. Some say that the girl drowned herself in its depths in order to escape the men who took her. Or perhaps it was they who drowned her, once they had finished with her.

Some say, in hushed whispers, that her spirit may still be seen ...

The rocks are larger now, the path steeper, sections of it crumbling, and Ethan scoops Libby up and carries her over them. Zack pauses and stares straight down into the drop, where a narrow stretch of woodland grows around the foot of the crag. I peer into it too, searching for what was once Old Bess Bowyer's home. After her death, her caves were apparently turned into a cottage, with rooms and walls built around them. It was named Rock Hall; I wonder if the stream still flows through it. These days, it's let out to parties of climbers visiting the crag. It might be right below us, but I can't make anything out through the canopy.

After another steep climb, we finally reach the top of the Roaches. A pale, gritty path heads over the line of the crag, between sparse clumps of heather clinging to the dry ground. To our left, the view is vertiginous. Huge jutting rocks give way to nothing but air. Far below, all the fields and farms formed by man are so tiny as to be insignificant. Pretty much everything is green as far as we can see, though miles in the distance is a single open stretch of water, a lake turned mist-coloured by the distance.

Up here, we are cut off from the world. It's of no surprise if stories were told of this place; little wonder if people thought anything could happen here.

We follow the path. The escarpment isn't that wide, and there's only one way to go. The scale of it is vast, though, and it seems an age before the path begins to open out into a flatter area, scattered with rocks. The ground between them is no longer parched but black and boggy, and at its centre lies Doxey Pool.

It is smaller still than Blake Mere. If it were anywhere else it would surely be so insignificant it was soon forgotten, but here, it seems improbable, even impossible. Like Blake Mere, its surface reflects back the clouds, the sky inverted, everything out of place. It gleams all the colours of the inside of a shell, until a breeze ruffles the water and turns all to grey, as if to say, *No more*.

The wind stills and the water settles, until it cradles the sky again. Libby steps closer, already under its spell, and prods at the water with her boot. She pulls a face at the mud and says doubtfully, 'I *suppose* we could bath.'

Ethan grins. 'Why not? It can't be that deep.' He points to where a clump of weed juts from the surface. Not bottomless, then; not even close.

Libby frowns, as though the magic has faded a little. At least she isn't keen on swimming, not today. It's cool up here with the wind sweeping over the rocks, and I wander away from the others and put my back to the pool. Looking towards home, I can just make out the course of the road, its edge marked by the stolid right angles of the Mermaid Inn. I scan the land around it and see only purple-brown moor, yellow-white sheep, grey rocks. I can't see Blake Mere Pool at all. If the sister mermaids wished to see one another, they'd need their watery tunnels. Or perhaps, on clear, moonlit nights, they'd be able to listen to each other's songs.

Zack is standing at the opposite side of the escarpment, his head tilted, as though listening. Then I hear it; not a human voice but sweet birdsong, rising from the woods below. The sound is so eerily clear it seems almost ethereal. Each note reaches us pure and whole, and it's easy to imagine travellers pausing here in times gone by, puzzled to hear a young woman's song haunting these rocks.

'Mind if I head off?' Zack points towards another path, rocky and narrow, almost like a staircase leading down to the foot of the Roaches and into the woods. There, I see three lads standing at the base of a huge boulder, another suspended halfway up, hanging from a rope that appears from this distance as no more than a wiry red thread.

'I could go and watch them for a bit,' Zack suggests, his face awakened with interest, like a flare of sunlight. This is how he was in Sandsend, always rushing off with his mates, searching for adventure. I find myself thinking in Ethan's voice: *Ordinary people can do extraordinary things*. Why not? Perhaps he'll discover rock climbing as he once did surfing.

He reads my expression and a grin animates his features. 'Great!' he says, before I can change my mind. 'See you back at the car.' In the next moment he's bouncing down from rock to rock as if they're nothing but pebbles.

I walk back to the pool's edge where Ethan and Libby stand side by side, motionless, entranced by the mirrored surface as though under a hypnotist's spell. Then Libby's arm twitches and something flies into the water. I recognise the friendship bracelet she'd been wearing – it was always her favourite. It rests on the surface a moment before being sucked under without a sound.

'Now we're friends,' Libby announces, and she reaches out and grabs my hand. I hold on to her tightly, and with Libby satisfied with her afternoon's adventure, at last we leave the pool behind us.

19

A postcard.

A mother and daughter walk hand in hand along the beach, under a grey sky. I'm taking Libby to hunt for hag stones. They're not difficult to find on this shore, especially down towards Whitby. There are lots of them – stones of dark grey basalt with natural holes all the way through. Many assume those holes to be worn by the endless grind of the sea, but basalt is igneous. It's more likely that bubbles of gas passed through the rock while it was molten, aeons ago.

It's early in the year, barely springtime, and we're wrapped up warm, with wellies on for wading through the regular outfalls and streams that come down off the cliffs. The breeze whips incoming waves into a cappuccino froth so the shoreline is speckled white right along the coast. On the strandline, knee-high banks of foam shiver in the breeze. Breakers curl and crash onto the sand, like spilt milk. Occasionally waves cross and collide, sending fountains of spray airborne, like angry bursts of words that can't be taken back.

Jasper loves it. He chases the whips of froth blown from the crests of the waves as they're carried off down the beach. He pounces on a clump, snaps his jaws to find there's nothing he can grip before starting again. For Jasper, it's the chase that's important.

We're approaching a promising section, stony and rough, rumbling like thunder as the waves drag rocks over one another. As it ebbs, the sound gives way to a lighter rattling of pebbles and the hissing of bubbles from fissures and pinholes in the sand.

We begin our search, scanning the grey shales and slates, red and pink sandstones, ochre-seamed quartz, mottled pudding stones. Sometimes there's pure black jet on this coastline, this area being famous for it, but that's a much rarer find. Libby squints against the grit blown up by the breeze, before frowning in concentration. My heart clenches. Sometimes, I catch flashes of my mother, but more often she reminds me of my gran. She's present in a quirk of my daughter's mouth or a pursing of her lips; even a certain expression in her eyes. As if to underline the similarity, she pushes her friendship bracelet more firmly up her skinny arm as she stoops. I'm wearing one too at her insistence, a zigzag of blue and yellow, and I wonder what happened to Gran's wooden beads.

Libby squeals in triumph and holds up a stone: a perfect hag, a little smaller than her hand, with a circular hole at its centre. I admire her prize as she pokes her fingers through it.

Missing Gran more than ever, I tell my daughter what she'd once told me. 'There's an old story that says if you look through a hag stone, you'll have enchanted sight. You can see fairies and other magical creatures. Why don't you try it?'

I laugh as Libby peers through the hole, staring out at the restless silvery waves.

'What do you see?'

But Libby doesn't answer. She's too busy looking. She scarcely needs magic to picture such things anyway. She loves all such fairy tales, perhaps even more than I once did. I've promised her we'll hang any hag stone she finds in her room. Gran would have said it was a charm, one that would protect its owner against any harm befalling them – not that I believe in such things, but who knows? Perhaps it will be a charm, of a kind. Libby's hag stone will hold this day within it, a precious memory to make her smile; a simple, everyday kind of magic. The kind I can believe in.

On the way back home, I decide to buy a latte for me and an ice cream milkshake for Libby at Tides Café. I whistle for Jasper, who's busy worrying at a root of oarweed as if it's a rodent in need of killing. Libby skips along, her hand on the hag stone in her pocket, and I gaze at the endlessly shifting sea. Zack is out there somewhere. I tell myself he'll be warm in his wetsuit, safe with his surfer friends. They know what they're doing, and he's promised to stick to quieter waters. Ethan's out there too, somewhere. He was just as mad as Zack, wanting to go to his wild swimming club despite the changeable conditions. Odd that they still committed, and I wonder if maybe they've secretly gone for a pint instead.

For now, there's no trace of either. The sand is covered only in footprints left by gulls, little arrows that point in every direction, impossible to follow where they have gone. Waves keep on rushing in, each leaving behind a bubbling, fizzing backwash and a thousand tiny rainbows.

We're sitting outside at the café, overlooking the beach where the beck flows through it, when Ethan sits down next to us. He's wearing his wetsuit and a broad grin and his eyes are shining brighter even than Libby's, which are widened with sugar and delight. By now, I recognise this glow he has. It's the remnant of his swim, he's been out there after all, and I know it will stay with him for the rest of the day. I'll catch him smiling in odd moments at the memory of being in the sea, just him and the elements, as he would put it.

'That was amazing,' he pronounces, pausing to kiss Libby. She pulls a face, wipes her cheek as he takes a sip of my latte. 'You wouldn't believe it, Ellie, I'm telling you.'

I just nod. I have plenty of excuses ready, if he ever asks me to join. Most of their meets are in Whitby, for a start, and I don't have time to trek there, plus there's Libby and Zack to consider. Ethan has taken Lib along a couple of times – not to swim, he swore she wouldn't, without me – he'd said the organiser, Rob, has a lovely wife with a little boy Libby's age, that she and some of the other family members enjoy sitting on the beach with the kids while their partners are in the water. He'd said she'd love it and she did, but anyway, I'm not sure I'm a strong enough swimmer to join a wild swimming club. I might have been once but I don't trust myself now. I glance into the grey and almost see her, the shadow of that girl I used to be, the one who loved the water. I shiver, telling myself it's only the breeze.

'Who went?' I ask, breaking the silence between us. 'Who'd you find that was mad enough? Old hands? Or newbies who don't know any better?'

'Oh, well there's—' He hesitates, then goes on. 'There's someone fairly new who managed it fine, actually. She joined not long ago. She's pretty brave.'

That's strange, because he's not mentioned anyone new.

'She was like you,' Ethan carries on, oblivious to my reaction. 'You used to love running, remember? So did she, but had to pack it in. Plantar fasciitis. It got really painful for her even to walk. She doesn't let it stop her, though. She's taken to the water instead. A bit nervous, but she did it anyway. She loves it now.'

'How nice,' I murmur. 'Who is she?' I'm unable to keep a note of sarcasm from my voice, as if to add the unspoken words: *this woman who's so much braver than me.*

He waves my question away. 'Didn't catch her name. It doesn't matter.'

And that's the moment I know my husband is lying to me. But I also know he's doing it for the right reasons. He wants to tell me he's really not interested in this woman; that he's only thinking of what I could do, if I actually wanted to, that is. He's lying to me out of love, but still, annoyance prickles under my skin. That, and I can't help being wounded a little, diminished in comparison to this brave, suffering, beautiful creature.

Of course, he hadn't said she was beautiful. But somehow I know that she is.

We walk home together along the coast road. Ethan is still glowing from his swim when we let ourselves through the front door, talking about how gloriously alive the sea makes him feel. It's starting to irritate me. Is he somehow *less* alive when he's with me? Still I nod and make the expected noises, and we walk into the kitchen and find our son, wetsuit stripped to the waist, rubbing Savlon into the red streaks scraped down the length of his arms.

'Zack, what happened?' I take the tube from him and examine his skin. The grazes are wide rather than deep but some are bleeding and he'll be covered in scabs over the coming days.

He shakes his head and salt water from his hair spatters my face. 'It's nothing,' he says. 'Don't be *extra*, Mum. I shouldn't have opted for short sleeves. There were some big rollers. I tried to stand up and wiped out, that's all. Got pulled under, knocked along the bottom a bit.' He grins, as if what happened is a rite of passage, a badge of pride. 'I got *rinsed*.'

'Zack, you *promised* me.'

He shrugs from behind a wall my words can't penetrate. I hand back the antiseptic, noticing for the first time that my son is taller than me. For now, all I can do is ensure he covers every scrape. We can save the argument for the next time he wants to brave the waters; the next time the winds are whipping up the waves of a wild sea.

Then comes a loud wail and we turn to Libby, holding out the source of her sorrow: her hag stone, the charm meant to protect her from any misfortune, made fragile by the hole that gave it purpose, has shattered into so many useless teensy pieces.

'It doesn't matter, Mummy,' she sighs, as if she's the one comforting me. 'I can still see the mermaid, any time I like. I can see her *all* the *time*.'

She reaches out and tips flaking shards of basalt into my outstretched palm.

20

Slowly, I lie back and allow myself to slip under the water. It creeps upward, submerging my cheeks, eyes, nose. My hair floats free. I stay under for a few long seconds, then sit back up. The bath is luxuriantly full, the air writhing with steam, a candle sending shadows flickering around the room. My back and shoulders ache, not so much from the walk as lifting Libby down sections of the rocky path. I'm not as fit as I once was. I run my hand down my body, over the spare flesh, silvery stretch marks from the kids gleaming under the water like tidelines. Unlike Ethan's *brave* friend, when I gave up running, I never pursued anything else. Children meant no free time. Naturally, their needs came first. I think of Ethan's hands stroking this same skin, rubbing in the coolness of aloe vera, when I was swelling with his baby.

I comb my fingers through my hair, a little too dark to be described as blonde anymore. Back in the day it was mermaid-long, right down my back, but it was such a pain to wash and detangle and dry. Then when we had Zack, he was forever grabbing and pulling at it with sticky little fingers. I'd dismissed Ethan's protests and cut it off. Now my boy is almost grown. He wants to hurl himself from cliffs on a thin red thread.

I can hear him rustling around in his room. He's playing music, and for once I don't mind it; at least it's not his usual frenetic rock. I sip crisp wine from the glass balanced on the side of the bath and lie back. I can't quite bring myself to move. The tune lulls me with a melody that's lilting and low, almost hypnotic, and I find myself trying to follow it. At that moment, I seem to hear a woman's voice snaking across the hall, through the steam.

I slip deeper into the water although oddly, I can still hear the music beneath the surface. There are words in it, though now it sounds like a single word being repeated over and over, albeit through a mouthful of water: *Lib ... Lib ...*

Something brushes against my arm. The touch is fleeting but distinct, like tendrils of long hair snaking across my skin, a momentary caress; but my hair isn't long enough for that. I push myself up. Now all I hear is water sloshing around the tub.

The bathroom is empty. The door is locked. No one's in here with me, or could be. But the unsettling thought lingers within the walls of my mind: someone *touched* me.

Or some*thing*.

I shake my head, though the voice I'd heard still echoes around inside it. My daughter's name, or something else – only an indeterminate, choking, *drowning* sound?

The voice I *thought* I'd heard.

I couldn't have heard anything, I reason with myself. I'm just an idiot who'd fallen asleep in the bath. I'd been lulled by warmth and wine and the water, and drifted off with mermaids in my head, and stories, and memories.

But that music, plaintive, alluring, strange, isn't just an echo in my mind at all. It's still playing, and it's coming from outside the room. There's sorrow in it, and something else. It doesn't sound like anything Zack's ever played, or would.

I climb out of the bath, wrapping a towel around me. Water trickles from my hair down my back, cold air following in its wake, like icy fingers brushing my skin. I knock and when there's no answer, push open Zack's door. His headphones are on the bed, but no tinny percussion spills from them. The room is silent, as is the whole house; the music has gone, and I feel oddly bereft. Still, I'm perplexed as to what I was hearing and keep on surveying my surroundings, as though my son will emerge from the shadowed corners. Or am I trying to conjure that sound again? Outside the window, the moon is full and yellow and low in the sky.

Zack must have gone downstairs to watch TV with Ethan. Possibly they've fallen asleep too. But something is tugging at me from deep inside, as if an invisible cord connecting me to my son is being pulled elsewhere. I tell myself I'm being ridiculous. I assure myself this isn't a mother's instincts, or even more than that, my grandmother's, trying to tell me – what, exactly?

I do hear something, but not from inside the house. There's a *scratch, scratch, scratching*, at the front door.

I clutch the towel tighter and rush downstairs. I'm already picturing Jasper waiting there – my lost, hungry dog come home at last. I yank open the door, so sure he'll be there that for a moment I almost see him, but then reality intrudes: an empty step. A garden filled only with moonlight.

A hare, however, is perched by our hedge, staring at me with bright little eyes. I still can't make out their colour, but its gaze seems almost human.

I picture it loping up to the door, setting claws to wood, demanding to come in. I know the thought is pure madness. This is a wild creature, nothing that belongs in my house, with my family, but rather with the earth and the moor and the dome of the sky. I probably never even heard a sound at the door. It's not as if it would be the first thing I'd imagined this evening.

My gaze falls to the bowl of water placed by the step. The hare might have come to drink and brushed against the door accidentally. There was nothing strange about it.

It still stands there by the hedge, motionless, staring back at me.

I step inside and close the door against the sight. Before I go up to dress, I check on my husband.

Ethan is in the lounge, just as I'd thought. The TV is on with the sound muted, and he's sprawled full length on the sofa, fast asleep.

There's no sign of Zack.

Perhaps he'd taken himself off to bed while I'd been standing at the door like a fool, and I'd never noticed him pass by. Still that cord inside me is tugging again, telling me he hasn't. I *know* he hasn't. I think he's outside. He might have sneaked out to have one last look for Jasper – or was it something else he sought? I try to stem the image of Zack wandering on the moor towards that yellow moon, reflected in a mirrored pool ...

A pool with the moon reflected in its surface is a gateway.

The voice is my gran's.

If anyone enters such a pool, they'll end up in the land where it is always summer. The place where enchanted creatures live ...

I shake my head. Gran used to say a lot of things. And Zack is not a little kid. He's fifteen, and sensible – most of the time, at least – and what's more, he's *fine*.

Behind me, the front door opens. Then comes a soft shuffling, as of something moving across the tiles. A lolloping, irregular, unrecognisable sound, and my mind insists on picturing a hare, walking into my home. An insistent, *watching* hare with bright blue eyes – warding off evil, or casting a spell?

The nape of my neck feels terribly vulnerable. I wish I had more than a clutched towel around me. I picture myself trying to catch the creature, the elasticity of its body, its warm weight. Muscular limbs scrabbling, claws raking my water-soft skin.

When I turn, the front door is open. There is no hare, nothing there at all, only a line of black, muddy footprints leading towards the stairs.

I close the door then follow the trail. On the landing, I pause to listen. Libby's soft breathing emerges from her room and I peek in to see her sleeping sweetly, honey-coloured hair strewn across the pillow. Zack's door is closed. Did I close it behind me? I can't remember. I stand there a moment, not sure what I'll find when I open it, then shake my head and push the door wide.

Zack is sitting on the bed. I can't make out his expression. He's staring down at the floor, or perhaps at his trainers, caked in mud. I'm not sure he's seeing anything at all because he seems oblivious to the mess he's made. He doesn't even seem aware of me.

'Zack?'

He still doesn't stir. I clutch my towel tighter with one hand, and with the other I reach out and touch his shoulder.

For several long seconds, he doesn't move at all. Then slowly, as if sleep were clinging to some deep part of him, he shifts his head and looks into my eyes. His expression is as wild and unreadable as the hare's.

'Zack, it's late. Where have you been?'

'You know where.' His voice is his own, yet it isn't. The thought comes to me that some part of him is missing, still out there perhaps, wandering the moor, and I force myself to swallow it down.

'The pool?' I ask, already knowing that of course it was the pool. How could it have been anywhere else? What did he seek there – and what did he find? Did he wish to stare into its glimmering surface when midnight struck? For now, he doesn't answer.

'Zack, what did you see?'

'See?' His echo strikes oddly upon my ears. *Sea? Sea?*

I take a deep breath. 'Zack, that's enough. You should have told me you were leaving the house. You shouldn't have been wandering around in the dark. You're just tired – go to bed. Trainers off. I'll clean up the stairs, okay?'

He kicks his shoes into a corner, rolls onto his side and wraps his arms around himself. He should brush his teeth, wash, change, get under the covers, but it's been a long time since I had to tell him to do any such thing and I don't tell him now. I'm still unnerved by the way he looked at me, or rather the way he didn't. The way that, for a second, he hardly seemed to know me at all. But everything tonight seems to have turned strange. It's as if the world has melted a little, nothing solid remaining. I remember the music, the scratching – was that *Zack?* – the night air, the moon, the hare. Those strange, wild eyes looking back at me.

For now, there are practical things to do. I fetch the dustpan, brush and a cloth to clean up the muddy footprints as best I can. It's not perfect, but I don't want to wake Libby with the Hoover – or Ethan, who is still sleeping downstairs. I don't want him getting angry with Zack. Our son is obviously more upset by the move than I'd imagined, and that isn't his fault. He doesn't need a dressing-down from his dad on top of it all. Ethan doesn't need the hassle either. He doesn't even need to know that Zack was gone; probably he'd prefer not to. It's easier just to clean up the mess.

We'll all go to bed and catch up on our sleep. Tomorrow will be another new day, another new start, everyone safe and happy at home.

After I've finished, I wake Ethan. He scowls when he opens his eyes, too bleary in his tiredness to notice the traces of peat on the stairs. I don't bother to dry my hair, just quickly towelling it off before slipping into bed beside him. He doesn't even murmur goodnight before he's drifting off again.

I, on the other hand, am wide awake. I almost feel untethered to the real world, about to float away. Or perhaps I've slipped under the surface of my grandmother's moon-haunted pool, and reappeared – I'm not sure where.

I slip out of bed and walk over to the window. The moon is still riding high, clothed in shreds of wind-torn cloud. Beneath, the whole land is a silvery expanse appearing more than ever like the sea. Darker forms swim within it and I tell myself they're simply trees or drystone walls, though I can't altogether make them out. I think of the lonely pools out there, glimmering under that same moon, their depths lured by its tidal call. What else is stirring there – what might answer its summons?

I look down at our lawn and see a woman staring back at me.

Her head is tilted back, as if she's standing at the bottom of an undersea garden, and something inside me goes very still.

The youngest and most beautiful of them all, I think; and she is.

At this angle, in this light, her features appear painfully young, yet full of sorrow. Her hair, darkened by shadows, flows loose, tangled by the breeze. It makes her skin appear pale, moon-white and flawless. There's something draped around her. It must be a coat but I can't make it out and instead my mind goes to fishing nets or seaweed …

A mermaid. Is that what I think I'm seeing outside my window in the middle of the night? I close my eyes. *What does that make me?*

Am I eccentric or just mad?

Ethan shifts in sleep, muttering something under his breath. Is he the prince in this story? If he is, he's made his choice. And it isn't *her.*

'Ethan.' My voice is louder even than I'd intended. 'You need to see.'

Sea. Sea …

He gets to his feet and walks towards me like a man in a dream, and perhaps he is. He stands at my side. Here we are: the two of us together, Ethan and Ellie. Even our names sound as if they belong together. When we met, *I* was the youngest and most beautiful of them all. That's what he always told me.

The loveliest. The greatest. The best.

You're the most beautiful girl on campus, Ellie.

He'd pursued me with the dedication of an Olympic athlete aiming for a medal. *I know what I want.*

He was keen and impulsive and generous. Not to mention so handsome. Other girls had watched with envy as I'd walked across the quad drowning in the flowers he'd given me. I remember what Ethan always said when I'd pointed out that people were looking at him.

They're looking at us, Ellie. And why not? We look perfect together.

I wonder if we still look so perfect together now.

'What on Earth, love?' Ethan seems to wake at last. 'I don't see anything. Again.'

'There.' But I peer down into the garden and see that he's right. There *is* nothing there.

Again.

'Were you having a bad dream? Poor baby.' He turns towards me, reaches out to stroke my forehead, but I push his hand away. 'What's wrong? Did you hear something? Maybe it was a fox. Or the house settling. We're not used to things around here, that's all. Come back to bed.'

'I saw someone.' But I'm no longer sure what I saw.

'What?' Ethan looks as if he doesn't have the first clue what I'm talking about. Or who. 'There's no one there, love. You must have dreamed it. It's just stress, that's all.'

A short while ago, I thought I'd heard music coming from out of nowhere. A voice, calling my daughter's name. A *siren's* voice. I'd felt a mermaid's hair, wrapping itself about my skin.

If I'm not careful, I'm going to be the one to ruin this. My vision of a new morning, all waking together safe and happy, will be spoiled. I must have somehow fallen asleep on my feet, even as I was standing here by the window. I'd dreamed up a presence, one drifting too often through my mind, swept away by stories and wishes.

I lean in towards Ethan and he wraps his arm around me, just as if we're Ethan and Ellie once more, as we always were. As we *are*.

Ethan kisses me on the cheek and whispers soft words in my ear. He is warm and insistent, murmuring that he loves me, I'm all he wants, and he presses his face into my neck as if those words are everything, and suddenly they are. He guides me away from the window, back to our bed, back to him. This time he doesn't fall straight to sleep or turn away from me. He wraps his fingers around my shoulder, runs them down my back, making me shiver the way he always could. He puts his lips to mine, lightly and then deeper, and I let him and then I kiss him too.

21

A postcard.

It's a bright, sunny day early in the spring, just a few wisps of cloud drifting amid the blue, but I have lesson prep to finish and so I'm shutting myself inside despite the lovely weather. Zack's already gone to hit the surf and Ethan's supposed to be watching Libby, so I'm surprised when he appears in the doorway with his wetsuit and tells me there's a swimming meet starting soon at the lifeguard hut.

'Don't worry,' he says. 'I'll only be quick. Rob's wife is going along, with her little boy. She'll have a natter on the beach with a couple of the others, and watch the kids. Libby will love playing with them for a bit, won't you, Lib?'

I don't realise she's standing behind him, listening to every word, until I hear the 'Yaaaaaay.' My lips are already pressed tightly together. I'm not even sure why I'm irritated, or if it's about only one thing. Don't these women have names? Is Ethan just presuming he can dump his child on them while he goes off and does whatever he likes? Anyway, he's supposed to want to spend time with his daughter. Not with his club, with that beautiful, *brave* woman …

Ethan shakes his head as if he already thinks I'm being daft, countering my objection before I can voice it. 'Really, they're lovely people, Ellie, they'll enjoy it too. And then we're going for a walk, aren't we, Lib? Just you and your dad. Who's the best dad?'

'You are!' Libby's eyes sparkle and I swallow my worries. I know what will happen if I say no. He's the best dad, but I'll be the worst mum. Ethan will argue that I'm being over-protective and spoiling her fun, in front of Libby. The shine in her eyes will turn to tears and there'll be screaming and sulks, and I'll get no work done at all, and no one will be happy. I tell myself to stop being stupid and let them get on with it. If Libby will be looked after, that's all that matters.

When I finish work and they still haven't reappeared, I decide to go and greet them. I'm also curious to meet these mums and their kids. We might become friends, which could be nice. Maybe I'd like to sit on the beach and natter too.

There's this woman who's joined. She's really brave …

Well, *maybe* we'll be friends. I push that thought down, telling myself it's ungenerous. Perhaps I'll even like her – whatever her name is – as long as she's not too busy being so brave and beautiful all the time, and – *admired by my husband.*

Stop it, Ellie.

Anyway, I'm likely too late for that. It'll just be Ethan and Libby by this time.

I walk down to the sea, ready to meet my husband, to kiss his salt-crusted lips and grimace at the cold of his wetsuit, but before I find him, I see Zack. He's a speck out on the water, but even from here I can tell he isn't daunted by the breakers rolling in. He adjusts his board, aiming it towards the horizon, and awaits his moment. Then he pushes out, leaps up, and he's riding the surf, straight towards me then twisting aside to follow the shallow angle of the wave as it heads into the shore. The lip starts to curl under him as it nears the shallows, where he jumps neatly onto the sand.

I'm still smiling at the sight when I turn and see Ethan. He isn't swimming or out for his walk. He's sitting on the beach with a bunch of others, Libby a short distance away, intent on burying her legs in the sand while a little boy helps her. Ethan's fellow swimmers have cast off their neoprene gloves and goggles, along with the brightly coloured caps that make them more visible in the water. Some are still wrapped in towels or changing robes, sipping hot drinks from flasks, warming up after their dip.

I'm reflecting that Ethan must have headed out far too early for the meet when I see the shine of golden hair, long and loose, as it lifts on the breeze and drifts towards him, wrapping itself about his arm.

I know at once that it's her. This woman with long, golden hair is the brave, beautiful one, the one whose name my husband pretended not to know. She's sitting right next to him, so close they're almost touching. I don't know her name and I can't see her face because her head is bowed. There is only the impression of smooth skin, an averted gaze, a shy smile.

Ethan sees me and the spell is broken. I tell myself it's all right, of course it is, though I'm suddenly conscious of my heart beating too hard in my chest. He's grinning at me, his usual grin, and there's no hint of guilt in his expression. I hear their casual goodbyes. He jumps to his feet and pulls Libby up too, sand scattering from her legs, and he walks away from the others without looking back.

I forget about introducing myself to them as his lips brush my cheek. Ethan has that glow about him, the one he only gets from swimming in the sea. From feeling *alive*. I put my arms around him and give him a long, lingering kiss, ignoring the salt on his lips, as if to say, *Mine*. I know I'm being stupid, I can't even be sure she's watching, but Libby is. She tugs on my top and squeals, 'I saw a mermaid!'

She's glowing too as she starts to babble. 'It hurts her to walk, Mummy, it stabs her feet, just like the little mermaid. But she can swim ever so fast, and she's got mermaid hair and she's so pretty. Oh, but—' She mimes zipping her lips tight closed, presses them together, as if remembering that mermaids don't talk. That they keep their secrets.

Of course she's pretty, I think. *What bloody mermaid isn't?* But I nod and smile, not wanting to spoil her excitement. Ethan picks her up and whirls her around, then he takes both our hands as we walk away.

As we head for home, I find myself thinking of Hans Christian Andersen's *The Little Mermaid* again. Things strike upon me now as they never have before. Why is it that the heroine is always the youngest and most beautiful of them all? Why does that mean she is also *good*, that she deserves to have everything she desires? I had so wanted her to find love, that poor, suffering creature who had given up her voice and felt every step on land as if her feet were being stabbed with knives. I had loved that tale as a girl. I never knew if that was in spite of the heartbreak or because of it, only that it filled me with a wild kind of yearning for things beyond my reach, coupled with a despair I was probably too young to feel. Love unreturned. That was the worst tragedy of all, wasn't it? A heroine who couldn't find her happy ending, who gave up all she had for love yet failed to win her prince.

Now I think, *Why should she?*

He simply didn't love the little mermaid. That's not something she could wish into being. Even when I was a child, my mother had pointed that out:

Well, you can't just make them, sweetie.

Because love doesn't work like that. The prince simply didn't feel the same way. He married the princess and never regretted his choice for a second. He gave the little mermaid his kindness, because she needed it and because he *was* kind, but that was all.

I suppose Libby would think differently. She's a child, and it's a mermaid. She will think that such a creature should win the prince, should always have love, the whole kingdom, anything and everything she wants. I suppose she'll think the mermaid deserves it, no matter the cost to anyone else. As the youngest and most beautiful the prince should be hers by right.

Not this time, love, I think. *Not when he's mine.*

Then something else occurs to me. The mermaid wasn't even all that lovely, was she? She wasn't all sweetness and light. At the start of the story, she rescued the prince from drowning – but what about the crew of his ship? No one ever thinks of them, do they?

The little mermaid might have saved her prince, but she never had the slightest compunction about letting everyone around him drown.

22

'Watch out for the Winking Man, Libby!' I call from the front seat. 'There he is. You see that rock, jutting from the hill?'

I turn to see her peering out at the boulder with a hole right through it: a giant hag stone. Ethan glances aside too as we head along the A53 from Leek to Buxton. The sky is visible through that hole, a bright blue eye in a rocky face, but as we drive, something behind it blocks the view and the eye closes for a second.

'He winked, Mummy!' Libby squeals, laughing.

Today, we're not hunting for Jasper, not pining or thinking of him. Over the last few days, Ethan's been going off in the car, Zack exploring the moors on bike or foot, and Libby and I heading out on shorter jaunts. But this is still our summer holiday. For once the sun is showing itself, and we've decided to forget everything and visit Buxton – its grand Opera House, Crescent, Museum, Pump Rooms and wells.

Zack hasn't joined us. He wanted to continue the search for our dog. The car feels a little empty without him, but the simple normality of a family outing lets me breathe more easily. It's good to remember the outside world is still there. I reach across and place my hand on Ethan's thigh. He twitches a smile. He's been so distracted, we both have, but he's right: this will be good for us.

We luck upon a parking space near Pavilion Gardens and soon arrive at Saint Anne's Well. Water pours from a bronze lion's mouth, the top of his head worn shiny by the touch of many hands. An inscription reads, *A WELL OF LIVING WATERS*. We wait for a lady to fill a plastic canister, her young son pleading for a coin to throw in. Then I lift Libby so she can dip her fingers in the flow.

'It's warm!' she says, and it is: blood-warm. Libby squirms, as if she's touched something unpleasant. 'Is the water alive?'

We laugh and Ethan explains about the geothermal spring far below us in the rock. 'This whole place was built on water, Libby,' he says. 'People came here to bathe and drink and visit the spa. They thought the water would cure all their ills. Make them better.' He gestures towards the grand crescent opposite. Libby shields her eyes against the sun, viewing the imposing edifices all around. Ethan begins telling her about the local festival when each well is decorated with flower-petal pictures. He doesn't mention its pagan roots, offerings to bless the life-giving water and the spirits that dwell there. The well dressing has become something else now, but I remember the boy tossing in a coin – an offering in exchange for a wish. Just like Libby, throwing her friendship bracelet into Doxey Pool. Perhaps something pagan remains in all of us, no matter how we like to believe otherwise.

We're a little too late in the season to see the well dressings, though I think of the water trickling beneath us as we meander through the Pump Rooms and then onto the Colonnade. Now a fancy shopping arcade, signs remain of the Colonnade's history as the famous thermal baths: tiled walls, an empty plunge pool, and an old bathing chair suspended above it. Beneath our feet, water percolates through the earth, carving out hollows and caverns, finding new ways through the dark.

There's a display about the landscape at the Buxton Museum and Art Gallery, and we wander through it as if travelling back in time. Aeons pass before us, until in the far distant past, we learn this whole place was once under the sea.

Libby's getting bored, hanging on my arm and swinging her leg like a ballerina, huffing at the display cases and stuffy old paintings. In the next room, we find a gentleman's study, perhaps Victorian or Georgian. Dark wood, bookcases, antlers over the fireplace. It's as if some bewhiskered, waistcoated fellow might walk in at any moment to light a cigar. At last, something captures Libby's interest. She rushes to a glass case and stares up at a peculiar figure.

It is no surprise to see she has found another mermaid.

This one is about forty centimetres tall, and she isn't young or beautiful. Her skin looks like desiccated, cracked, grey-brown leather. Her eyes glare, pale globes in dark sockets. Her mouth, fixed in either a smile or a leer, is so crammed with teeth it's grotesque. Her nose is just a bony cavity, reminding me of the zombie movies Zack likes but I would never allow Libby to watch.

The mermaid's left hand is raised as if to comb the wisps of her hair. The other is positioned over her heart. It looks as if she ought to be holding a mirror, but perhaps it's a mercy for her that it's missing. I peer closer. Her fingers are surprisingly delicate, each one tipped with a tiny white nail. She's shrivelled, ancient, and creepy as hell. I wonder that anyone ever wanted to bring *this* mermaid home from the sea.

With a start, she reminds me of something: the carving hidden behind our staircase, hacked insistently into stone – ugly, barbaric. She's posed the same way.

Libby stares, entranced, as I read the history. The Buxton Mermaid has teeth of bone and eyes of mollusc shell. Her hands are of wood, her fingernails slivers of mother-of-pearl. Her tail is fish skin. Her hair is human. She was likely made in the Far East by fishermen, sold to western sailors who would bring such things back as souvenirs, or put them on display in exchange for coin, passed off as real.

I scan the ingredients again: bone, wood, shells, skin, hair. A witch's brew. Because that's what she is, isn't she? Not a mermaid at all, she's too ugly for that. She's a sea witch.

Now Libby has wandered away, so I'm standing alone, transfixed. My daughter is with her dad, examining fragments of skull placed on a desk. Ethan points to the most intact, playfully: 'A tourist, do you think? Got lost in here.'

Libby doesn't laugh. She slips back towards the Buxton Mermaid. I watch, unsettled, as she whispers to the figure, though I can't hear her words. It's almost as if she's offering up her voice to the sea witch – but in exchange for what?

You will have your wish, for it will bring you sorrow, little princess.

'Come on, Lib.' I make my tone bright. 'Time to go. We're hungry – what would you like to eat?'

The mention of food distracts her and I'm more than happy to agree to her demands of fish and chips and ice cream. Anything to get her out of here.

Ethan casually spears the white slippery flesh of the squid he ordered instead of fish, crushing it between his teeth. I've lost my appetite. I just want to go home. I wonder if there's been any sign of Jasper so I text Zack, hoping for news I know he can't have – he would have told us. But my son doesn't bother to reply.

23

A postcard.

A beautiful spring Saturday in a seaside town on the Yorkshire coast. A family walks down the street: a man, a woman and a little girl. The man and woman are close, her hand tucked into his arm. The light catches her hair, making it gleam. The man leans towards her, smiling and attentive. It's a lovely picture. It speaks of happiness and sunshine and holidays. It's perfect – or would be, if the woman on my husband's arm were me.

I'm hiding in the doorway of a nearby florist, concealed behind banks of fragrant petals and the bustling tourists that have already descended on Whitby.

I lied to Ethan. I'm not proud of that. I told him I was visiting an old friend who's moved to Pocklington. His eyes lit up, so happy to be free for a space of time he didn't even ask who this mysterious friend was, or what we planned to do.

Zack is at the beach, back home in Sandsend. He's busy, throwing himself into life and the sea with his friends. Jasper is with him. I'm surprised Ethan didn't insist he bring Libby too. That he didn't nags at me – can he really be doing something wrong if he has no problem taking our daughter along? Wouldn't he be worried she might spill his secrets, since she always tells me everything inside a minute? And yet my husband has stopped talking about the woman in his swimming group, the oh-so-brave and beautiful one. I've tried to convince myself that's a good thing, but part of me is horribly afraid that it isn't.

Each time Ethan heads out for a swim, already glowing with anticipation, I tell myself I don't *know*. And yet when he returns and I kiss him – sometimes I can't detect the faintest trace of salt on his lips at all.

My doubts are like waves. No sooner do I ride one out than the next arrives, deeper and stronger. A tide that won't be halted and won't turn.

Today, he boarded the coast bus to Whitby, just like I'd thought. I raced back to our car, which I'd already told Ethan I'd need for the day. I yanked up the door of our rental garage at one end of Sandsend's car park, leaving it swinging open behind me. I knew roughly where he'd be heading. I was manoeuvring into a parking space just as they alighted. The rush of Libby's bright chatter went to my heart. She sounded so happy.

Now she takes something from her pocket. It's a hag stone, new and intact. I don't know where she got it. She lifts it to her eye and stares up at the woman beside her, and I remember the stone that once broke in her hand.

It doesn't matter, Mummy. I can still see the mermaid, any time I like.

Is that what she's seeing now – not just any mermaid, but *Daddy's* mermaid?

She's always so excited after outings with Ethan. So full of chatter about mermaids, which I'd disregarded, laughed at even, assuming it was a child's make-believe. I remember how she'd glance at her dad and catch her breath, closing her lips tight on her words, because mermaids don't tell, do they? They don't because they can't.

I had thought he'd filled her head with fairy tales. But he had, hadn't he? Libby's, and mine too.

I feel stupid and hollow as I trail in their wake. Ethan was always my prince, but my prince has lied to me. He lied to our daughter. He took her longing for magic and turned it into something ugly, a cursed gift for a little child. Libby may only be four but she has a voice, and Ethan couldn't take that from her – so he did something else. He blinded her, and he'd used her own dearest wish to do it.

He blinded me too. Now there's too much truth in front of my face and I can't look at it. My vision blurs. Pain radiates through my chest, as if my heart's been ripped out. Ethan's mermaid smiles. So beautiful. Happiness shines from her, making her appear even younger than I suspect she is. But she has no worries, does she? No kids hurling themselves into the sea or worrying over a school project or crying because a friend doesn't like them anymore. No little girl screaming at bedtime because again, like every day, it has come around so very soon. There are no such problems to wrinkle her forehead. There's been no childbirth to thicken her once lithe waist.

And me? I'm the biggest fucking cliché of all. Of course, my handsome husband chose the younger and more beautiful model. All the stories warn of this, don't they?

The woman limps slightly as they walk. She leans on Ethan, letting him take her weight. So brave in her suffering. She's clearly the heroine of this story. I wonder what Libby thinks, skipping beside this astonishing, magical creature. This mermaid. Does my daughter think *she* should have the prince? That she deserves to win him from the bride he chose – her own mother?

The three of them are walking away. *She* is leaving, and taking my family with her. The air is suddenly too warm and suffocating. I can't draw enough of it into my lungs. I bend, resting my hands on my knees. Someone touches my shoulder – an older lady with silver hair and kind eyes. 'Are you quite all right?'

I say what I'm supposed to say, that I'm fine, just having a little turn, that's all. I rearrange my expression into something she can accept. She nods and walks away, pleased to have helped.

People swarm down the street around me, most headed for the sea. It's lunchtime, so they'll be in search of cockles and mussels, or fish and chips from Magpie's by the harbour. The wheeling shriek of gulls rises above their chatter, an alien, unfathomable sound.

For a moment, the crowd parts and I see them again, paused outside a shop. The woman is holding something out to my daughter: a doll. It has shiny blonde hair, clamshells for a bikini top, and instead of legs, a shimmering fishtail. The scales catch the sun: periwinkle, lavender, aquamarine. A mermaid doll. It is all the colours of the sea.

24

The morning after our trip to Buxton, there's no more making the most of our holiday. Ethan heads out before I've even finished breakfast, cramming a slice of toast into his mouth as he grabs the car keys. There's a sense of purpose about him as he plants a kiss on my cheek. 'Are you okay staying in with the kids? I might head into Leek, ask if anyone's seen Jasper. Get some shops to put up posters.'

I can't imagine our dog heading for a noisy town with busy streets and traffic, but it's hard to protest when Ethan's trying so hard. I nod and kiss him back. His idea can't hurt, I suppose. Maybe someone has seen something, though I can't shake the feeling that the answer is closer to home.

Zack comes in, shoving a slice of bread into the toaster and grabbing juice cartons.

'Morning, love.'

He grunts. He came in later than we did yesterday and vanished into his room. When I asked what he'd been doing, he muttered something about friends and shrugged, as if to say all the teenage stuff: that I wouldn't understand, didn't know anything about anything, etcetera, etcetera. I'd told myself to let it lie, to allow him space to settle before bombarding him with questions, but now he's heading out again and clearly we're not going to have the talk I'd hoped for. 'Jasper or friends?' I ask, and he replies with the usual monosyllable, 'Both.' I ruffle his hair, remind him not to miss lunch. A few more grunts and he's heading out onto the moor. He doesn't look like a boy off to meet his friends. He appears as a small figure, entirely and utterly alone.

Zack doesn't return for lunch. Nor does Ethan. At least my husband shoots me a quick text: I'll grab something on the go. See you later. Looks like rain again. Stay in and keep warm!

Keep warm – as if I'm ninety and this isn't the middle of summer. I shake my head and text Zack, yet again. He's been out for hours by now. Call me, I write, but he doesn't. I scowl at the screen. My son may think he's too cool to ring his mother the minute she asks, but vanishing without a word – again? That's not happening. I start considering punishments – chores, or grounding him, even confiscating his mobile for a while if he can't be bothered to use it – when I hear an odd sound.

It's clearer at the top of the stairs. A soft, constant whisper, echoing faintly around the walls. The sound comes from below, though I don't know where until I lean over the banister and peer straight down.

Libby is crouched at the bend in the staircase, tucked into the little hollow where the stairs turn. She's staring at the carved figure in the slab of stone, her fingertip tracing its lines. I can't make out what she's saying. I creep downstairs, move to stand behind her, but she doesn't stir and doesn't stop whispering. Earnest sibilant words, running together. *She's too deep*, I think, and don't know why.

'Libby, what are you doing?' My voice is sharper than I'd intended.

She jumps, startled, as if unsure where she is or who's spoken. Then she blinks and finds me. She still doesn't reply, though. She's *too deep*.

'Sweetie, why don't we go out for a bit?' I soften my tone and hold out my hand. After a moment, she grins and springs to her feet.

I get her ready and she's back to being Libby again, my little girl. She was caught up in some story, that was all. Now we focus on the practical. I promise her we'll put up pictures of Jasper along the way, grab some tape and plastic wallets to waterproof them, but there are no posters. Ethan must have taken them all this morning. I boot up my laptop, connect it to the printer and run off a few. The photo isn't as sharp as the ones printed in town, but it's better than nothing.

That done, we set out onto the moor. Libby skips along in her yellow boots, the ones that match her rainbow-haired doll. The sky glistens, pale and delicate as mother-of-pearl, and the view is endless.

The thought of this land being under the ocean gives me vertigo. Now there's barely a trace of water in sight, though I know it's there, beneath. In White Peak it trickles through the limestone, finding every crack and fissure, dissolving rock, carving out new caves in the dark. In the geology of Dark Peak, it vanishes into the porous gritstone or is absorbed into the surface peat. There's rarely open water at this altitude; the lake I saw from the Roaches turned out to be a reservoir constructed by the Victorians. Not so mysterious after all, that the Peaklanders gave every pool its own legend, its guardian spirit.

Is the water alive?

Of course not, Libby, we'd told her. But it strikes me now that it's not altogether dead.

And the old stories: are they still breathing, too?

'I'm swimming, Mummy!' Her voice rings out.

I turn to see her doggy-paddling through the air and I sigh. I don't want her within twenty miles of Blake Mere, though I recognise that my fears border on superstition. I don't have to let her see them; and that's where Libby wants to go. She loves stories as much as I ever did, she needs the stories, and I'm not a monster. I won't deny her what she loves.

'Come on, then.' I hold out my hand and she runs to take it.

We take the same route as our first day. From the pool, we can follow the road back, putting up posters wherever we can. Cars zip by too fast to see them, but maybe walkers and cyclists will take notice. Libby will like that we're doing something to help. For now she shakes me off and runs ahead, kicking at the heather, which springs back as if untouched.

It doesn't take long until we reach the pool. For a moment we stand and stare at the water, sweetly dreaming in its hollow. Clouds gather on the surface, just as before. But something's strange. Above us, the clouds drift in the breeze, but in the pool they appear perfectly motionless. They could almost be painted, eternal, as though there for centuries.

I think of our old home by the sea. The water there was never still, always tumbling, relentless waves breaking over themselves. Here, it's the escarpments in the distance that appear to be breaking. Nothing at all stirs the glasslike water. I look beyond it, to where the heather is ruffled by the wind, around the jutting rocks. Then I see it. A figure nestled among them, dark against the gritstone – heavy, unmoving. Or it is only the drifting of dark brown hair?

Everything stops. My mind narrows to the memory of the touch of my fingers against the screen of my phone, texting Zack. **Where are you?**

He still hasn't replied. Now I see why.

He's sleeping. He's drifted off right here, among the heather. He doesn't appear comfortable – his body twisted, one arm flung towards the pool. I worry he's cold, lying on the ground like that. Why hasn't he pushed the curls from his face? His hair is too long. It needs a cut. I'll need to take him into Leek or some other town. I'll ask him about it in a moment, when he stirs. He'll be embarrassed. Caught cat-napping like a much younger child. I'll tease him about it. Laugh. We both will.

Posters slip from my hands, Jasper's face fluttering to the ground. MISSING. MISSING. MISSING. I run across the space between us but I sink into the peat, wet earth opening beneath my feet, revealing glimmers of water, eager to rise. It's like sand, damp and shifting. I think of a mother running across a beach, her face stricken. There's a little boy afloat on the sea, his arms outstretched. She can't run fast enough. Her feet sink into sand as choppy and treacherous as a bog. Everywhere, people stare. Children pause building their sandcastles. Parents take off their sunglasses, then wish they hadn't. *Thank God that isn't me.*

Please God, don't let it be me.

I kneel beside him, saying his name, a single syllable that vanishes at once and completely into the chasm that's opened at my feet. *Don't let it be him.* Don't let this be my punishment, the one I've feared since I was fourteen, when I watched a boy drown and a curse wove its way into my bones.

I stop.

It isn't Zack.

His hair is a shade too light. His face is more rounded, his cheekbones less prominent, his lips not as full. This isn't my beautiful boy. Tears spill from my eyes. I know this is someone else's boy, but the relief is electric, flooding my body and making my hands tremble. Now I've focused on the things that make him not my son, I see what was right in front of me: there's something wrong with his skin.

One side of his face has been clawed. Scratched and furrowed.

I shake my head in confusion. *There's another version, though that one's not so nice …*

The words come to me, disembodied and disconnected, until they snap into place. This is where I'd heard them. The cyclist had wanted to tell us a story, but I hadn't let him. I had shut it out but now it returns to me: Joshua Linnet, the man who drowned the beauty who scorned him. Cursed by her final breath. Found here, three days later, *his face disfigured with claw marks.*

Fear washes over me, sudden and cold, as if I've stumbled over something that shouldn't be possible – a story brought to life.

Or rather, dragged back into *reality*. There's no life in him.

I notice my hand hovering just above his hair and snatch it back. Did I touch him? I don't even know. *Mustn't touch the body.* DNA. Evidence. Contamination. A more rational part of my brain takes over, preventing me from disturbing the scene. Perhaps this is the result of an argument with a woman who'd scratched at him with her nails. Or someone swung some spiked object, catching his face. I try to think logically, to dismiss the image rising: a lone traveller wandering too close to the pool, Jenny Greenteeth reaching up with long green arms tipped with cruel green claws to drag him under.

It will turn out to be something innocent, and a wild creature had happened to come along afterwards and find him here, a hare perhaps, and *scratch, scratch ...*

A wild creature, or a lost dog.

No. Not that.

Jasper would *never ...*

A small sound reminds me I'm here with Libby. She's crouched at the water's edge, one hand extended over the pool. She's holding some sprigs of heather, plucking the tiny flowers and scattering them over the surface. Despite their weightlessness, they do not float. They rest for a moment then vanish without a ripple. An offering, claimed.

Libby turns to look at me but her face is as still as the pool. She doesn't smile, nor does she look away. She doesn't even seem to notice the boy sprawled at my feet.

What was I thinking? My daughter shouldn't be here, not within sight of this. I have to get her home.

I stumble towards her, falling to my knees in the mud and gathering her up in my arms. She's warm and alive. I clutch her and tell myself Zack is warm and alive too, somewhere. As if only now realising something is wrong, Libby starts to wail. She clings to me and I whisper that it's all right, dabbing at her eyes with my sleeve.

I don't know what she's seen or what she thinks she has. I don't know how much she understands. I tell her we're going home. Even though I know I should call the police right away, I don't, because my daughter comes first and I don't want her in the middle of this. Before we leave, as the sky starts to spit with rain, I scoop up the posters, keen to absent my whole family from this place as if we'd never been here.

We walk back along the road as fast as we can, me dragging her by the hand. All I want is to be inside, the door shut, locked and bolted against the world. The rain falls in earnest now, pattering against our coats like tapping fingers. To distract her, I raise my voice and make up a new story.

'Someone left a coat on the ground up there, Lib. A gift for the mermaid for when she gets cold, isn't that nice? I suppose she must be cold, out there all alone at night. Did you see?'

See? Sea … ?

A shiver passes through me. I should stop talking, stop lying to my child. This is what Ethan used to do – convincing Libby that the reality in front of her eyes was nothing but a fairy tale. Now I can't seem to help myself. I hold her hand, offering what warmth and comfort I can, and try to convince her she hasn't seen anything at all.

25

Later that afternoon, there's a police officer sitting on our sofa. He doesn't look much older than Zack. He has traces of acne along his jaw and a mop of curly hair, shaved at the sides. PC Jackson nudges his cup of tea, testing the temperature, but doesn't drink. He's puzzling over why I hadn't reported the body straight away. Why I'd left it up there on the moor a moment longer than I had to. It's raining hard now, the sky gloomy despite it being the middle of summer. I tell him I'd forgotten to take my phone. That's a lie, and I feel my cheeks flush. I'd even texted Zack on the way home – **Call me NOW** – and tried ringing him, though he still hasn't answered. Too busy off being a teenager somewhere.

I hope PC Jackson won't ask to check my messages. Is that something the police are likely to do? I'm not in a police drama on TV and I'm not a suspect, I reason. I don't know what happened to the man by the pool, what it is I'd even be suspected of. But I can't tell this officer that I wanted my daughter to believe in fairy tales for a little longer. He saw Libby when he arrived, but I sent her to her room with my iPad as a special treat. I can hear the happy little beeps and chirps as she plays a game.

I suppose the police will have descended on the pool by now, investigating the scene. I suspect that's where PC Jackson would rather be too, judging by his shifting feet and restless glances at the window. 'This lot won't help,' he says, 'with collecting evidence.'

He means the rain; the rain that began just as I left the pool – the *scene*. The rain I'd walked home in, let fall for long, precious minutes before reporting what I'd found. Of course, I hadn't known what damage it could do. I'm no expert. I hadn't been sure it would matter.

His words tell me two things: one, that it does matter. Two, that *I* don't, or he wouldn't have said it so casually. He wouldn't have given me that comfort. But of course, I'm not suspected of anything other than being foolish. Neglectful. Of failing to *see*.

'And how did you know he was dead, Mrs Kellaway?'

I stare at him. What kind of a question is that? I *knew*. 'I—' is all I can muster, then I ask my own question, one I'm half-afraid to have answered. 'Wasn't he dead?'

'I can't tell you that. It can be difficult to ascertain, until the doctor arrives.'

I battle to control my expression. He *was* dead. This is about the technicality of a doctor's pronouncement, nothing more. Still, I have to smother the hope that stirs at the idea the boy might not have been. But I *knew*. I hadn't left him there, alive, in the cold and the rain—

'And you didn't touch the body?'

I flinch. 'I don't think so.' My voice is too fast, too breathless. 'I'm not sure. I hope not. I have a son about the same age, you see, and for a second, I thought—'

PC Jackson consults something on his tablet, tapping the screen, so casual and unconcerned that I hate him for it. 'And your son is—'

'Out with friends.'

He sighs. 'I meant how old is he?'

'He's fifteen.'

He frowns, shakes his head, and I want to shake him too, shake some sense into him. I want him to confirm what I saw – that the boy was dead. But I remember he hasn't even seen the body, so how can he know? Seeing it – that's exactly what he wants and can't have, and I hate him a little bit more.

I just want him gone. If he wasn't here, I could call Zack. *Out with friends,* I'd said, the words automatic, but I don't even know where Zack is, or who these new friends are. I haven't the faintest idea what he's doing.

What does that say about me as a mother? At least I can be glad he's not involved in any of this. It's already bad enough that Libby was there.

PC Jackson keeps typing, building or adjusting the witness statement on his tablet. 'I'll ask you to read this over in a moment and sign it,' he says. 'We may need to come back and take your fingerprints, maybe a DNA sample for elimination purposes.'

He appears a little bored as he passes it over – already done with me – and I sign.

'Fine,' I tell him. 'Whatever you need.'

'Is there anything else you want to tell me?' he asks. 'Anything we should know?'

There's a mermaid who lives in the pool, I want to say, biting back the burst of laughter that rises in my throat. *She cursed a man with her last breath as they drowned her, didn't you know? Three days later they found him there.* Dead.

Instead, I stay silent and listen for Libby's game but can't hear it anymore. I remind myself this is reality. The dead boy's story is probably all too prosaic. An aneurysm, or a hidden heart condition. Some ticking bomb inside him, which meant his time had come. There was nothing I could have done. It's sad, yes, but not unnatural that he died at the pool alone, where any animal could have—

No. I don't want to think about that either.

I glance towards the kitchen and realise I'm listening for Jasper, *scratch, scratch, scratching* at the door. The gouges left by his claws are still in the other side of the wood, the paintwork ruined. I haven't had time to paint over it yet.

PC Jackson gets up, pausing by the framed photographs on the shelf. He tilts one towards him: our whole family, the Kellaways, Jasper curled up in the middle of us. 'Cute little feller,' he says.

'He's gone now,' Ethan tells him, appearing in the doorway. He's holding Libby, her legs wrapped around him, her hair hanging over her pensive face.

I open my mouth to say something, to correct PC Jackson who is making *sorry* noises, assuming Jasper's dead rather than missing. I don't know whether to protest that Jasper isn't *gone* or to wonder how Ethan appeared without anyone hearing.

'Is Mummy going to prison?' Libby pipes up before I can say a word.

'Oh, love.' I reach for her but Ethan twists away, holding her tighter.

'Mummy's fine, sweetheart,' PC Jackson promises gently. 'She's just helping us, that's all.'

'Helping?' Ethan's voice is tight, holding back a tide of emotion. He must be wondering what happened – why the police are here, why Zack isn't. What I had to do with any of it.

'Everything's all right, darling,' I force myself to say, though my voice doesn't sound like mine. 'We're all fine. I found something on the moor, that's all. I'll explain in a moment. PC Jackson's just leaving.'

Ethan nods. He doesn't look at the officer, staring into Libby's hair and whispering, 'It's okay, it's okay,' comforting her as I should have done. I wonder when she stopped playing on the iPad, what she might have heard.

I show PC Jackson out. He says they'll be in touch if they need anything and I say again that's fine, eager to be cooperative. As he leaves, I find myself wondering if he'll be the one to inform the dead boy's parents – yes, *dead* – that their son isn't coming home. I push the thought aside. This isn't our story any longer, it belongs to someone else, and I can't deny I'm relieved to let it go.

'What's going on?' Ethan speaks quietly when I return. He's rocking Libby like a baby, though she wriggles in his arms. After a moment he puts her down, and I kiss her cheek and ask if she wants to play one more game before I make hot chocolate. She nods and runs back upstairs.

Haltingly, I tell Ethan what I found on the moor. As I speak, I start to shake, brushing away the tears that come. Ethan's expression is so tightly closed I can't read it, and I wonder if he blames me – not for what happened, he could scarcely do that, but for bringing us to a place where such a thing could.

'A *boy*, you say? That must have been – that's awful, Ellie. I'm sorry you had to see that.' He reaches for me, kisses my cheek, then my lips, gently, harder, wrapping his hands into my hair. He draws me close and I hold onto him a moment before stepping away.

'I have to call Zack again,' I tell him. 'He's not replying.'

'He's not here? Where the hell is he?' Ethan's expression darkens, tension returning to his jaw. I know it's a sign of concern, but I'm dismayed. I don't know whether to be glad I never told him about Zack's last disappearance or if that would have made this easier somehow. I grab my mobile and wander upstairs, listening as it rings. Zack's room is empty and quiet and still. I need him to be here, blasting angry music or glued to his Xbox. I need him to walk through the door, safe. The phone rings and rings, then goes to voicemail. I tell myself that doesn't mean anything. Zack's always on his phone, but like any teenager, he hates actually talking on it. If he's with new friends, he won't want to look uncool by chatting to his mum.

I send a text. **Call me now, Zack. It's urgent.**

His curtains are half drawn, casting a dim shadow. A hoodie's slung over a chair, socks jut from an overstuffed drawer, a pile of rolled-up posters waits to be hung. Two bodyboards lean by the window, one blue and one red. No surfboard – he gave that away before we left. At first, I'd wondered if that was in protest, but Zack did it quietly, without show or fuss. I'd eavesdropped from the next room as he passed it on to Nuggie, who insisted on paying for it, even though Zack didn't want anything. I peeked in, saw him staring at the notes in his hand as if it were blood money, unsure how to spend it, this cash that came in exchange for his precious board.

Now he's out there somewhere, in a place he doesn't know, without the things he loved. Without even his dog. He's cast adrift and I can't reach him no matter how hard I try. This is all my fault. Because I couldn't forgive. Because I just couldn't – keep – quiet.

There's a shell on Zack's windowsill, which didn't come from Sandsend. It's a conch, a perfect whorl of pearlescent pink and white. I reach for it, already knowing the sound it will make, the whispery echo of the sea. Of course, I know that's not what I'd be hearing. Not even the blood rushing in my ears, as many people imagine. Simply air passing through the shell's hollow spaces, resonating in empty chambers, as indifferent to humans as the sea it came from – but I never do hear it. Ethan enters and sees me with my hand on the shell, a sign of my wasted time. He exhales sharply. 'It's about time Zack took some responsibility—'

I can't reply because perhaps this is the correct response, the way I should be feeling. But Ethan's next words land like a slap.

'What did you take Libby up there for? You should have stayed in, like you said. Why would you expose her to that?'

I don't know where to begin. One moment his arms were around me, the next he's looking at me like I'm a stranger. Worse. I never even told him I'd stay in; that was *his* idea. 'Sure, Ethan,' I say, 'because I knew he was up there all along, didn't I? I thought it'd be just the thing, taking Libby for a walk to see a *dead body*.'

A noise behind him makes me realise my mistake. He turns and scoops Libby into his arms, our daughter who must have been standing there all along, listening to every word. She's crying now. I glimpse her tears as he carries her away, murmuring words of comfort to a little girl who surely cannot believe in fairy tales any longer, even if her dad still gets to swoop in and be the prince.

26

A postcard.

The sea; always the sea. A woman surfaces from the blue, shaking back her golden hair. She's beautiful. Droplets adorn her skin, glistening along long, smooth curves. The water clings, reluctant to let her go. Another form bursts from the waves beside her, a man with a slender body and toned limbs. They look perfect together.

The man slicks his hair back, and I recognise the watch on his wrist. I should; I bought it for him when we moved to Sandsend. I'd chosen it so carefully, making sure it was waterproof so he could wear it anywhere he went, whatever he did. I see the engraving on the back as if it's before my eyes:

For the years to come. All my love, Ellie.

Ethan is swimming, he's wild swimming, and he has that glow about him, the one that only comes from the sea. Unless, of course, it doesn't. Unless he already had it when they entered the waves; before they even reached the beach.

Libby is at a friend's house. Zack is out in Sandsend with his mates. And I am here, watching from a distance, unseen. In Whitby – always his territory, not mine. That was never said aloud, just something I felt. Ethan must have felt it too, because he seems entirely at home as he moves into deeper water, reaching for her, drawing her after him as if teaching her to swim. When she's close, I picture her legs wrapping around him. He flashes that smile of his, wide and white. Handsome. People are watching, tourists all around, and he doesn't even care. Always so confident, my husband.

I don't understand how he can be so unafraid. People here know us. Someone might recognise him – a colleague or a pupil, a friend of Zack's, even. Does he count on not being seen? Or perhaps he has some excuse ready? Or does he simply never admit the possibility of failure, of crashing down to Earth? But then, on the surface, there's nothing to see. They're just swimming; wild swimming.

They dive into the depths. No words exchanged, only a glance, but it's as if they had the exact same thought at the exact same moment. They stay under for ten seconds, twenty – longer, a minute – before they surface, face to face. Their glow now is luminous, brighter for being reflected in both their eyes, and suddenly I know deep and sure that they've been kissing under the water. Right in front of me. In front of everyone. And no one saw a thing.

I've been trying so hard to convince myself it wasn't true. Even after I'd seen them wandering through Whitby arm in arm, I'd persuaded myself there was no proof. He might have bumped into her accidentally. He was just being kind to her, offering his arm because it hurt her to walk, because he *is* kind. She'd even bought my child that doll as a thank you.

Libby came home beaming, chattering about how it was good but not as good as a real live mermaid. Ethan had been smiling too, relaxed after their great father-daughter day in town. He didn't mention *her* – because she didn't matter, or something else? He asked after my friend and I couldn't even explain where I'd been. Ethan barely noticed. He kissed me, gazed into my eyes. His were the clearest blue, never blinking, never breaking away from mine. And all the while he looked at me, I told myself stories: that I couldn't be sure, that I needn't feel the pain of it, the fucking *betrayal*, not yet. That I didn't have to break my family apart, wipe the smiles from Libby's face, destroy Zack's faith in his dad. I told myself I didn't *know*.

Now I do.

Ethan left this morning with his sports bag, packed with towels and warm clothes and a flask, all ready for the sea. But he hadn't gone to the beach. Not at first. He went to a side street and knocked at a nondescript door in a row of identical ones, and when the door had opened, she was there. She wrapped her arms around him as he stepped inside and less than a minute later – *fast work, Ethan* – the curtains upstairs were yanked closed. Two shadows moved together.

I know because I followed him. I watched them from my vantage point further down the street. I didn't even try to hide. If he'd turned his head when he knocked at the door, he would have seen me. But he never did look back.

I walked on legs that didn't feel like mine. I stood in front of her house, staring up at what must be her bedroom. No one looked out of the window or saw me there, watching.

At least today he'll only have to tell me half-truths instead of full-on lies. Today, he's had swimming *and* sex. Lucky old Ethan. I suppose he'll have a double glow about him when he comes home, tasting as he should, of salt. He'll feel properly *alive*.

They float in the sea now and he smiles at her. She looks so happy and so does he. They don't even glance in my direction.

I'd left her doorway before they emerged, but I'm standing here now, right on the beach among the tourists. Easy to spot, if they ever looked away from each other. I'm the only one not doing anything: strolling up and down the sands, or playing with a dog, or building a sandcastle with a child. They might not look but I do. I see everything.

I remember his words. *You'd love wild swimming if you got into it, Ellie. It's just you and the elements. You and the water, in the moment, and nothing else. It makes you feel what it's like to be completely alone.*

That's what Ethan told me. And all the while, he's been fucking someone else: the oldest story of them all.

27

Despite the drizzle in the air and the lateness of the afternoon, the laybys remain full. No matter the weather, hikers are still trekking up the field, eager for the view from the Roaches even through the gathering mist. An older couple, the man with a floppy hat and walking stick, the woman with a bright red fleece, emerge from the gate and head for their car. I manoeuvre mine around in a five point turn, blocking the road until I can take the space they've left behind.

I took the keys and slipped out right after the policeman's visit; after my row with Ethan. My last view of my husband was a sliver of his face in the window, half obscured by clouds reflected in the glass. I couldn't make out his expression. I hadn't cared. I'd guess he was angry, but so am I. And I can go for a sodding walk if I want to.

Except that's not what I'm doing. I'm searching for my son.

It's madness to think I can just pick a place and stumble across him, more like something my grandmother would have done, but there's a logic to my plan. This is the one place where I glimpsed the old Zack. The one with glimmers of excitement in his eyes when he spotted that group on the rock. *Mind if I head off?* He hasn't told me anything about these new climber friends – hasn't even seemed interested, beyond the odd monotone grunt – but he was always that way with surfing too: full of laughter and life with his friends, eloquent in his movement on the waves, yet inarticulate and muted when he tried to express his feelings to me. Now I curse myself for not making him tell me more. But this is where he met them, and this is where the rocks are. There isn't much else to climb around here.

I check my phone. One missed call from Ethan. He hasn't left a message and there's still nothing from Zack. I picture my son's empty room as I head into the field, that pink shell whispering to itself on the sill, strange voices coming from the sea.

There's a family by the Bawdstone. A little girl, not much older than Libby, is stooping to peer beneath, surely too young to need to scrape the Devil off her back. Children are innocent; everyone knows that.

I don't head for the top of the crag because I can look for climbers just as easily from the bottom, so I cut diagonally across the field instead. When I reach the woodland that grows around the base of the escarpment, it feels like I'm the only person in the world. There's no lovely birdsong, not today; no hikers' voices or brightly coloured waterproofs dotted about. It's a little eerie to find everything so still. It wouldn't altogether surprise me if, instead of silence, I heard strange, melodic singing drifting out of the past – a maiden mourning the life she lost as she was carried away.

I pass a tall boulder with footholds cut into it, a practice climb that at least makes me feel like I'm on the right track. Soon after, I see Rock Hall. As expected from a structure built around the caves that were once Bess Bowyer's, it hugs the rock – no bigger than a cottage, yet resembling a miniature castle. The roof is crenelated, the windows mere slits. It appears tinier still next to the crag, dwarfed by the trees growing around it. Little wonder I hadn't spotted it before. I might have been looking straight at it and never noticed a thing.

There's no road leading to the door, barely even a path, so I pick my way through the woods. A little gate marked PRIVATE bars the way. After a pause, I push it open. The path leads around the building, neat but narrow, as if for a doll's house. I knock loudly on the front door, three times.

There's no sound of movement from within. I suppose the climbers are out on the crag, but the place feels empty and abandoned, as if everyone has long since bundled all their kit down to the road and returned to their lives. I peer into the woods, searching for movement. A vision of Zack, disappointed, trying to scale the crag alone with no ropes or helmet, his fingers slipping from their grip and skittering down the rockface flashes through my mind. I try to shake it away. *He wouldn't.* They must be here somewhere.

The trees loom over me, some kind of conifer, their limbs twisted and contorted by lives spent searching for light. The ground is a tangle of fallen branches, similarly twisted and pained. I step over and around them, scanning the crags for specks of coloured jackets. No helmets, no ropes – no sign of civilisation at all. There's nothing but rock, nothing but silence. I could almost be back in Bess Bowyer's day. There's even a dark fissure at the base of the crag that reminds me of her famous tunnel, where she's supposed to have harboured smugglers and other criminals – perhaps the same who later carried off her daughter.

Before I know it, I'm clambering over fallen branches and toppled rocks, heading towards the cave and leaving the path behind. My mind tries to assure me that there's sense in my actions. Lads who like climbing might like caving too. That's why there's no trace of them on the crag; they've burrowed into the earth. I glance up at the Roaches, huge, indifferent. The thought of disappearing into their darkness makes me shiver, but I can't turn back now because I feel *something*.

A vibration. An aura. An energy. Gran's face flickers through my thoughts, her lips moving as she tries to tell me some new story, her blue eyes wide. I shake my head, unable to hear a word; but of course I can't. I don't believe in vibrations or energies. It's been years since I imagined feeling any such thing. Just the echo of something pagan inside my mind, as it always was – although I'm still not going back. I'm determined to see this through.

Because I can sense that Zack's in trouble. I don't know if I'm being neurotic or if it's some stronger, more visceral kind of magic, a mother's love perhaps, and I don't care. I need to find him. I have to *see*. I look up at the cliff above and around me, and for a moment, the whole massy edifice seems to vibrate with some sympathetic resonance, urging me on.

The cave mouth offers no secrets. The opening is just the right height to let me in, but it appears to end quickly in solid rock. Still, something makes me reach out, and from somewhere inside the stone, cool air caresses my fingers. I squeeze into the gap and realise it doesn't end there after all. It twists around; there's another opening, concealed from view.

I picture myself walking inside and the gap squeezing closed behind me. Vanishing, just like that. A foolish, pointless end. I think of the way these rocks must have folded and shifted and tumbled over centuries. They could do so again. All that would remain is a car in a layby. Zack's probably already back home. They'll be sitting down to eat, wondering where I am.

Nobody knows where I am.

A line from one of my grandmother's fairy tales comes back to me, as if she's whispering it to me now.

Be bold, be bold – but not too bold,
Lest that your heart's blood should run cold.

I shake my head. *Foolish*. I haven't come all the way here to turn back without even looking.

I take out my phone and touch the screen to summon its torch. It doesn't help much yet; I hold it in my left hand while my right feels the way, skittering over jagged edges. I inch deeper into the nothingness inside the crag, feeling my way through darkness, the chill air growing cooler still. I sense the space opening around me. It smells of sour, ancient stone.

'Hello?' My voice is small against the dark. I wait for an echo, even a reply, but none comes. The torch-light reveals a patch of scuffed earth at my feet. I'm strangely reluctant to shine it around. I'm no longer certain I want to *see*.

'Zack?'

My voice is an intrusion, quickly swallowed up. The sound of my breath is like air resonating in the chambers of a shell. This place feels just as empty, and every bit as indifferent. The air wraps about my arms, like the cool beads of a wooden bracelet.

Be bold ...

I raise my phone towards the wall at my right shoulder, sweeping it in an arc. There are cracks and fissures, odd shapes revealing and concealing themselves, and plenty of shadows, but I don't think there's a tunnel. Then there's *something* – there and gone. It resembled a figure, but not quite. It almost appeared to be floating, as if submerged in water, and never making a sound, no voice at all ...

I direct the beam back.

The light finds a shape that is rippled like the rock, that merges with the rock – and yet isn't rock. It is paler than that, drained of colour, like – *like a dead boy's face*. A gasp slips from my throat. My hand starts to shake. If my son were here, he would have said something when he heard my voice. He wouldn't just be crouching there, clinging to the rock. I'm imagining a human form where none can be, where there is nothing but gritstone and time. I blink, expecting it to vanish – but the shape doesn't disappear. Instead, it flinches. The movement is more animal than human.

'Zack?' His name slips from me again even though this cannot be my son, won't be my son. I'm not sure it's even a person at all.

The shape unfurls and turns towards me. Torchlight reveals skin, dark eyes, the flick of hair. It moves, raises a hand to shield its face from the light.

'Who are you?' My voice sounds hollow, even though I'm trying not to betray how scared I am. As if only now finding the cave's echo, it returns to me from the walls. *Whooo ... whooo.* It sounds like mockery, like something from one of my grandmother's tales, and I'm glad when silence takes its place.

Then I hear a voice. 'Mum?'

'Oh my God, yes, it's me.' I shuffle forwards, feeling my way over loose stones and grit. 'Are you hurt? What are you doing here?' *How are you here* is what I want to ask – it isn't possible, but there's no time to dwell on it further because my son needs me.

He doesn't answer; I'm not sure he can. I lower my phone's dazzle and his face retreats into the dark. I see now why he appeared to be floating. His chest is bare, his shirt rolled down to his waist like a wetsuit. His skin is very pale in the glare of my torch, but his jeans blend into the shadows.

'What is this place?' He scarcely sounds like my son.

'Where do you think you are, Zack?'

I hear him swallow. 'I remember going to the pool.'

I reach out, hesitating before brushing the dark curls from his forehead. His skin is clammy, his hair damp. I find myself scanning for a tunnel once more. There's nothing obvious, but that doesn't mean there isn't one. I picture Zack stumbling through the dark, pulling himself through squeezed, narrow spaces – but why would he? And the tunnel here is supposed to pass under the crag. It would need to be almost vertical to lead to the top of the escarpment and Doxey Pool.

'Zack, you're at the Roaches. Don't you remember how you got here? What happened?'

'Is Jasper here?' He blinks, still confused. 'I need to find him. I think it will be all right if I bring him home.'

'No, son. He isn't, not yet. We *will* find him, but for now we need to get back. Your dad and Lib will be worried.'

'Lib.' He frowns, as if the name means something to him, something I can't guess at. 'Libby. She's safe. She'll be fine, Mum. Won't she?'

The question is like cool, clammy fingers, a mermaid's fingers, running over my skin. A sound echoes in my ears: *Lib ... Lib.* 'Of course she will, Zack. She *is* fine.' That voice I thought I heard wasn't real, just as the stories aren't real, the woman standing outside my house wasn't real ...

And Zack?

It half feels as if Zack isn't real either. I offer out a hand to take his arm. His skin feels cold, like the stone surrounding us. 'Come on, love. We're going home.

You're shivering.' I edge backwards, pulling him with me. It would be easier to turn around, but somehow I don't want to lose sight of him. It feels like he'll vanish if I do. With my free hand, I angle the beam of light down at his feet. My son isn't wearing any shoes. His feet are skinny and pale and bony, smeared with black, peaty mud.

I don't let him see my shudder. I guide him out, back into the daylight. Now I'll have to get him through the wood, across fallen, twisted branches, and over the long field covered in tussocky grass and sheep scat. I stoop to pull the shoes from my own feet and realise he'd never fit into them. I could go alone, fetch some for him, but I won't. I'm not leaving him here. I still feel like he'll melt into the air the moment I stop looking at him.

'Pull your shirt on, Zack.' I help him to roll it up and over his body and find his mobile jutting from the back pocket of his jeans. I pull it free and see the trail of missed message notifications decorating the screen. I don't say anything, just hand it back to him. We take it slow, Zack holding onto the sleeve of my shirt as if he were a little boy afraid to get lost. His movement is unsure. Awkward. It seems a cruel contrast to the old Zack, balanced so gracefully on his surfboard. He walks as if he might break, but it's still *him*. He's my son. My chest aches at seeing him like this. All I want is to get him home. I will wrap him in blankets, feed him hot soup, and bring the life back into his eyes. Libby will leap on him and he'll call her *Lippy* and tease her into overexcited shrieks, and I won't mind a bit. None of us will, because we'll be together again. A family.

There's an oddly distant expression in Zack's eyes. It's the same look he wore when he snuck out of the house at night, when he'd heard the call of that magically dreaming place and its dreams had got into him; as if he'd slipped under some spell and didn't quite know where he was anymore, or who, or how he'd come to be there. The same look that shows he has no memory of what it was he's seen – or what he might have done to end up like this.

28

Once in the car, Zack begins shivering in earnest. He doesn't answer when I ask if he's cold, but I grab a picnic blanket off the back seat and wrap the rough plaid around his shoulders, ignoring the curious glances of a couple just getting out of their car in waterproofs and hiking boots.

I steal sidelong glances at my son as I drive, taking in his hair, his eyes, his lips, as if to reassure myself it's really him. I don't like it when I have to focus ahead and he becomes a blur in the corner of my eye. It's feels too much as if he's been snatched away or turned into something unrecognisable, glimpsed in the darkness of a cave.

Gravel grinds under the tyres as we pull into the drive. I go round and open the car door for Zack, practically dragging him towards the house. He stops halfway over the threshold, like a vampire in a horror movie who needs an invitation to enter, so I grab his sleeve and help him over the step. I don't care if his feet are grimy. He's getting straight into a hot shower, even if I have to shove him in there.

Ethan appears in the hallway, brows drawn, lips tight, eyes full of storm-clouds. He barely looks at me, just takes in the sight of his son. I know he'll be angry and have questions. Why was Zack so late? Where the hell was he, and why didn't he call? What *happened*? They're the same questions I want answered, but now isn't the time.

Then Libby flies out of the lounge, grabs her brother around his legs, and sobs into them. 'I'm sorry, I'm sorry.'

Zack stands there silently. Places one dirty hand on her honey-coloured curls.

'Zack's fine, sweetie,' I say. 'Just a little bit tired, love. And he's lost his shoes. Haven't you, Zack?' I speak as if this is all perfectly normal. I wonder where his trainers are, when he lost them – whether they're half-buried in some peat bog between here and the Roaches, or up on the crag. *I was at the pool.* There was black peat around Doxey Pool too, like at Blake Mere. But why wouldn't he pull his shoes back out of the mud, if they had been sucked from his feet? Unless he took them off on purpose. Had Zack been *in* the pool – not the same dark water Jasper drank, perhaps, but so very like it ...

'We'll talk later.' Ethan at least seems to realise Zack needs time. He reaches for Zack's shoulder – but stops short of touching him, as I had earlier. He spoke softly, though, and guilt thrums through me that I hadn't called him the moment I found Zack. He's been worrying longer than he needed to. I open my mouth to apologise, but before I can speak, he sweeps Libby into his arms and vanishes into the lounge, closing the door behind them. My apology dissolves on my tongue.

Thanks, Ethan.

I take Zack's shoulders and guide him towards the stairs. I help him up, open the bathroom door, start the shower running and feel the water begin to warm. 'I'll let you clean up, love. I'll put some fresh clothes for you by the door. Okay?'

After a long pause, he nods, finally seeming to understand where he is and what he needs to do. I leave him, grabbing clean things for him to wear as I said, but instead of going back downstairs, I just slump onto a step, all my energy gone. I hear Zack moving around in the bathroom. I wonder if he still has that empty expression in his eyes.

The events of the last hour replay in my mind: finding Zack crouched against the cold rock in the dark. Zack speaking to me, but all wrong, bewildered, lost. How had he got there? It's miles on foot to the Roaches. And why was he so confused?

I find myself thinking the words spoken to my daughter by the man we'd met in Leek.

Some say all three of the mermaid pools in the Peaks are connected. They say they're bottomless, with watery tunnels running between them and all the way to the sea ...

I shake my head. That's impossible. The pools aren't really magical; they aren't bottomless. They're connected by stories, and nothing more.

But Zack was gone for hours. He's been fascinated by Blake Mere Pool, as is Libby; as, I suppose, am I.

Was that the pool he meant? If it was, then Zack would have been the one to find the body, not me.

Could that be the real reason he's shut down, the cause of the haunted expression in his eyes? He'd seemed half bewildered the first time he went there alone, and there had been no body then, only the pool. Perhaps, this time, he found something worse waiting for him on the moor. And on top of everything else, he lost it for a while. Maybe he wandered in a daze, walking straight through bog and heather, losing his trainers along the way, not stopping until, miles later, he reached the crag – and then wandered further, around it, or under it—

I get up and walk down the rest of the stairs, wanting everything to be normal again. Wanting Zack to turn back into something resembling normal, too. As soon as I walk into the lounge, I know it won't be that easy. Ethan is perched on the edge of a chair, facing the door, clearly waiting for me.

'Do you want to tell me what on Earth's going on, Ellie?' he asks. His tone is mild, I imagine for Libby's sake. She's occupied with some toy on the sofa, her back turned to us both.

I'm already annoyed. It's as if I'm supposed to have all the answers to all the questions. I just dragged our son out of a cave. I don't even know what led me there or how I found him, not really, apart from a feeling that something was off. And I can't explain, not with Ethan looking at me like this. So I give him an answer he might begin to accept. 'Zack got lost at the Roaches, that's all. He must have been trying to find his climbing friends. Trying to find Jasper, too – he's been working really hard at it, more than any of us. If you could try to be nice to him, instead of—'

'Instead of?' Ethan's eyes are wide, the colour of clear water; almost transparent.

'You mustn't be hard on him, Eth. You keep pushing him, you know you do—'

'*Pushing* him?' Ethan draws in a breath. 'All I want – all I ever want – is what's best for Zack. What's best for us all. This hasn't been the greatest time, Ellie, you know? What with finding the police in my house. Moving here in the first place. With the dog going missing.'

Libby stirs at that, or perhaps at Ethan's tone, then bends lower over her toy, murmuring words I can't quite hear. That doesn't mean she isn't listening. Ethan's face is as still and unforgiving as a carving, and I can't control my anger any longer.

'Just try being a little kinder, can't you? You shouldn't expect so—'

'Of course I expect so much, Ellie. What's so very wrong with that, do you think? I always support our kids, help them to do well, achieve whatever they want to do. Whereas *you*—'

'Me?'

He sighs and holds out both his hands, lets them fall. 'Look, okay, I'm sorry. If that's what you need to hear, I am. I didn't mean anything. I know I've done things, Ellie, but we both said we'd move on, and somehow I get the feeling you haven't.'

I stand there frozen, not knowing what to say.

'We moved here, didn't we?' he goes on. 'You chose where and the house and the school and I agreed to all of it, for *you*. You got your wish, didn't you?'

'My *wish*?' I choke on the word, staring at him. What I want to say is, *I didn't wish for you to fuck someone else.* But Libby is right there, and besides, he's right. I had wanted to leave. And that part of it wasn't down to Ethan – was never anything to do with Ethan. This landlocked place is what I wanted, even when I pretended I didn't. I'd wanted it even when I tried to persuade myself I was happy with the life we'd built together. So I did get my wish, in a way, though Ethan's indiscretion was the price of it.

You will have your wish, for it will bring you sorrow ...

And it has, hasn't it? It's brought sorrow to us all.

I remember how the four of us were in Sandsend: a picture-postcard family on a picture-postcard beach, a happy family. But even then, the cracks were always there. Now dark water is seeping into them, down into the bedrock, finding every fault and fissure, forcing those cracks wider. It's inside me too, in the bitterness that flows through my veins, tainting my blood with salt.

'Jasper was back,' Libby announces, and I stare at her. She doesn't look up. She's teasing out the braids in Barbie's hair with a little comb. She has dressed her in aquamarine.

When Ethan speaks, he sounds very tired. 'You just thought it was him for a minute, didn't you, sweetie?'

I shift my gaze to him, and he waves my hope away. 'No one's seen the dog. We didn't see anything. There was just this scratching at the door, and Libby got all excited. I opened it but there was nothing there. It must have been a twig or something, that's all.'

Ethan comes over and places his hands on my shoulders, leaning in, but when his forehead is almost touching mine he steps back and walks away. He leaves the room and is gone, and there is only cool air where he had stood. I realise there are tears in my eyes and wipe at them with my sleeve before Libby sees. She still hasn't moved from her place on the sofa, intent on her task. Her hair is loose, hanging in her face, so I reach out and tuck it back. Her lips are pursed with concentration, and she still doesn't look at me, doesn't even twitch. She lifts her doll for me to see. It's not the one I gave her. This one has a body that ends, not in two shapely legs, but a curving fishtail.

Libby tilts her head, resting her face against the doll's. The toy is as clean and shiny as it was before I shoved it into the rubbish bin outside our cottage in Sandsend, down, deeper, before leaving it a hundred and forty miles behind us. It's as clean and shiny as if *Daddy's mermaid* had just this moment put it into her hands.

'I asked for my dolly back,' she says, and smiles.

There is silence. I find myself listening for the sound of the sea, that constant presence, but of course there is nothing.

'You *saw* her?' I can't bring myself to say who I mean, even to Libby who doesn't understand, who never really did.

She nods. 'The sea witch.'

My skin prickles. I reach out and stroke Libby's golden hair, as if to assure myself she's really here. I wish I could take the mermaid toy from her and tear it into pieces, but I can't. What kind of mother steals their child's favourite doll?

'In the museum. And here, on our wall.' Libby flashes her teeth in a sudden grin. I remember that desiccated thing in its glass case in Buxton, like an old leather bag. Libby whispering to it, telling it her dreams, her wishes.

Now her doll has reappeared, the one she has loved since the moment it was given to her. I haven't the first idea how it came to be here, and I can't demand the explanation I need from Libby. She's only seeing something wonderful. The granting of a wish. I reach out and brush the soft skin of her arm with my fingertip.

Then something else occurs to me.

'What did you offer to the witch, Libby?'

Because that's the thing with sea witches, isn't it? They always want something in return, even in a child's imagination. Doing favours isn't in their nature. No: they make deals, and with a sea witch, there's always a catch.

Libby's face crumples. She turns away from me, just like she does every time she knows she's been naughty. 'I'm sorry,' she mutters again, and I think of the way she threw her arms around Zack's legs. The way she cried when he came home.

'Your brother,' I say. 'You said she could have Zack, didn't you?'

Her head moves against my arm as she nods.

'Well, that wasn't very nice, Libby. But I dare say it doesn't really count. He came home after all, didn't he?'

I feel her nod again. Then she adds, 'I said he's hers now.'

'Well, of course he's not,' I smile.

Words burst from her. 'He is, Mummy, because I asked for my lost things to come back again, and I got my mermaid dolly, and Jasper was scratching at the door, he wanted to come in, only that must be when you got Zack cause he went away again.'

I let out a soft laugh and shush her, as Libby sobs into her mermaid's hair, inconsolable. And I think of Zack – the way he'd felt so strange, not there, not *mine*, when I found him. As if I was taking him from something. I can't help picturing Jasper too, before he ran away from us; his head lowered, eyes glaring, as if he no longer recognised us as his family at all.

I shake my head, trying to remind myself that even though things are strange, that doesn't mean they can't be explained away. That it won't all feel better after a good night's sleep.

Libby's growing tired already. She snuggles against me and I kiss the top of her head, telling her I'll make her favourite tea, chicken nuggets and chips. She brightens. She's forgotten her doll. It's slipped to the floor, gone, and soon Zack will come downstairs, looking the same as he always has. My children will be fine, knowing they belong to this family, to nothing and no one else, and Ethan will remember that this is about *all of us, together*. We will try to forget that vows have been broken; that our dog is gone; that Libby tried to exchange her brother for a doll; that anything in our home was ever missing at all.

29

A postcard.
This one isn't such a pretty picture. The aftermath never is.

I'm telling Ethan it's over. There's no changing it. I'm angry and humiliated. My heart hasn't been so much broken as wrenched from my body and trampled to a bloody pulp. I tell him we're going to separate, that I'll have custody of the kids. I picture driving away, just the three of us in the car, leaving Ethan and Sandsend behind and never looking back. I won't be a Kellaway any longer. I suppose I'll have a different name from my own children, but we'll go somewhere green, I promise myself that. Somewhere we can't even see the sea, where it's nothing but a memory.

The kids are in Libby's room. I made sure Zack put some music on and I can hear it now, the volume louder than our hissed words. They'll have to find out soon enough. I know they'll be crushed. They'll miss their dad every day, will cry and rage or worse, be silent about it all. I think of Zack, torn away from his surfing, his friends, his school. Libby leaving behind her precious mermaids.

Fresh anger rises inside me. Ethan should have thought of that. I should never even have come to Sandsend in the first place, never given him his way, never been with him at all. Now it's plain: I can't be here any longer. I won't spend my days in this house, listening to the sea whispering in my ear every damned moment.

I poke the hurt inside me, which simmers still, despite the weariness dampening it down. I picture Libby in a new bedroom, clutching that horrid doll to comfort her as she cries. She's probably playing with it now – she's decided it's her favourite, her very best possession in the world.

I've been such a fool. I'd tried to convince myself I was wrong, seeing something when nothing was there, denying the knowledge I could sense just beneath the surface. I've skirted and dodged it, built flood barriers against it, but still it's here in front of me, finding me after all. I was the one who'd been viewing life through a hag stone, seeing what was lovely and magical rather than reality, and it didn't protect me. It only ever protected Ethan.

Now my husband says, *I just couldn't help myself.* He says he felt adrift, that it made him vulnerable, and she was *right there.* He claims, *I didn't know what I was thinking.*

He was powerless, afloat, taken by the tide. Seduced. Bewitched. He must love Libby's idea of magic. Was his mermaid so incredibly alluring, so siren-like, that she cast him under a spell? Why, then none of this is Ethan's fault. Her perfection means he can be perfect too.

Or *remain* perfect. He always wanted to be the best, didn't he? To be the best and *have* the best – whatever or whomever that was at the time.

Adulterer. Such an ugly sound. Not like *adulteress*: that's a dangerous, romantic, scarlet word. An adulteress does not do the dishes or pick up Lego or wipe snot from children's faces. No, mermaids are too busy being tempting, aren't they? I wonder what Libby would think if she knew the real story, if she knew mermaids could lure men to their doom. But that's not a tale fit for a child's ears, is it?

And Ethan did this. There was no enchantment in it. He schemed and lied and cheated. He threw all of us aside for her – this perfect woman. Once upon a time, he thought *we* were perfect; that was the story he told me ever since we met. Now that seems like the worst of lies. I gave up everything for my prince, and what did he do? He fucked up our happily-ever-after, threw it into the sea. Is it any wonder fairy tales stop at the wedding?

Now it's over, THE END, and Ethan looks at me helplessly as if he's hoping I'll relent. I wonder if he thinks I'm supposed to feel sorry for him. Does he imagine I can't blame him, now that I've seen her slender body, her golden hair, her pretty face, as if those things gave her the right to have him? Ethan, who has a lovely family, a great home, a life to be envied. Ethan, who never had a fault in his life, who can't admit them in himself, who chose never to see them in me.

That's the moment when Libby, breaking her promise to stay upstairs, *Mummy and Daddy need to have a little chat*, pushes open the door. She stands there, the mermaid doll tucked under her chin. Her hair has pulled loose from its scrunchy, so she looks nothing less than a mermaid herself: golden and lovely. Only her reddened eyes betray her all-too-real emotions.

Zack hovers behind her, his expression tight. They can see we've been rowing plainly enough, if not by the looks on our faces, by the tension in the air. He puts his hand on Libby's shoulder, but she isn't comforted. Little girls aren't fooled; they know heartbreak when they see it.

'Hey,' Ethan says softly. 'Everything's okay. We're just having a little disagreement. Aren't we, Ellie?' He leans across and kisses my cheek. I can't pull away. The kids' gazes, fixed on me, willing Ethan's words to be true, mean that I can't.

I stare at him, into him. I'm the cusp of a wave about to break. I'm the highest point of the tide. I am foam rushing against the cliffs, making them crumble. The power of the sea wells somewhere deep inside me, though I don't know if it's going to carry me onward or pull me under and see me drown. Words are welling at my lips, all the words I want to say, but for now, I swallow them down. Sometimes, not having a voice is the most powerful thing of all. On the surface: calm, still waters. Underneath: a whole fucking sea of rage.

Ethan holds there for a moment, his hands gently cupping my face, his forehead resting against mine. Then he murmurs, 'You know, I'd do anything for you. The three of you – you're the most important things in the world to me. I'd do anything, go anywhere, as long as it means my family is together. To make you happy.'

Water glistens in his eyes. He's crying. For the first time, he's crying in front of the kids, in front of me.

He says, 'I love you.'

Those three little words, full of magic. Words to convince me this is not THE END, but a new beginning.

And suddenly I know what is going to happen. I know what we must do, all of us, together. Where we will go. I know exactly how our happy ending is supposed to turn out.

This time, when Ethan kisses me, I kiss him back.

30

I sit in the lounge while Ethan puts Libby to bed. I'm surprised she didn't protest more, but all is quiet. I assume he's telling her a story. Zack is already asleep, early for him, but he'd looked even more tired than his sister. The reason I expected protest sits on my lap. The mermaid doll's tail is curled against my body, her hair brushing my throat. There's something grotesque about her. What if the doll were brought to life? Would Libby still want to touch her, run her fingers over cool, hard scales and a soggy, tangled mass of hair? To see her rows of shiny sharp teeth?

Or perhaps Ethan's right. I'm the one who just – can't – let it go.

I know I've done things, Ellie, but we both said we'd move on, and somehow I get the feeling you haven't ...

I thought I had, or at least I've been trying to. I imagined I'd left mermaids far behind me, but they are in front of me and everywhere I turn. *Here be mermaids*, even in this green landlocked place, so far from the sea. And mermaids have curses as well as blessings to give. They can save a man from drowning or drag him down. They can give him immortality or steal his life away, calm the waters or raise a storm. They are everything a woman can be and all that she should not. They are young and lovely. They're hideous creatures with scales for skin and a tail where their legs should be. See her teeth; feel her claws. Take the punishment she offers – especially you single men, or those who merely behave as if they are.

Lust. Caprice. Malice.

She's practically human.

When Ethan returns he doesn't look at the doll, doesn't show any surprise to see it at all. There's a brief glance and his eyes slide away, perhaps to deliberately mask his expression.

'She gets worse,' he says. 'She wanted two stories. I'm afraid I gave in. Tomorrow, it'll be three.'

I don't reply to that. I run my hand through my hair, cut short so long ago, and ask, 'Did you bring this doll here, Ethan?'

This time, he's forced to see it. 'Where'd you find that old thing?'

It's hardly old, but I don't point that out. 'I didn't find it,' I tell him. 'I threw it away. I put it in the bin in Sandsend and buried it in rubbish.'

His forehead creases. I'm waiting for him to tell me I'm a bad mother for doing such a thing, but he doesn't.

He knows where Libby got the doll as well as I do. He was there. 'Well, you can't have, love,' he says. 'You must have packed it in a box and forgotten about it.'

'I could hardly do that, could I?'

Now he looks away.

'So can you tell me how it got here, Ethan?'

I want him to tell me the truth. I want him to admit he must have seen *her* again, that he's seen her since we moved here. I know Libby's story – that she made a deal with the sea witch and got her wish, hey presto. Perhaps that's the real purpose of magic: not to make dreams come true, but to simplify everything. But we're no longer children and those are a child's dreams. If anyone knows the truth, it's Ethan. If she followed us here, leaving the sea behind her just as we did, he must have seen her too. Maybe he's even met up with her on purpose, coming home late, claiming to have been searching so hard for Jasper.

There's nothing there, he had told me when I'd seen something outside our window. He'd put his hand to my forehead as if I were imagining things, as if I were going mad.

'Does it even matter?' he says. 'Maybe Lib had another one of those dolls, love. You know how crammed her toybox is. Or maybe she found it herself, have you thought of that? Or yes, maybe I found it and forgot all about it. You know what? I probably did. I was kind of busy, you know?' He grimaces. 'There's been a lot going on, moving here, where you wanted us to be, so it slipped my mind, okay? Is that what I need to say? I don't know what you want from me. Maybe let this go, Ellie. What does it even matter where that thing came from?'

I stare at him. What does it *matter*? 'It matters, Ethan, because she's *here*. I think she brought this to Libby. Either she bought another doll just like the first one, or she went through our bins to try and trace where we'd gone and she found it. And you know what, Ethan? I think she took Jasper too.'

He sucks in his breath, squeezes his eyes closed for a moment, as if gathering himself. 'Ellie, that's insane. Why on Earth would she even want to do that? Do you really think I could go on seeing her, *and our dog*, and keep that from you and the kids? Do you think I'd *want* to – that I've moved all this way for nothing?'

I press my lips tight together.

'That woman was a mistake, all right?' he goes on. 'A fucking *curse*. And now what? You think I'd have let Zack go wandering all over the moors searching for the dog, if I'd known where he was – that I'd have watched Libby cry?'

He waits for me to answer, but I'm thinking of something else Ethan had said to me: that if anyone was there, Jasper would be barking. But Jasper only barked at strangers. Ethan had let our daughter see her. It's not such a stretch to think she'd also got to know our dog, perhaps even well enough to lure him away. 'I've seen her, Ethan. More than once. You promised me it was over, but it isn't, is it? She followed you. She's been standing outside our house. Watching us. Watching the kids.'

'What the hell, Ellie? That's madness. It all is. Jesus: coming here – *everything*. All of this.'

'Every time you went off in the car, were you even looking for Jasper? Or were you—' *Fucking her*, I want to say, but can't. When I close my eyes, all I see is her hair, golden and lovely, blowing and twisting in the breeze, wrapping itself about Ethan's arm.

'*What?*' he knows exactly what I mean; his voice is half stricken, half furious. 'Ellie, of course I haven't.' His eyes are innocent, wide as a child's, so blue, like sunlit water. Or are they only the surface of a pool, concealing who knows what secrets?

My chest tightens. I want to say she wants everything he has, everything we are. That she hasn't stopped and likely won't. My whole family: that's what she came here for. *Ethan's* family. She wants to steal them away, one by one. The dog was first, an easy place to start. Libby's already half enchanted with her. And Zack – will she try to confuse him too, tell him stories about herself and Ethan, about me … ?

'Ellie, for God's sake. If I'd seen her and she had the dog, do you not think I'd have brought him home to us, if I could?'

Again, *the dog* – as if Jasper were luggage, not a part of our family. I feel suddenly very tired, my limbs weighed down like lead. Or perhaps I can't answer because there's no answer to give. The doll is here and I'm freaking out but perhaps the answer is as simple as Ethan says. Surely it must be, because Ethan *would* have brought Jasper back if he knew where he was. Even if she was here and had taken him, Ethan would have done that much. It's not as if he'd have had to tell me where he got the dog; he could have said he'd found him on the moor. Where would she even keep him out here? In her car? A hotel? My arguments topple in front of me, leaving nothing but a dull ache in my chest.

Perhaps Libby really did have another mermaid doll. Maybe Ethan found it in the bin, and thought it a mistake so threw it in the washer when we got here. It's only in my head that everything comes down to *her*.

'Ellie, this is ridiculous and you know it. There's no wonder you can't answer me. There *is* no answer. Sienna is—'

Sienna.

Everything inside me goes still.

I had once asked my husband to name the new woman in his swimming group, the *brave* one, the *beautiful* one, and he had pretended not to know. *It doesn't matter*, he'd said. Later it did matter, but by then I didn't want to know. All those times we'd yelled and stormed over her, all the times I'd cried because of her, and I never had allowed him to say it. I'd cut him off if he seemed likely to blurt it out. I didn't want her name on his lips. I didn't want him to *taste* it again. So I'd insisted I didn't want to know one more damned thing about her, and she had remained nameless – just as a mermaid should.

I want to laugh in his face at the irony. *Sienna.* Ethan's mermaid, whose every step on land pains her, who has learned instead to love the sea, was named for nothing but the earth.

I can't look at him any longer. When I turn away, I see something else that doesn't belong here: the cold gleam of water, reflecting clouds that don't move, that seem never to have moved. I blink and it comes into focus. Blake Mere Pool is on the television.

I kneel in front of it and turn up the volume. The image gives way to a live shot, and the pool is changed after all. When the camera pans back, it reveals police tape cordoning off the side nearest the road. The water flickers unnaturally – not magic, only the reflected blue lights of police vehicles pulsing over the bank, rain rippling and stirring the surface.

'The man has been identified as a resident of nearby Thorncliffe, a Mr Andrew Gregory, thirty-four years old,' a newsreader says. 'The cause of death is as yet unknown, though it seems likely he had fallen from the roadside onto rocky ground. Facial injuries suggest there may also have been some accident or attack involving a large dog. Anyone with any information is urged to contact ... '

Then the pool is gone, as is the story, as the news moves on to something else. The words sink into me: *a large dog*. I think of Jasper, wandering the moor on those short, not-quite-collie legs. PC Jackson's comment: *Cute little feller*. I'd been afraid our dog might have stumbled on the body – on Andrew Gregory – after he was dead, but it sounds like that couldn't have been the case. Gregory might have still been alive and standing when those wounds were inflicted, if the police were making assumptions about the animal's size. A small dog like Jasper couldn't jump high enough to scratch a man's face, even if he'd wanted to, even if he was ill and not behaving like his usual self. I'm so busy feeling relieved that it takes a moment longer to consider what else they'd said – and then I don't know what's real anymore.

Thirty-four years old.

Ethan hasn't missed it, though. 'Didn't you say you'd found a *boy* – someone Zack's age?'

I had. For those long, horrible moments, I'd thought it *was* Zack. And there's no explanation for that other than I'd been wrong, as I have been about so many things. Blinded by fear for my son, distracted by those scratches marring the man's features, I'd seen only what was in my mind.

If that's the case, what else have I only imagined?

I'd heard a voice singing to me while I took a bath. Heard it calling my daughter's name. Felt hair brushing by me when none was there. I'd imagined a hare, a blue-eyed, unearthly hare, loping up to our door. I'd looked into my son's face and felt like I didn't know him at all. And when I was fourteen years old, I had watched a child playing in the sea: floating, serene, safe.

'Thirty-four,' Ethan says. 'You heard them, Ellie. He wasn't a kid. All of this – where have you *gone*? And now you think there's someone following us, lurking outside our house? Look, I'll show you.' He grabs my hand, pulls me towards the hall, starts lacing his trainers, then gestures at mine.

'What are you—'

'You think she's here? There's nothing and nobody, El. I'll prove it to you.'

'What? No, I— Ethan, don't.'

He's at the door in two strides and pulls it open. Cool air hits us and then he's standing on the step, calling, 'Hello?' He strides into the garden and walks the perimeter, makes a point of peering into the hedge, staring across it and into the field – where a hare sits motionless, watching us both. He vanishes around the back of the house and the hare and I remain perfectly still, regarding each other.

'Nothing here ... or here. Nothing. Nothing.' I hear Ethan's voice as he searches, as if I'm a child and he's proving to me there's no monster, nothing hiding under the bed. But I know there's no monster. There's nothing here, not now. I wonder if Ethan knows that too, through some means of his own. Has he told her not to come tonight, and that's why he's making such a show of this? I'm clinging to something I know isn't solid, it can't be, and suddenly I'm swaying. It's as if my feet have been lifted from the sand and I'm floating, nothing to rest on at all.

Ethan catches hold of my shoulders and waits until I meet his eyes. I look back at him, but I can't give the acknowledgement he wants, can't say a word. His face is so familiar, the line of his cheek, the jut of his forehead, his clenched jaw, yet it feels as if I hardly know him either.

He's silent. He's waiting for something from me. He wants me to take back everything I'd said; he's waiting for me to be his wife. Or perhaps he just wants me to stop acting like I've lost my mind.

A moment ago, it was the ground I couldn't trust. Now I know it's really me.

Ethan sighs, gesturing towards the landscape and dismissing it all, as if he regrets ever seeing it. 'Ellie, you made a mistake,' he says. He brushes my tears away, his voice becoming softer. 'We agreed to forget this, didn't we? I know that what happened was down to me, but it can't be now, Ellie, not any longer. This isn't just about me anymore, is it?'

He pauses and I give the faintest of nods. 'I'm sorry. I'll always be sorry, but I can't take it back. We have to move on together, or this will be over. I don't want that, do you – El? We chose *us*. We both did. We decided to leave all of that behind. I can do that – can you?'

I feel the light touch of a kiss on my forehead and realise my eyes are closed. I open them and look into his. I weave the fingers of my left hand into Ethan's right. My fingers are cold and he kisses them, then rubs the back of my hand to warm it. The pictures in my mind, however vivid, start to dissolve. Ethan's arms are strong around me, drawing me back inside. He made a mistake too, but it's over now. And he's ready to forgive me mine; to forget.

I put my arms around him and try to be the person he believes in. 'I'm sorry,' I whisper, but my voice barely carries. Ethan sighs into my hair, resting his head against mine. I realise I'm still holding the mermaid doll in one hand when it slips to the floor. I feel it fall, just shiny fabric, stuffing, and thread. Nothing that should matter. Nothing that does.

And yet—

'That's my Ellie,' Ethan says, smiling. 'This is our life, El. That's what matters most. You know that, don't you?'

—I can see my grandmother again. Her lips are moving, as if she's trying to tell me something. And I see Zack hunched over in a cave; impossible that he should have been there, where I'd sought him on little more than a whim, but there anyway. Just as the doll is here, something else that's impossible too.

My instincts keep chiming, like *energies*; like *vibrations*. Everything wrapped up in each other. Is that what Gran would have wanted to show me? She'd never tried to make me believe in all the things she had. I think in her own way, she'd just tried to make me believe in myself. Now I sense the connection in our blood, spreading to my children, binding us together with invisible cords. And behind us – for a moment I'm caught between Gran, who'd told me stories, who never turned from me, never questioned her trust in me, and my mother, whose lips are pursed in disapproval. But I realise I never had to choose between them.

'You know, Ethan,' I say, 'sometimes two things can be true. And maybe two people can be right in their own way, even when they're saying opposite things. You're asking me to trust you and I will. I do. But I need you to trust me too.'

I see the exasperation in his eyes; the disappointment. The realisation that I won't be exactly what he wants, when he wants it: that I can't be his perfect wife.

'You say you haven't seen her,' I continue. 'All right, I believe you. I'm sorry if I didn't for a while. But I *have* seen her. It may be an odd thing for her to do, even unhinged, to follow us here. But people will do crazy things for – for someone they care about.'

I should know, after all. I'd followed Ethan to Whitby, hadn't I? I'd stalked him, stood outside *her* home, stared up at *her* window. And neither of them had suspected me for a second.

'That doll is here, and I refuse to believe you plucked it out of the bin and forgot about it. Someone else did that, and it wasn't me. And our dog is gone. He went running off from us, all excited, as if there was someone out there he knew.

'So I need you to accept that it's at least a possibility, Ethan, and I need you to fix this. Maybe the way you finished things left some room for doubt. Maybe it didn't, but she couldn't accept it anyway. So you need to talk to her.' I pause. 'Make things clear. Make sure she stays away from our kids and stays away from us. Then we can start over again properly. We can move on, together, like you said. We'll leave all of that behind for good.'

Ethan goes on staring at me, his eyes paler than ever. After a long moment, he nods. He puts his arms around me. He holds me a little too tight, and I no longer know if he's trying to draw me back – or if he feels like he's drowning too.

I pull free and go to the door. Before I close it, I see that the land is almost the same colour as the sky and the moon is high and yellow and there is no one to be seen in the entire world. The hare has gone. Even the lights from Thorncliffe have vanished. A soft mist has swallowed them all. It's a perfectly still evening and no one is out there watching us. The whole place is as vast and empty as the sea.

31

A memory.
There's a letter in my hand, although I don't understand what it says. The words are there in black and white, but they feel far removed from reality, nothing to do with what he told me. They can't be right.

Ethan's in the bedroom, getting dressed. We were up late last night, celebrating some good news in the best possible way. My skin still tingles from where he touched me: pretty much everywhere. The worries crowding my brain have evaporated into the air, the ones about where we would live in London, how things would be in the city with a child, how we'd afford everything we'll need. It's not as if I can start work for a while, not now. I'll be able to graduate but after that I'll be getting used to life with a baby before I can think about a job. I knew I'd find a way, as so many people do, but Ethan's ambitions were pulling him in another direction. The moment his last exam was over he'd got on a train to take up an internship at Canary Wharf. Stock market trading, dealing in futures. Thirty interns, and only one job at the end.

He wasn't even daunted. 'You can lose big if you get it wrong,' he'd said. 'But I won't get it wrong.'

Now he's here. He's come back to me. He'd missed me so much, he realised none of that was what he truly wanted. His thoughts are focused on the two of us now. He'd packed up his stuff, abandoned the room he'd taken for the next couple of months and got on the next train north. He'd presented me with flowers he bought at the station, pressing them on me as if they meant everything he wanted to say, and I knew that we'd be okay; that everything would.

'London won't do for us,' he'd murmured, as we cuddled on the sofa. 'We need something better. A different kind of life. I've looked into post-grad teacher training. Who better to raise a kid than a couple of teachers? And raising a kid is the most important thing anyone can possibly do, right? More important than making cash with those empty, pointless, spineless idiots I was working with.

'Being the best dad – that's what matters in life. What matters to me.'

He'd kissed me then, before adding, 'And the best husband, of course. Ellie Kellaway sounds good, doesn't it? Ellie Kellaway, forever.'

I'd laughed, still a little worried that he was trying to convince himself more than me that this was all he really wanted. 'Maybe. When you actually ask me.'

Images had flashed through my mind: an archway made of flowers. A flowing white dress. Would my bump be showing? No: we could have the wedding after the baby's born. When he or she can hold the ring, tucked in the pocket of a teeny little dinner jacket or a princess dress, so cute, either way. I pictured Mum wearing a pastel blue twinset and a pillbox hat, nothing I'd ever seen her wear in her life, but the most important thing was the expression in her eyes: pride, simple and pure, for her lovely daughter and handsome son-in-law and beautiful grandchild.

'I'd better get thinking then,' he'd said, laughter in his voice. 'No boring proposal for *my* woman. It'll have to be good.'

'A fairy tale,' I'd agreed, though I didn't care about any of that. I didn't need that big white frock or the flowers or a whopping great diamond or a grand gesture. All I wanted was the happy ending.

And that was now in front of us.

I was awake before Ethan the next morning. His things were still scattered around the flat from last night and I started to clear them away. When I scooped up his jacket, thrown over the arm of our little two-seater sofa, a piece of paper fell to the floor. A sheet of A4, folded into three. The paper was thick and creamy. Straight away, I sensed something about it. I didn't know why, or what; perhaps it was what Gran would have called an aura. There was just – *something*.

I knew I shouldn't unfold it, but what would Ethan care? We didn't have secrets. This fell out of his pocket. It could have unfolded all by itself.

I go on staring at it now. The letter is from the company he'd been working for, his fancy internship. But what it says still doesn't make any sense.

Employment terminated.
Trial period unsatisfactory.
Conduct unbecoming.

The words are in black and white, clear enough, but they swim together in front of my eyes. If Ethan had been fired, the vision he had spun for me last night was never his choice at all. A part of me had felt so guilty that he was ditching the life he wanted for himself, for me and this baby we hadn't planned for, but was that only what he wanted me to think? *Conduct unbecoming.* The worst words of all – because I can't know what they mean. I picture the kind of things they conjure: paunchy old men groping young female colleagues or sending suggestive images over email. Ethan surely wouldn't have done any of those things. He's a decent guy. He never oversteps the mark; if anything, he keeps people at arm's length. He likes to keep everything on a professional footing, even with our friends. Had Ethan simply screwed up, added the wrong column of figures, messed up a deal? *You can lose big if you get it wrong. But I won't get it wrong.*

He'd been so very confident. Just like he always is. I've always loved the way he seems to breeze through life, making it straightforward in the best of ways, everything so simple. He's never told me much about the placement other than it was hard work and long hours. A little bit cutthroat, he'd said, but nothing he couldn't handle. He'd said it was going great. Now

I remember the words he'd used last night when he spoke of his colleagues. *Empty. Pointless. Spineless.*

Spineless?

Had Ethan taken greater risks, flown too high, and come crashing down?

Or – and the thought makes me feel sick – perhaps I *should* feel guilty, maybe *am* guilty, because what if they found out about me? They might have dismissed him as a candidate because they thought he'd never manage the workload with a new baby. If so, there's little wonder he hasn't told me the truth. He must be hiding his disappointment, his hurt – to protect me.

I close my eyes, wondering what to do. I want our future with our baby. I want us to be together, his thoughts all for the two of us, just like he promised. I fold the letter once more and replace it in his pocket before draping his jacket back over the arm of the chair. I can hear the shower running. Soon we'll have breakfast together. Ethan is putting in his teacher training application this morning, plans that have come together so quickly he must surely have been considering them long before any of this happened.

Now we'll just have *a different kind of life*, that's all. The best thing I can do for him is to make sure that I – we – make him happy.

And I know that we will.

32

Ethan leaves early the next morning, while it's scarcely light and I'm half asleep. He murmurs something into my hair – I catch *for us all*, though I don't know what he's talking about. I think I'm still dreaming, and it's easy to drift again, to sink back into the dark. It's not until later that I awake properly and find he hasn't come back to bed. There's an empty space beside me, the sheets on his side long since turned cold. He's gone – to talk to *her*. The fact that I asked him to do it doesn't make it any easier.

You will have your wish ...

I've pushed him right back towards her. I picture him sitting in the car with his phone pressed to his ear, listening to her voice, letting her in. I tell myself it doesn't matter what she says or how she says it. She can't have any power over him any longer. She doesn't have the voice of a siren, no matter what Libby thinks. I'm secure in my family, and there's no room for doubt or worries any longer. He chose me once and he's made it clear he'll keep on choosing me. If I can't learn to trust him again, what we have will be over anyway. Still, I can't stop the images of them together circling in my mind, never settling. Like birds wheeling. Like swallows swooping over a pool …

I make the kids breakfast. Potter aimlessly around the house. Tell myself he can't be talking to her right *now*, this moment – or *now*. It's been too long. I don't even know what time he left. The car is gone. Did he need to drive away from me, to create distance, before he rang her? I picture him sitting in the car, having made his call, staring and staring into space while he thinks of her. Or perhaps he's only been out looking for the dog again, and not even thinking of her at all. Maybe it's only me doing that—

Finally, my phone rings, and I jump.

'Hey,' Ethan says casually. There's a background noise, a harsh whistling wind, amplified by the speakers. I imagine it sweeping over the moor; then comes a sharp, high cry, one I recognise, and I go still.

'Guess where I am?' he asks me.

I can't speak. I can't speak because I already know, even before he adds, 'Ellie? I'm here. In Sandsend.' There's a brightness in his voice. The expectation of shared reminiscences. I stare out the window at the miles of green between us, feeling more distant than ever. 'Ethan, what are you doing there?'

'What? We agreed, didn't we? So I came. I thought I'd put some posters up for the dog, while I'm here. In case he comes home.'

Home.

'I called by our old house. It was nice, seeing it again. I spoke to Kath. Mel, too. I might go and see some of the other neighbours. There's no sign of him, but who knows?' Ethan's voice trails off. 'I've already done that other thing you wanted.'

He mentions it like he's posted a letter or put the washing on. Anger shifts inside me, a rising tide. 'You've *seen* her?'

'Of course. It's what we agreed, isn't it? I went to Whitby before I came here. What did you think—'

'What did I *think*? Jesus Christ, Eth. You didn't have to sneak off before the crack of dawn. All you had to do is call her.'

There's nothing on the line but the sound of the wind. Or was it always the sea? When he speaks, he actually sounds hurt. 'I couldn't do that, love. Look, I came here for *you*. You told me to fix it. It was you who pointed out that our break-up didn't seem to stick. Wasn't enough, is what I mean. I had to make it clear. You wanted me to make her understand.'

'You didn't need to go rushing back—'

'I had to do it face-to-face, love. It was the only way to be sure.'

I sense anger rising in him too. Waves meeting, sending bursts of spray into the air.

He speaks slowly now, as if to a child. 'I had to do this properly, El, not just be a voice on the phone. And it's all right. She's not in the Peaks, she's here. She's fine. I think she's over it, you know? Just like I am. Look, she never even left Whitby. She said she hasn't been to the Peak District since she was a kid. She didn't know we'd moved.'

The thought of them, chatting together, so amicably ... my rage surges and churns inside me. He makes her sound calm. Independent. *Brave*. He makes it sound as if she doesn't even care about him any longer – he would, though, wouldn't he? To convince me it's all over.

Now I picture her, so beautiful, so young, roused by her phone and seeing her ex-lover's number on the screen. Ethan wouldn't have driven all that way without knowing she was home. And at that unearthly hour of the morning – what must she have thought? Whatever it was, Ethan must have been pretty sure she'd answer his call. That confidence of his again – or something more?

When he speaks again, Ethan doesn't sound confident at all. 'I'm sorry, love,' he says. 'I just thought I'd try to put your mind at rest – and look for the dog while I was at it. I wanted to show you I'd do everything I can, *anything*, for you and the kids. To make you happy. It's all for you. I thought—' a pause. 'I'm not sure what I think any longer.'

My anger crashes down, shattering on the rocks. Perhaps that's what I've been hearing all along in the background; perhaps it's all I ever heard. I close my eyes and picture Ethan's expression at this moment. *I'd do everything I can,* anything, *for you and the kids.* And he has, hasn't he?

When Ethan told me there was no one outside our house, I should have listened to him. None of this had been necessary. Even his other reasons for being there – going to see Sally, for goodness' sake, even Mel – were pointless. Hadn't I told him I'd called them already?

It's as if Ethan reads my mind. His tone grows warmer and I know, if he were here, he'd be sliding his arms around me. 'It's a good job done in the end, you know? She knows how things are now. There's no way she can misunderstand, even if she wanted to. She knows I don't have any feelings for her any longer. I've sorted it.'

I nod, though he can't see.

'We're okay, aren't we, Ellie?' he says. 'Isn't this what you wanted? Please tell me I did the right thing. I love you, El. I always will.'

He needs to hear something, anything, so I say the only words I can.

'Of course, my love. Of course you did.'

33

A postcard.
   This one is blank.

I check twice but Libby isn't in the lounge, which is strange because her favourite film is on, belting out that chirpy song about the sea. She's not posing in her mermaid blanket as she was a minute ago, waving her arms in time to its beat, nor has she sneaked off into the kitchen in search of a snack. There's only Jasper, gazing up at me with soulful eyes in the hope that it's time for food. She isn't on the stairs or in her room, or ours, or Zack's. Everywhere I look is empty. Zack's out surfing. Ethan's gone to fetch cod and chips from Fish Cottage. We're all going to sit down to eat, as soon as he's back and Zack comes home, except that Libby is *gone*, vanished into thin air.

My hands shake as I open the back door and run out into the garden, calling her name, hoping she's just playing a silly game of hide and seek. A herring gull, huge and impertinent, sits in the middle of the grass, picking at something red and wet. It doesn't fly away until Jasper flurries after me, pleased something is finally happening but still *hungry*.

All I can hear is 'Under the Sea', looping in my head, swimming around and around. I run back inside and check the sofa again, where my daughter was sitting. Her blanket is gone too. That splash of aquamarine with its fish scale pattern is missing, and my gaze goes to a little ceramic plaque hanging on the wall: LIFE'S MORE FUN AT THE BEACH.

I can hear the beach now, or rather the sea. Its voice finds its way around the walls and through the windows and down the chimney to where I am.

I check the front door, which is closed and still on the latch, although it isn't locked. We never lock it when we're inside. Our home is safe. Our friends live here, all around us. There's always someone about.

Always someone about.

But not Libby. Not now.

Feeling as if I'm trying to swallow sand, I grab my keys and run outside, not pausing to grab a coat. I almost collide with Sally, who's walking up the court, laden with supplies from the general store around the corner. Libby likes to sit on the benches outside and eat ice cream, but I know she won't be there now. Of course I do: I'm her mother.

'Whatever's the matter?' Sally asks, reading my expression.

I explain quickly, my voice tight, all my constricted throat will allow.

'Oh my God, Ellie. Wait one second. I'll dump these and come with you.'

I don't want to wait while she stows her bags, her *one second* feeling like forever, but then she's back, barely keeping up as I run down the wide, shallow steps of the court. I'm already scanning the sea. Is that a child floating there, the water lapping at their lips like an invitation? But it's only foam on the water. *Drowning doesn't look how you think.* I want to tell Sally so she'll know what to look for, but I can't speak. Can't even formulate the thought.

I rush to the edge of the sea wall to scan the most northerly section of the beach. It doesn't stretch far, petering out into rocky slabs terminated by cliffs. Libby isn't there. In the other direction, the sand stretches for miles. At low tide, it's possible to walk all the way to Whitby.

We race down the concrete slipway by the car park and onto the sand. A mother going in the other direction must see something in our faces because she grabs her own children by the hand, pulls them close and holds them tight.

The dry, soft sand slows us as we sink into it. We stride onward until we reach the beck, and even though we're not wearing wellies, we wade through, the cold water rising to our ankles. It's a clear day, spring tipping into summer, and children are everywhere around us. They love this part of the beach. They paddle in the beck, skimming its surface with colourful fishing nets bought from Tides Café. Libby isn't among them. She isn't anywhere. I let out a strangled sound – a drowning sound.

Sally squeezes my arm. 'Keep calm and think, Ellie,' she says. 'I'll help you. Where would she go?'

Here, I think. *Here.* Libby was watching her favourite film about mermaids, playing at mermaids. I scan the waves again, trying not to picture her wrapped in that aquamarine blanket as it grows waterlogged and drags her down, down …

There's no one in the sea now, not that I can make out. Not so much as a dog chasing a ball into the waves.

We jog along the main front. 'I'll ask if they've seen anything at the lifeguard's hut,' Sally calls out, waving me on, and I keep going. There are more children here: flashes of armbands, parents rubbing sun cream into soft skin, a toddler toppling into the sand, unsure whether to cry. Still no Libby. She might have vanished into one of her magical stories.

Sally catches up with me, breathing hard. 'I don't see her, Ellie. Perhaps we should call—'

The police. That's what she's going to say, and a chasm opens in front of me. One more step and I'll fall in. I pat at my jeans pocket, find it empty and realise my phone is still at home on our kitchen table. I didn't even pause to grab it, can't even call Ethan. Soon he'll get back home only to find the house empty and all of us gone.

Then I remember where he went, and hope washes over me. It might not be what I'm thinking, nothing to do with mermaids, and I grab Sally's arm, explaining that maybe Libby went to meet her dad.

'She'll be home before you know it,' Sally says. 'I'll head back along the beach, in case we missed her. I'll meet you back at yours. If she's not there, then we'll call.'

I hurry towards a set of steps that lead up to the coast road. There's only one main route through Sandsend, no other that Libby could take, and as soon as I reach the top, I see my daughter.

Libby is walking beside a tall, slender woman who moves awkwardly, limping as if every step pains her. Her hair drifts in the breeze, bright gold, as does Libby's, only a shade darker. There's an aquamarine blanket slung about her shoulders, one corner trailing behind her on the pavement. Libby is clutching an ice cream from the shop. It's melting, dripping down her fingers, but Libby doesn't notice. She gazes up, enchanted by the woman alongside her. A mermaid, in Libby's eyes anyway, is here in front of me after all.

I see, with rising fury, that they're holding hands. They look like a mother and daughter, this mermaid and my child; like a fucking postcard. They look so perfect that any casual observer would think *she's* her mother.

The thought turns me hollow. Libby's name bursts from me, but it's the woman who glances around. Then she keeps walking away, towards Fish Cottage, where Ethan is. Does she think they'll meet him together?

I call again, louder. The woman tugs on Libby's hand, but this time my daughter has heard my voice; and mother's voices have power too, perhaps as great as the magic of mermaids. My daughter twists, peering over her shoulder as I run straight across the road. I'm dimly aware of a car heading my way, a sudden deceleration, a loud horn blaring. I don't care about that. Libby is in front of me and I reach for her. She beams up at me, sticky with sauce. 'I've got mermaid ice cream, Mummy!'

There's nothing mermaidy about it, it's her usual toffee flavour, but I suppose it's who bought it for her that counts. I straighten and look into the face of the woman who's been fucking my husband. She's beautiful, but not how I'd imagined; not quite perfect. Fine lines bracket her lips and there's a crease across her forehead, as if she's puzzled that things aren't going the way she'd thought.

'What do you think you're doing with my daughter?' I demand to know.

She lets go of Libby and raises her hands, as if surprised – as if she's the innocent one here, under attack. 'I was just taking care of her,' she replies. It's the first and only time I hear her speak, and her voice is low and sweet. She even sounds a little hurt. *Suffering*. It makes me yet more furious even before she adds, 'Lib came out to me, didn't you, Lib? And – well, I said I'd help her find her dad.'

'You so much as touch her again,' I say, 'and I'll have you fucking arrested.' I snatch Libby's hand, sticky ice cream and all, and clasp it tightly.

'What? I didn't *take* her, did I, Lib? She came to me. I was—' she hesitates. 'I was just there, in the court. Outside your house – I'm sorry for that. I—' There are tears glistening in her eyes, *tears*. Even the thought of her standing in our court makes me want to slap her. At least when I stood outside her house, I had good reason. I had a *right*. Dimly, I see shadows gathering – onlookers, drawn by the scene. Watching.

'I was still there when Libby came out,' she explains. 'I suppose she must have seen me through the window. She said she wanted to meet her dad, so I asked where you were, of course I did, and she told me Mummy wasn't there—'

'Liar.' *Mummy wasn't there?* Like hell. More words rise to my lips, hard, unpleasant things I shouldn't say in front of Libby, who's too shocked to cry but still listening. Always listening. They spill out anyway.

'You stay away from us. If you even look at her again, I'll kill you.'

Then Libby starts crying, and I'm bending down, saying 'I'm sorry, I'm sorry.' I want to tell her I didn't mean it, but how can I?

I meant every word.

The woman, *Daddy's mermaid*, hurries away, leaving Libby and I alone. I hug my daughter, holding her little body close. I tell her the two of us will go and meet her dad, and remind her we'll have a lovely lunch together, and after that I'll buy her another ice cream, all that she wants. After a while, she starts to sniff and I straighten. People have paused on the pavement, but now the show is over, they likely think it was simply a toddler tantrum. I focus on one woman – a stranger, probably a tourist – and glare until she looks away.

Thank God Sally went home. If she hadn't, the whole sorry tale would have come out. Not of *Daddy's mermaid*, but Ethan's lover. I hadn't told any of my friends what had been going on, not wanting to be the object of their pity. I couldn't bear to see my humiliation reflected in their eyes every time they looked at me. I couldn't face that. I decide I'll tell Sally that Libby was off searching for mermaids after all, playing pretend. That's the fantasy Ethan spun for my daughter; well, I'll use the story now.

Later, when Libby is settled in the lounge tucking into a plate of chips, Ethan and I talk. Our own chips sit abandoned on the table, filling the room with the sharp tang of vinegar.

'Are you sure?' he's asking me. *Are you sure my unhinged ex-lover came and stole our baby away?*

'What do you mean, am I sure? I found them together. Eating ice cream.' I tell him.

'You said they were walking towards Fish Cottage.'

'I did, didn't I?'

'So she wasn't running off with our daughter. She was coming to meet me. Like she said,' his voice fades away.

'You think that's okay? She *took* her. She took Libby. I'm reporting her to the police, Ethan. I don't care what you—'

'And tell them what? Look, I'm not saying you did anything wrong, but I know what it's like. You get distracted, your back's turned for a second – just a *second* – and what does Libby do? She wanders off.' He shakes his head, as if this is somehow my fault, that the police will think I'm a bad mother. 'I know you were busy. You didn't hear her. You didn't *see*.'

My mum's voice, echoing in my ear. *Didn't you* see? *Sea ... sea.*

A child floating on the surface, staring at me, his lips dipping in and out of the water. A child I was caring for. Another child I was supposed to be *watching*.

'Did you even lock the door, El?'

I can't speak, shocked at how he's turning this around. I'm not sure what will break between us if I do.

'She shouldn't have gone off with Lib, of course she shouldn't – she can't really have imagined you'd leave her on her own. But then, she doesn't know you. It's only – I'm just saying, love, that maybe, just maybe, what she said was true.'

Liar. I spat the word in her face. I still want to rip out her tongue. The fear I'd felt: that empty sofa, where my daughter had been.

'The thing is, if you report this to the police, they'll ask questions. That's all I'm saying. About her, of course, but you too. What if they get social services involved? It won't look great, will it – a pair of teachers who can't even watch their own kid?'

I glance towards the lounge. 'Under the Sea' is playing again and I feel sick to my bones.

'We don't want to freak Libby out, either, do we? We don't want her growing up jumping at shadows. Scared of what's on her own doorstep. Not when there's nothing to be scared of.' He softens. 'I know you're angry, love, but I really don't think she would've just taken our daughter. Why would she? She'd never mean any harm to Libby.'

I think of the way Libby had cried. The things I'd said in front of her. And Ethan's words have turned to honey. He's stroking my arm. 'I think we can safely keep this between us. *All* of it, you know? Telling everyone our business – it won't help. Us or anyone.'

I should have known Ethan would have thought of that too, the way the whole sorry tale might come out. *Who's the best dad?* That image he's built so carefully could just as easily be torn into pieces and trampled underfoot.

But I don't want that story to be told either. I can imagine the pitying looks, hear the whispers: not only about him, but about me. Perhaps people might even laugh, thinking it's not surprising he'd want someone better than me. Ethan has picked apart my anger like a gull shredding its next meal. I don't want to permit the slightest possibility that that woman can hurt us again – but she can't, can she? We're *leaving*.

We've already found the perfect place. The right house appeared almost the moment we started looking, as if it was meant. As if it was waiting for us.

She'll be left outside for good, forever stuck on someone else's doorstep, looking in. We're the ones who'll be inside. Together. A family. And if she ever shows her face – if she goes anywhere near Libby again – I've already warned her exactly what I'll do.

34

Libby is sitting perfectly still, staring with unblinking eyes at the mermaid carved into the slab of stone set into our wall. The little mermaid had a marble prince at the heart of her home; now we have this monstrosity at the heart of ours. Libby isn't playing any game that I can see. She only stares in wonder. When she senses me behind her, she speaks without turning.

'He's still hers.'

It's Ethan that comes to mind. Ethan slipping through another woman's door, diving beneath the sea, the two of them surfacing from the perfect blue. My husband still isn't home. He'd said he'll be a while yet, before he even starts driving back again. *He's still hers.* I can't speak, even though I know that Libby means her silly wish, her offering to the sea witch. She means Zack, not her dad, who she still thinks is perfect. And how can I shatter that illusion?

I take a deep breath before I say, 'Not really, love. That's just pretend, isn't it?'

'No. He's hers, like the other one.'

'What other one?'

'The *man*, Mummy. The one who had mortality.'

She means *immortality*, but I don't correct her. *There were an old feller from Hayfield used to visit her, and he lived ever such a long time.* That story wasn't even from here, it was the one from Kinder Scout, miles away. It was about the mermaid who could grant men long life, if she chose to. Libby's mixing up her tales, getting confused and putting the wrong pieces together. Of course, they all seem to run together anyway. All the mermaids are sisters, all the water spirits one spirit … meeting and merging like droplets in a stream.

'She doesn't like to be on her own,' Libby murmurs, running her hand over the carving, her little fingers slipping into the grooves, and I resist the urge to drag her away.

No, love, I think. *Women like her never do.*

'She lives forever and ever. The man doesn't, though. She doesn't like them when they're *old*.'

No, I don't suppose she does. I huff. She never has to grow old with anyone. No doubt she'd simply pick someone else's husband. Or maybe she'd just help them *feel* young again – the only kind of immortality she has to offer.

He lived ever such a long time, that's what the man in Leek told us. I frown at the memory. And how had she done that? By sharing a little of her magic – making him stay looking younger than he was, years after he should have grown old? The youngest and most beautiful of them all would want her man to be young and beautiful too, at least as long as the enchantment between them lasted.

Thirty-four. You heard them, Ellie. He wasn't a kid.

A man I'd taken for fifteen years old. But that was surely more down to me than him. I shake my head. It's as if strange ideas are emanating from that carved slab of stone along with the chill that permeates the air, touching Libby and reaching me too. She twists her head towards me and smiles. It's not her usual smile. I don't like it; I find myself staring at the tips of her small white teeth. I reach out and stroke her hair, just Libby, my sweet girl. 'Hush,' I say. 'That's enough stories for now, Libby.'

Lib ... Lib ... My voice seems to echo from the stone.

'She'd need a new one,' my daughter carries on. 'Even if the old one doesn't like it. He didn't like it, *not at all*. But he went away.'

'What do you mean?'

'He went away, Mummy, like the others. She's got Zack now.'

'*Like the others?*' I repeat the words. Who does she mean: the sailor from Thorncliffe? The old feller from Hayfield? Any lone traveller wandering too near the pool? But the image in my mind is of Andrew Gregory, staring out at the moor with sightless eyes, my hand suspended over him. Thirty-four, but looking, for a moment, so very much younger. Andrew Gregory, who had *gone away*, who couldn't have gone further if he'd tried ...

'The ones from *here*.' Libby sighs, as if Mummy's being stupid. Then she jumps to her feet and asks, 'Are we going swimming now?'

It's as if she's forgotten the last few minutes, but I can't. 'No, darling, we're not going swimming. We could maybe go for a walk in a bit.'

'The pool!' Libby is all excitement as she stomps off upstairs. At least she sounds like herself again, like my little girl. And I'm left staring down at the sea witch carved into our home like a spell. I try to think of the way that everything is connected: the mermaids and their men, the pools at Blake Mere, Doxey and Kinder Scout. Different places, different names, but all of their stories are really the same story, aren't they? Joined, not by watery tunnels, but by words.

I reach out and touch the cold stone, sensing the connections running under the earth beneath our feet, the tales buried there, layered into the earth like sediment, as solid and present as the rock. They are in the water too, of course. Everything is connected, but nothing more so than water; the droplets percolating through these hills must have seen the sea. They have *been* the sea.

She'd need a new one. Even if the old one doesn't like it. He didn't like it, not at all. But he went away.

I shake away the images conjured by Libby's words: Andrew Gregory, in love with his own mermaid, walking to the pool to visit her. And finding someone else there – a younger, more handsome man, scarcely more than a boy, also in love with what he'd found there, half hypnotised by the creature he'd fallen for, or been *given* to ...

And then what? Zack and Andrew Gregory – fighting over some magical creature?

Stop it, Ellie. I rub my eyes, trying to come to my senses. *Stories. Stories for a child.*

Still, another image rises: Zack standing in the sea, past where the breakers meet the shore. His back is turned. He's stripped to the waist and staring out at the horizon, waiting for – what? When he turns, he looks just as I expect, his face young, but he isn't young at all because this is years in the future and even he's *old*. Somehow I know I'm long dead, Ethan and Libby too, and only Zack remains. Yet still he appears just as he always did. Except perhaps for his eyes, because *everything* is in his eyes. The things he's seen, the things he's *done* ...

A soft sound comes from somewhere above me and I stir. I look up to see Zack on the landing, peering over the banisters, watching me. I don't know how long he's been there. It feels as if he's reading every thought running through my head. I suddenly come over dizzy, putting out my hand for balance. I find myself leaning against cold stone; the slab with a mermaid carved into it, inescapable, *here*.

'All right, Mum?'

'Yes, I – of course I am. Sorry, love. I was just playing Libby-games, that's all.' That's all it is, I tell myself. He doesn't ask why I'm standing here playing them on my own. I glance at the mermaid again, or rather the sea witch, carved – *scratched* – into our home, a part of it. I should have it removed. Get rid of her for good. But Libby would never forgive me, and it's the heart of the structure, where the supporting walls meet and join. Would the centre hold if we tore her out, or would everything fall around us?

'Everything's fine, love,' I say, hoping the words might make it true. Although it's hard to believe, with Ethan miles away, instead of here. With *us*. With his son, who's staring like he doesn't know me. His daughter, who speaks of nothing but mermaids.

Zack barely looks at me. It's as if he's listening to something I can't hear. I speak more firmly. 'I'm taking Libby out for a walk. I think we need some air. Why don't you come with us?'

He grimaces. 'I think I'll stay in my room.'

'Really, Zack? This isn't like you.'

'How would you know, Mum?'

My mouth snaps shut. I should tell him off, but something in the way he's looking at me stops me. I soften my voice and try again. 'A walk might do you good. Maybe we'll see some of those friends you made. You can introduce them.'

His gaze drifts and he shakes his head. 'I'm fine,' he says. 'I don't want to go to the pool. Not right now.'

'I never mentioned the pool, love.'

'But that's where you're going, isn't it?'

I begin to protest, but he's already gone. His bedroom door closes; the space where he stood is empty.

Well, at least that disproves my own thoughts – my mad, eccentric thoughts. A part of me is relieved that he doesn't want to go near Blake Mere. If he's taken some aversion to the place, I can't say I'm sorry.

He's hers now.

Libby's games have struck too close to the truth. But at least she was wrong about that.

35

Libby tugs at her coat, pulling a face. She looks as if I've dressed her for a storm in her raincoat, hood and bright yellow wellies, rather than a changeable August day where the sky could go either way. She's carrying her mermaid doll. She'd asked if she could bring her for a walk, and I'd forced a smile, reminding myself she's four, and none of this is her fault.

I send Ethan a quick message: We're fine, Lib and I are heading out. His reply is prompt:

Almost done. Sorry it's taken so long – I put up a lot of posters! Have fun. We should stay away from that pool – doesn't seem a good place. Don't want Lib getting ideas.

I shake my head. Why does everybody assume that's where I want to be? And Libby's always getting ideas. Shouldn't Ethan be heading back to me by now, instead of giving me advice on what to do?

'This is the stile,' Libby says to her doll as I help her over the stone steps. She jumps down hard with both feet. 'This is the path.'

Across the blue-green swathe of land, the outcrops of the Roaches and Hen Cloud look like tidal waves frozen in the act of rushing towards us. I point down towards where Thorncliffe is tucked into its refuge between the hills. 'How about that way, Lib?'

Her face crumples like a discarded drawing and she pulls away from me, letting her legs go loose so that she's half sitting on the ground. I lean back, holding her up, but she won't stand on her own. 'The mermaid, Mummy,' she huffs.

'There is no mermaid, Libby. There never was.'

I snap out the words without thinking. Libby looks stricken as she clutches her doll tighter. My daughter, who wants to believe in magic. Who loves to have blue eyeshadow brushed across her cheeks and an aquamarine blanket wrapped around her legs. 'Sorry, Libby. Mummy's tired, that's all.'

And I *am* tired. Tired of waiting for Ethan to be done chasing around where he has no need to be. Tired of all the stories and make-believe. But Libby isn't. She's a little girl; they're hers by right. It's no good me insisting there's no such thing as magic; I don't even want to. It's no good trying to pretend the pool doesn't exist when we live here and she's seen it with her own eyes. If I don't take her, I worry she'll sneak out one day – not tomorrow, perhaps, but sometime soon. I can imagine her wandering the moor, clutching that blanket. Gazing into the pool, entranced. Wading in.

The blanket growing waterlogged and heavy, restricting her movements. Dragging her down, deeper, until only her hair floats …

I blink the image away, dismissing it not as a premonition, not even a mother's intuition; it was nothing but fear, and fear can be banished. Ethan was right when he said, *She has to be able to handle what's on her own doorstep.*

I crouch down in front of her. 'Do you remember going to the pool last time, sweetie? What did you see – can you tell me?'

'A coat,' she says promptly. 'And Mummy was scared, but Mummy is silly.'

I look into her eyes, seeking some sign in their depths that she's okay. They sparkle back at me, proof that nothing untoward is hidden there. I smile and stroke her cheek. I don't tell her off for calling me silly; right now, I'm glad of it. She isn't upset or hurt. She's my forthright, guileless little girl, nothing to worry over, nothing wrong. If she was damaged by the sight of Andrew Gregory – by me, *exposing* her to *that*, she'd surely show signs of it, but this proves she's all right.

'All right, Lib, we'll go to the pool.' The words slip from me in a rush almost before I know what I've agreed to. It's still not where I want her to be, but if Blake Mere is forbidden it will only grow more alluring, weaving an ever-stronger spell over her. I don't want it to ever lure her in; better that it should be familiar, with boundaries that are set down and understood. That way, sooner or later, it will lose its magic and she'll lose interest. Still, I can tell by her cheer that time isn't quite yet.

We head out, and I'm glad of our coats. There's a fine mizzle hanging in the air, droplets clinging to our hair and clothes. All the colours around us are drab, clouds sagging with their heavy grey weight, the heather an ominous dark purple. As we draw close, Libby rushes on ahead. 'Look, Mummy!' She's reached the ridge and must be able to see into the water, though I can't, not yet. I hurry to catch up.

The pool appears as it always has: a perfect mirror. Only clouds are reflected there, but it's odd; in its glimmer, they almost appear to be full of sunlight, rather than their current grey. They look like clouds from a different day, or another world even; a place where summer actually arrived, where mermaids gambol in the water. Then the wind shivers the surface, chasing tiny wavelets across its length, and the vision is lost. It's nothing but a pool once more.

Libby isn't happy. She takes picky little steps, using tussocks of grass as stepping stones until she reaches the edge. She pokes her welly into the murk, unimpressed; she starts to pout, and I'm glad to see her already falling out of love with this place.

I stare across the water, seeing again in my mind's eye that crumpled shape, too still, too quiet, lying on the ground. The one I'd been so certain was Zack. Instead, *thirty-four years old*. There are only rocks jutting from the grass where he had been, as grey as the shadow of the banking rising behind them. The cyclist had told us he liked to sit on those rocks and dry off after a dip, and I pull a face, wondering if he'll like it so much now. But there's nothing left of Andrew Gregory's story to be seen. The peat looks as it always has, betraying no memories within it.

Libby isn't interested in where Andrew Gregory was found in the slightest. She's staring down into the water. Without looking up at me she says, 'I think I can see her, Mummy.'

I'm walking towards her when Libby slips. One foot vanishes into the pool and I rush over ground that is half solid, half liquid, and reach after her and tug her back. For a moment, the mud holds on. I do battle with it, then she slithers towards me with a sucking sound.

She pulls a face as if she might cry and yanks her hand away from mine. It's her doll that comforts her; she clutches the mermaid to her, hugging it tight. Still, she doesn't argue when I say it's time to head home.

We're walking back to the house, looking down across the hillside, when I see him.

Zack is in the back garden, something beside him on the wall that doesn't belong there. For a moment it makes no sense – then he raises his hand to his mouth, and it does. He tilts back his head and smoke plumes from his lips before being lost to the breeze.

Libby's fingers twist in mine and I realise I'm squeezing them. I let go of her and pull my phone from my pocket. I'm going to ring Zack, tell him to *stop right now*, and I find there's already a message on the screen. It's from Ethan.

On my way. Back soon. I love you.

Zack picks up the object from the wall and heads inside, clearly done. No doubt he's going to replace it in plain view before I get home, so that no one suspects a thing.

I look down at Libby, but she's holding her mermaid doll against her face, oblivious to what her brother has been doing. She's whispering in its ear, the sibilance almost subsumed by the rustle and buffet of the breeze. The wind is growing stronger, plucking at our coats. Soon it will scour its way across the landscape.

We hurry home, the wind pushing against us. There's a sound in it, as if the sea has found us after all, tidal waves preparing to rush over the hills. As I open the gate, I notice that Jasper's poster has been ripped away, carried off by the breeze, leaving only little tags of paper behind. I don't even know how long it's been gone. The poster might have been MISSING for days, just like our dog, but I can't think about that now.

I'm due a little chat with my son.

36

I hardly wait to help Libby out of her coat before running upstairs to Zack's room. He jumps when I barge in without knocking. He pulls out his earbuds and a burst of tinny drums escapes before he pauses the track. He reeks of Lynx and toothpaste, but of course he does. My boy's not stupid. He just thinks I am.
This isn't like you.
How would you know, Mum?
Maybe I don't. Maybe I'm only now beginning to *see*. I stalk past him, not asking for permission, and go to his windowsill and snatch up the conch shell that's positioned there. The same one I'd seen a few minutes ago, balanced on the garden wall. It feels fragile in my hands, but I turn it over and shake it. A little plastic-wrapped packet flies out. It's pretty obvious what's in it. 'And the other stuff. Where is it?' I demand, my voice harsh.

He stares wordlessly, going to his wardrobe, where he rummages beneath the boxes at the bottom, hands me a pouch of tobacco, a pack of Rizlas.

'What the hell were you thinking, Zack?'

He doesn't meet my eyes. Are his glassy? They have been so often of late, but the reason wasn't so very strange, was it? It's right here in front of me. 'Well?' My question hangs in the air.

'Mum, I—' He scans around as if searching for a way out. There isn't one, not this time.

'Look at me, Zack. I want the truth. How long have you been smoking this stuff? Is that why you were in that cave, in that state? Roaches at the Roaches – *really*? Or was that something worse – are you on other stuff?' I try to lower my voice, not wanting Libby to overhear.

'I'm sorry.'

He's crying. Zack, my happy, carefree boy, is crying in front of me, and something in me breaks a little. This is not my son; my responsible, sensible son. 'What were you doing?' I ask again, and *fuck*, my eyes are stinging. 'Where did you even get it? Is that where those new climber friends of yours have led you? I don't want you seeing them. Never again, you hear? We're not doing this. I'm not going to watch you—'

'*No.*'

There's something about the way he says it and I stare at him. His face is distorted in my vision. Tears in my eyes; tears in his. 'Then what?' I ask.

'I don't have any fucking friends, Mum,' he says, and I don't tell him not to swear, I don't say anything, not yet. I'm waiting for something to spill from him, something I know is there, beneath, and it does.

'They brushed me off. Said I wasn't trained. Said I was too young. They didn't want to know me. I don't know anyone, not here. I don't have anything here.'

I stare pointedly at the packet in my hand. *You have this.*

'I got that in Whitby. Before we left.'

'You what?'

'Someone I knew from school. I had some cash from Nuggie, for the board. My surfboard. I didn't know what to do with it. So I thought, I might as well.'

'That's how you make your big decisions now? *Might as well?*'

'I know what he did, Mum.'

Everything goes quiet. Zack looks up at me, his eyes red and wet. I can only stare. I tell myself I don't know what he means; but I do.

'I know why we left. Did you really think I didn't? All that yelling, and times we're supposed to stay upstairs so we couldn't hear you arguing, and I'm not supposed to say anything, about him, about that *bitch*. I just have to babysit Libby, keeping her in the dark—'

'Oh God, Zack.' My voice is barely there. No more than a whisper.

'He's my *dad*.'

Who's the best dad? I suddenly feel sick. I can't believe he knows. I thought I'd protected him.

'And you're my *mum*,' he mouths, and I throw my arms around him. We hold on to each other, crying together. *I'm sorry*, we keep saying, both of us. *I'm sorry.* I'm sorry for everything, for all the things I can't change, that I can't take back, not now. I'm sorry for failing to *see*.

Eventually, I step away but keep hold of both his shoulders, looking into his eyes. 'First, Zack, I'm flushing this stuff. No more. Never again. Okay?'

He nods.

'Second, things will get better. Change takes time, that's all. I know you're a bit cut off right now, but school will start in a few weeks, and you'll make more friends. New friends.' *Friends who don't sell you drugs*, is what I don't say, deciding it will do no good. 'You'll find your feet, Zack. In a couple of years, you'll be thinking about university and you can go anywhere you like. It's not so long to wait, not really. But it's far too early to start ruining your life.'

I draw in a deep breath. *Third*, that's next: the whole sorry mess of it. 'Your dad—'

'I don't want him to know,' Zack says.

I'm unsure whether he means the drugs, or that Zack's aware Ethan screwed someone else behind my back. That wound splits open again, raw pain in my chest. I remind myself it's over. Ethan's *sorted it*. I focus on my hands gripping my son's arms, feeling the invisible cord that binds us, everything resonating with *energies*, with *vibrations*. I'm no longer sure if the pain is his or mine. I take a deep breath, pushing my emotions down beneath the surface.

'Your dad,' I start over again. 'People make mistakes, Zack—'

He grasps my words, suddenly eager. 'Yes, they do. Mum, they do. He doesn't need to know about me—'

I'm still not entirely sure which secret he wants me to keep. Probably both. What difference can it make? 'Zack, I can't.' I shake my head, realising I'll be the one in the wrong if I keep this from Ethan.

'Mum, *please*. You know what he's like.'

I open my mouth to argue, but I hear Ethan's voice as if he's in the room: *Ordinary people can do extraordinary things.* I picture his pride as Zack won a race, the cheers ringing out: *Kell-a-way, Kell-a-way …*

I know what it is to lose the faith of a parent. To know there are layers in their eyes, every time they look at you. Ethan's disappointment would be worse than his anger. He's dealing with a lot right now. He might not stop to think about what he should say to his son, might even say things he can't take back, no matter how much he wishes to. And really, there's no need for Ethan to be disappointed, not in any of us. He can go on believing in us and loving us and being proud of us, and Zack *will* make him proud. I know he will.

'Please,' Zack says. 'He'll just – he'll go *off*. I didn't even want to do it, not really. It's just kind of where I ended up. It's just, I don't belong. There isn't a place for me here.'

'Of course there is.' I give him another hug, breathing in the scents of cheap body spray and mint. I make my choice, deciding to hold onto this trust between us, and speak more softly still. 'All right, love.'

His arms tighten around me and we stay like that for a while. My throat constricts and I swallow back tears. I won't cry anymore. 'This never happens again, you hear?' I warn him. There should be more than that – I suppose I should ground him, but if I'm not going to tell Ethan, I can't explain why he's being reprimanded. And I feel like Zack's been punished enough. He's been through enough, and I've been blind to it. I should have *seen*. I can still sense the hurt in him, there, beneath, all bound up with a bright thread of guilt.

But *people make mistakes*. At least Zack can understand that too. We both can.

'Just promise me you haven't taken anything else, love. That you won't. You were in such a state, the other day.'

'Mum, I hadn't even tried it before then. The cave – I don't know. I suppose it was all a bit new to me. I was upset. Maybe it did hit me a bit hard.'

I frown. Zack had had that horrible blank expression in his eyes before that, hadn't he? When he'd been to Blake Mere. He'd come back confused, half in a trance, leaving those peaty footprints leading from the door. That was before the day of the cave; but then, he'd been tired. Worn out, in need of food, that was all.

'Come on,' I say. 'I'll make us something to eat.'

So that's what I do, leaving a plate for Ethan. It's raining outside, and I keep wandering to the window to watch for the car. He should be home by now. He'll look at Zack without a shadow in his eyes, whirl Libby in the air, hold me tight, and he won't have to know about all the things that have hurt us because they're already in the past. They're behind us, because I've *sorted it*.

The end of something. Another new beginning.

Ethan doesn't get back until I'm already in bed, half asleep. He strips naked and slides in next to me and wraps me in his arms and pulls me close. He kisses below my ear, the side of my face, my lips. His skin is freezing. He's as cold as marble, but I know how to warm him, and I do. And if it feels a little like saying, *He's mine* – why not? He *is*.

I never ask Ethan for any more details about what he said to Sienna, or what she said to him. I'm not interested in the way she looked or how she reacted when she saw him or what he saw in her eyes. I don't want to picture her face, or worse, to actually begin to feel sorry for her. I don't want to know if she cried.

That's already in the past, and I've decided to leave it behind me. This time, I will. We have our future now.

I've sorted it isn't much to go on, but it's enough, because that isn't the important part.

I love you. That's what matters.

37

The rain has finally passed – it lingered for four more days, then the sun revealed itself at last. It's shining as we drive through picturesque villages and over hills, deeper into White Peak. Outcrops of limestone gleam from the grass, boulders scattered about like pulled teeth. We pass a ridge signposted TOP O' TH' EDGE, then drop into another village. A pub stands ahead, moss growing on its roof, chickens clucking about the yard. It's the name that catches my attention. The pub is called The Quiet Woman. There's a painted sign depicting a flouncy blue dress, pink arms jutting from the sleeves, but the neck ends in nothing but a stump. Above the headless form is written, SOFT WORDS TURNETH AWAY WRATH.

'I don't think she has any feet,' Libby says as we get out of the car. 'Was she a mermaid?'

She's right – they can't be seen beneath her long dress, which flicks out, a little like a fishtail – and I laugh at Libby for being more concerned about that than her lack of a head. I google and find the story, which I recount as we go inside and order orange juices at the bar.

'The woman was a hopeless scold. She nagged and nagged her husband, day and night – even haranguing him in her sleep – until finally, he took an axe and cut off her head. Hmm. It says here the neighbours were so grateful, they had a whip-round to celebrate. Well, Libby, I suppose she lost her voice then, didn't she? So she is a bit like a mermaid. Clever you.'

'Take heed, Lippy.' Zack teases her, miming zipping his mouth closed. 'That's what happens to noisy little girls. Seen and not heard, yeah?'

He winks, and I'm glad to see him relaxed and joking, more like himself. I kiss Libby's head and tell her, 'You can say anything you like, sweetie. No, I don't think she was a mermaid, was she? She was someone whose husband was a very bad man.'

Libby catches her breath, then grins. 'They should chop off *his* head, Mummy.'

'Yes, they should.'

She giggles. 'She should have taken him in the water.'

My smile fades. For a while, no one says anything. Ethan stares out of the window, his gaze distant, as if he's not quite here with us. There have been moments like this since he came back from Sandsend – not sad, exactly, just distracted, as if he's holding onto something he can't say. I can't help being annoyed. Is he thinking of *her*? Was it so very hard to say goodbye – is it Ethan now who can't bear to hear talk of mermaids?

He frowns and rubs his face and I notice he isn't wearing his watch, the one I gave him: *For the years to come. All my love, Ellie.* I brush my fingers over his bare wrist, where the watch should be. He flashes me a smile, then turns to Zack. 'How about finding a bit of private land? We could start preparing you for when you can learn to drive officially. Give you a go behind the wheel.'

Zack jolts upright, sitting straighter. He looks brighter than he's been in days, any shadows of the past forgotten in a heartbeat.

Ethan grins at his expression, and also seems relieved. Maybe he's been worried about Zack too, even without consciously knowing what's wrong. 'When you pass your test, we could think about getting you a car.'

'Oh my God, that would be *sick*.' Zack's suddenly the one in chatterbox mode. 'I could go anywhere, whenever I want. Even back home.'

I can't help smiling, even if Ethan should have run this idea by me first. And I've kept enough things quiet from Ethan anyway, haven't I? Of course, Zack's only fifteen now and it'll be over a year until he can start learning properly, but I'm too glad to see him happy to point that out. It occurs to me how much Ethan would love to see his son passing his driving test before anyone else his age, his competitiveness rearing its head again, and picture the two of them united in delight.

Now Ethan's the *best dad* all over again, basking in Zack's gratitude. More than that, he's an *epic* dad, an *amazing* dad. They carry on talking about engine sizes and nought-to-sixty times and I let my thoughts drift while Libby sips her juice, both of us silent now.

'Why don't you sit in front for a while?' Ethan says to Zack as we leave. 'I can show you the whole mirror, signal, manoeuvre thing. You could maybe change gear when I press the clutch.'

I shrug and climb into the back with Libby. We're heading towards Chrome Hill, where the remains of coral reefs are still visible in the calcium deposits, a reminder that all this was once under the sea. And yet, after an initial demonstration, Ethan falls quiet. Zack gets twitchy, starts fiddling with the radio. It's as if he's deliberately trying to annoy his dad, shifting from station to station, brief, irritating snatches of voices interspersed with bursts of song.

Then a voice, hissing with static, says, *Concern is growing* – and cuts out.

'Stop messing about, will you? I'm trying to drive,' Ethan snaps.

'You're supposed to be showing *me* how to drive,' Zack bites back, and the two start bickering. The radio station doesn't get changed and neither of them are listening anyway, until the newsreader says a name, *Sienna Clarel,* and Ethan stops mid-sentence. The name hangs in the air, crackling like electricity, and the voice returns.

… missing for several days …

Ethan snaps out a hand and turns off the radio. Zack protests and Ethan says he won't ever be learning to drive if he's not careful, won't be getting behind the wheel until he's twenty, and Libby starts to wail, she's *hungry*, and I feel her looking at me but I can't say anything, can't even turn my head.

Sienna. It's not a common name. Of course, that doesn't mean it's the same person.

Missing for several days.

How many days could they mean?

It's been five days since Ethan went to see her.

I'm not sure where my mind goes for a few seconds. There's only a blank, then I remember something else Ethan said: *She's here. She's fine.*

So why is she missing now? Ethan had told me she'd never even been to the Peaks, that she was home all along. Or had his visit put the idea into her head to make one of her own? Perhaps she hadn't been quite so calm, so *brave*, in accepting the situation after all.

Or she could have been missing for longer than they claimed, and I really did see her here. She might have come to the Peaks to watch Ethan, to be close to him, and in shame at her own actions, had failed to tell anyone where she was going. But he'd sworn to me she hadn't.

I replay his words, trying to let them anchor me to my seat.

She's here. She's fine.

But she's not, is she?

Missing for several days.

And other words return, ones my husband said to me. *I've sorted it.*

38

A memory.

Ethan has told me he's going to be on that podium. He's done a few triathlons, placed high, but never taken the top step. Now, he says, nothing will stop him. He's determined to win, for our baby. Our child isn't even born yet and his father wants to grasp the moon and put it in his hands, to show him that ordinary people can do extraordinary things. 'Today will be great, Ellie,' he says. 'Everything will. Better than great. Perfect.'

This baby doesn't feel ordinary to me, having already taken over my world. I have a prominent bump which keeps me warm against the early morning chill, like my own internal radiator. It's a little before six in the morning and everything is ready. Ethan did a lot of prep yesterday: registering, stowing his cycling kit bag for after the swim, racking his bike, checking the transitions, eyeing the competition. I'm standing just up the hill from the harbour, a dark well where shapes move and lights gleam. The town is busy with tents, stewards, supporters. A changing station waits where helpers will strip off wetsuits so the athletes can don cycling gear. And there's an indiscriminate mass of competitors in matching race swimming caps, milling around ready for the start. Ethan's in the first tranche, but I've given up trying to spot the yellow shoulder bands on his wetsuit. Everything's lost against the first rays of the rising sun, appearing over the hillside on the other side of the harbour. That won't make it easy. The swimmers will be dazzled, struggling to spot the buoys marking the course.

Below me, the sea begins turning to froth. Ethan described it to me: bumps and punches, splashing and white water, swimming blind in what he calls a washing machine start. It sounded awful to me – no way I'd get in the middle of that – but he'd grinned at the thought. I can't make out individual arms or heads, only a tide of jostling and chaos, but I know Ethan will have positioned himself to be out front.

I catch a glimpse of those yellow bands, like a hornet cutting through the water. Ethan isn't right in the front, but he's not far off. Three others are just ahead of him, so tightly packed together they must be bashing elbows. Ethan is fenced in. He'll surely get kicked in the face, emerging with black eyes or worse, and I wish he'd drop back a little, but he doesn't.

I can sense his determination even from here. Ethan won't give up. It isn't in his DNA. I should know; I've benefited from it, after all. He was the same with me, with all those flowers and dinners and compliments – pursuing me with the same intensity, making sure he landed his prize. He hadn't needed to then and I wish I could tell him he doesn't need to now, but he won't let anything stop him. He's managed to find a gap between two of the lead swimmers, or forced one. Another stroke and he'll be on top of them, and he *is*. Ethan raises his arm; on the downward stroke, the foremost swimmer's head is in reach. Ethan pushes him under.

I freeze. It's surely an accident. Ethan must have been dazzled by the rising sun. He must have struck out blindly – yet he doesn't move away. He's broken his usual rhythm, his right arm still down, almost as if he's holding the guy under. In the next moment, Ethan pushes himself up – forward – over him.

He's spoken to me of this, one competitor swimming over another, but I've never seen it done and never wanted to. I certainly never wanted to see it done by Ethan.

The swimmer he pushed down hasn't come up again. His wetsuit had a broad blue flash right across the back and I wait uneasily until I finally spot it. He's caught by the onslaught of competitors, thrashing the sea into white water, and he's barely moving. The others are swimming through as if he isn't there. He takes a kick in the face and is under again. He doesn't even seem to be trying to swim any longer. Then he's gone, below the surface.

I close my eyes, but what I see in my mind is not a man but a young boy. He's floating, staring back at me as his hands pat at the sea as if it's his pet, his lips now in, now out of the water.

A boat begins to weave its way through the swimmers. The lifeguards have seen him; of course they have. They know what drowning looks like. Out here, I suppose it's pretty much as you'd expect. They're using a kayak – anything else would be too risky – and the tide of swimmers breaks and parts around it. They ease their way through, stow their oars and delve into the water. They are on him fast, dragging him aboard. The man slumps into a heap, but he's sitting at least, and I see him nod at something they say. He pulls off his goggles, cradling his face with one hand as they take him away and out of the race.

He's breathing. He's *fine*.

Ethan is still out in front, moving easily, sunlight glinting off his yellow shoulder flashes. He hasn't even realised what he's done. He can't have, otherwise he'd have abandoned the race to check on the guy he'd injured, to try and help. But Ethan doesn't abandon the race and he won't abandon the race, because he's winning. He's rounded the first buoy. He's keeping the promise he made. *That podium is mine.*

It turns out not to be, though. Ethan comes in seventh. It's a great result, but he does no more than grunt about it before he starts to wolf down a huge plate of pasta. He's jumpy and snappy, as if adrenaline from the race is still fizzing through him with nowhere to go. All I can picture is that blue-striped wetsuit, vanishing beneath the water. I'd half expected Ethan to be disqualified – *conduct unbecoming* – but he wasn't.

I ask him about it, hoping he'll say it was just a nasty accident. Does he even know how the man is? Has he checked? In reply, Ethan throws down his fork and draws a long, pained breath, as if I'm being tiresome. 'He was an idiot. He should have moved aside. I was faster and stronger. What was I supposed to do? There's no room for weakness. If it wasn't for people like him—'

I would have won: the words he doesn't say.

'I think he was hurt, Ethan.'

'What do you want from me, El? That's how it's played. He knew what he signed up for. It happens. I only did what he'd have done, given the chance. I did what any one of them would do. What they're supposed to do, if they want to get anywhere.'

Ethan stares at me, his eyes wide and unblinking. After a moment, I'm the one who looks away. I can't admit what this reminds me of: a folded letter falling from a jacket pocket.

I have to assume he's right. How would I know? I've never done a triathlon and never will. There's no way I'd get into the water – I wouldn't even if it was empty of crowds and flat as a millpond. Not that I'd tell Ethan that. I've never told him any of it. How could I?

There's no room for weakness.

I want him to have confidence in me, and he does. Just like he has confidence in himself.

You can lose big if you get it wrong. But I won't get it wrong.

I feel closer than ever to knowing what went wrong on Ethan's internship. Thirty candidates competing for one permanent position. I don't think that Ethan did get it wrong, not really. But did he try to make sure someone else did? Maybe he'd sought to pick off the competition somehow. Maybe he'd tried to swim over them.

I'm staring at the table when Ethan gently takes my chin and turns my face to his. 'I just wanted it to be special, you know?' he says softly. 'For *you*. When I asked you.'

At first, I don't know what he means. Then the picture snaps into clarity: Ethan on the podium, grabbing a microphone or loudspeaker, calling my name, beckoning me up to join him. Going down on one knee. Asking me to marry him. Everyone turned towards us, all smiling and cheering. Ethan joking that he'd won the very best prize of all.

Now his eyes are on me and I shake my head, meaning so much by it: that I didn't need the spectacle. I didn't need a grand gesture, didn't even want it. I certainly didn't want Ethan to do what he did to try and get there, nothing of the kind—

I can still feel the disappointment radiating from him.

'Ethan,' I say, 'this – it's enough, you know? *You're* what I want.' And to prove it to him, to show him this is all we need, I'm the one who drops to one knee, clumsy and big-bellied.

'Marry me,' I say. 'Marry *us*.'

His eyes go wide. A succession of emotions passes across his face before he pulls me towards him and kisses me. 'Of course I will, Ellie.' He throws back his head and laughs. 'Well, we've got something to remember after all, haven't we? *You* asking *me* – that's a story worth telling, isn't it?'

'Of course it is,' I say, nestling against him, and I know it's true. That's what we have, Ethan and I.

A whole, beautiful fairy tale.

39

We're heading home from our outing, the wheels humming against the road, a sound that might be in my head. We don't talk. We don't speak of all the things we so need to discuss, not in front of the children, though they must be able to sense the atmosphere between us, sharp with unasked questions.

Ethan had said that everything was fine. He told me he'd *sorted it*.

I google Sienna Clarel on my phone, glad I'm in the back seat where Ethan can't see. It's her. She's from Whitby. She was due to join Ethan's school in September as a science teacher – that comes as a dagger to the heart. I picture them passing in corridors, exchanging smiles, secretive glances, a touch of their hands. Closing an office door behind them. Having the whole day to be together, snatching moments in breaks and after school.

Her family haven't heard from her. They reported her missing when she failed to respond to their messages.

It might have nothing to do with us. Maybe she was sleeping around. She might have pissed off some other man, or his wife. There could have been other homes she wrecked. Maybe she'd taken off with someone else's child. Or more worryingly, it's everything to do with us. I close my eyes and see her again outside our bedroom window: a hazy form defined by the rain, there and then gone. Her pale skin, her floating hair. But that was only a dream I'd had, a moment of madness. I had so wanted to picture her that way, expelled from our lives, shut outside …

I want to turn off my phone and banish her, but the past won't be so easily forgotten. It's here, in every thought that passes through our heads, Ethan's and mine; it always was. No matter how I've imagined her, that doesn't mean she isn't here right now, in the Peaks. She could have lied to Ethan. He might have lied to me. Maybe she really has been here all along, having followed us when we moved, and it's just that no one noticed her absence until now. They don't sound altogether sure how long she's been missing. Maybe she hasn't contacted her family out of shame at her own behaviour. I don't suppose she'd have been keen to tell them or any friends she had why she was going away or what she was doing.

Ethan's hand shifts on the wheel, changing gear. One of Libby's friendship bracelets slides up and down his wrist. That same hand that had reached out to silence the radio – he didn't want to hear any more.

As soon as we get home, Zack slips away and takes Libby with him. There are things that need saying, and Zack can read that in the air as clearly as we do. He leads his little sister into the lounge and puts on her favourite DVD without asking and she cuddles up to him, enjoying time with her big brother. Ethan and I don't look at each other as we go upstairs and into our bedroom, closing the door behind us. That buzzing is still in my ears. It feels as if we're still in the car, everything around us shifting, nothing solid in this world.

'I know what you're going to say,' Ethan says.

Does he? Because I'm struggling to shape the questions clogging my throat. 'You *knew*,' I start. 'You knew she was missing. So where is she?'

He puts both hands in the air, his classic *Don't blame me* pose. 'I don't know.'

'Don't give me that. You're the one who was *fucking* her. You're the one who was playing happy families with her.'

'What? Of course I wasn't. I haven't—'

'You *have*, Ethan. Where is she?'

'I don't know, Ellie. I haven't seen her.'

'You saw her a week ago. Not even that: five days.' *Several*, I think. *Several days*.

He shakes his head.

'You said you'd *sorted it*. What did that mean? You never told me.' I can hardly get the words out.

'Ellie, listen to me.' He seizes my upper arms. I barely register that it hurts, that his grip is too tight. 'I didn't see her. I'm sorry I lied to you, but I didn't. I haven't. I have no idea what's happened. Please believe me. You have to, El.'

I can't even move. I don't know who he is any longer, this man I married.

Ethan is breathing hard. 'Look, I went back to Sandsend. I tried calling first, of course I did, but she never answered. She wouldn't even pick up. I figured she was done with me, that she didn't want to talk – so I just showed up. I was so sure she'd be there. She should have been there.'

I shake my head. I can't fathom this new story he's telling me.

'I had to do everything I could for you, Ellie, but the house was shut up and I couldn't hear anything inside. I thought she was in there, hiding from me or something. And I couldn't do anything else. If she wouldn't see me, let alone talk, I figured she must have got the message anyway, you know?'

'You lied to me.' I'm not sure why I'm surprised anymore. He's lied to me before; of course he has. He lied to all of us.

'I know. I'm sorry. But I only wanted you to know that it's over, El. And it was over. It *is*. I tried messaging her, I tried calling, I tried her door. I did all I could, for *you*, Ellie. Everything. I always will. You know that, don't you?'

'But you knew she was missing. The way you turned off the radio—'

'I knew. I saw it on a news site – *after* I'd been over there. After I'd got back home.'

I take a deep breath. 'So you didn't see her – but I did, Ethan. I must have. I might even have been the last. I saw—' *Something.*

'Ellie, for fuck's sake. No, you didn't.' He raises his voice, running a hand through his hair. 'You thought you did, that's all. I don't know what the hell you saw, but you've been exhausted. Not yourself.'

The silence hangs between us until he punctures it again.

'What do you want me to say? Okay – let's assume you were right, even though it's crazy. Is that what you want to hear? Maybe she *was* here. Maybe she was watching us. Maybe she's turned fucking invisible, so you can see her and I can't. Or maybe – just maybe – you imagined that part, because you can't fucking let this go?'

He takes a deep breath. There's a brightness in his eyes, a cold determination, as if he's in the middle of one of his races. Perhaps he's just swum over someone. Perhaps he's trying to swim over me.

'Ellie, I'm finished with her. You know that. I finished with her weeks ago and I'm finished with her now, like you wanted, like we both wanted. If she's gone off somewhere, it's nothing to do with me. She could have gone on holiday to get away from it all and not told anyone. Maybe she'll send me a fucking postcard.' He looks around, as if seeking the answers. 'I *don't know*. How could I? She was upset. She probably felt she needed to put some distance between herself and her life for a while. You'd understand that, wouldn't you? Running away?'

His words hit me like a flood of cold water and I flinch. We stare at each other. I wonder what it is that each of us sees.

'Look, I'm sorry. But this – what you're suggesting – it's beneath you, that's all.'

For a while, neither of us speaks. All I can think is, *What the hell* is *it that you think I'm suggesting?* He'd lied to me about seeing her. He'd dreamt up her state of mind, the *brave* one. He'd falsely claimed that he'd *sorted it*. I'm still picturing Sienna Clarel outside our house. Perhaps it's her who's not quite herself. She might be the one who's crazy. Maybe she likes to imagine it's her house, that Ethan is her husband, that she'll reach out to take Libby – *Lib* – by the hand and her little girl will smile up at her. That Zack will come around. In my mind, Jasper is already standing at her side, her faithful little companion. Or is all of that only because I can't believe she'll ever truly be gone?

'There *is* a possibility—' Ethan's voice is hoarse now. 'I don't think she ever came near the Peaks, El. Why would she? But – this might be about *us*. And I don't think she's coming back. That's a lot, you know? For me. I just can't—'

He scrapes at his hair again. Is he sorrowing over her – or is this something else? A feeling is closing over me, like a heavy blanket, dragging me down.

'I've been trying not to think about this, but I suppose I have to,' he says.

I feel the distance opening between us. I wonder how long we've been adrift. Can we even see the shore any longer? This sea is too vast, too dangerous, too ready to swallow us.

'I think she might be dead. And if she is – it's partly down to me, Ellie. It's just – she was – she was all alone.

They talk about her family, but she wasn't close to any of them. And then I broke up with her, on the phone, of all things. She begged me to see her, did you know that? To talk to her just one last time. She said she didn't have anyone else she could speak to.'

'You think she *killed* herself?' I ask, my voice no more than a whisper.

He doesn't reply or look at me. But of course that's what he's saying – that she went off on her own somewhere and set a blade to her wrist. Tilted back her head, swallowed down pills. That she walked into the sea.

He's saying she loved him that much.

Did she?

Is that where Ethan's mermaid has gone – vanished into that grey nothing, becoming foam on the ocean like in Andersen's story? If she did and her body hasn't been found by now, I suppose the sea will keep its secrets. We might never know where she's been, what she's done, what she thought, how she felt. That's what mermaids are like, though, aren't they? Voiceless. As unknowable and mysterious as the sea. Perhaps, now, she always will be. And there will be no words to spoil his image of her, this woman who'd died for the love of him. All there will ever be is remembering; all he can ever feel is longing.

Once upon a time, I hadn't known what drowning looked like. I never knew what it felt like either, even though Ethan and I have been doing it for months. Possibly years.

Now he doesn't need to put his fears into words. Ethan and I understand each other perfectly. I wonder if I should feel sorry at the idea of Sienna's suicide. I try, but there's nothing: only a grey, bottomless deep, vast and indifferent. Not so much as a flicker of light on its surface.

'I have to go, Ellie.' Ethan stirs, taking his gaze from me again, a light that I can't have. 'I can't do this anymore. We'll talk more later, okay? But for now, I need – some – fucking – space.'

Before I can protest, he strides past me and out of the door. His footsteps descend the staircase, the one concealing that carving of a mermaid or a sea witch, the one that has been here, at the heart of our home, all along. There comes a pause while he puts on shoes; the rattle of keys. The front door opens and closes behind him and just like that, my husband is gone.

I go downstairs and into the kitchen. I stand there for a long time, staring out of the window. Ethan is missing and so is the car. The drive is empty and the gate is wide open. Beyond that is the *nothing* that I came here for. Clouds roll on forever above the grey-green land. If Ethan needed some space, he's found it. He hasn't left a trace of himself behind.

40

I don't know how long I stand in the kitchen. Eventually, I flick the kettle on, though I'm not even sure I want a drink. I keep returning to the fact that I don't know why Ethan left: whether it's because we rowed, or because of his feelings about Sienna's possible death.

His tragic, beautiful mermaid – killing herself because she couldn't have her prince. She always was the heroine in this story, wasn't she? And I'm just the wife, though I'm the one who's left feeling the grief, not for her but for myself. For my empty driveway and quiet kitchen and the way my kids don't want to come out of their rooms and for all the hollow resonating spaces inside of me.

I'm not just going to stand here waiting for Ethan to come back. I pick up my phone and google Sienna once more. Maybe, while we were arguing about her, *again*, she's been found. She might be safe and well and if she could see the two of us now, she'd laugh.

But there are no more updates on her disappearance, only the same unanswered questions. Instead, I google Andrew Gregory. There are some new details.

The cause of death has been confirmed as a head injury, consistent with falling from the banking onto rocks below. Alcohol levels in his blood suggest a level of intoxication that may have contributed to an accidental fall, though DNA recovered from scratches to his face has been confirmed as canine, and it remains possible that the wounds were inflicted shortly before death ...

This time there's a photograph to accompany the story. Andrew Gregory doesn't look anything like Zack now. How did I ever think he did? I can't believe how I'd reacted, reaching out to touch him, so stupid, the last thing I should have done. The police haven't been back for a DNA sample from me, though, so perhaps I hadn't; unless any traces I'd left on the body were washed away by the rain. I don't suppose that really matters, though. The police understand how I'd found him. They already know I'm just some foolish woman who'd been in shock and lost her head, who'd mistaken a man of thirty-four for her teenage son ... *Worn out, not yourself. In need of rest. Quiet.*

Maybe I *am* losing my mind. Hearing voices, seeing things. Telling myself stories.

The police have obviously had long enough to decide, anyway, since they've already tested the canine DNA. Now I'm relieved about that too. It would take a much bigger dog than Jasper to inflict those wounds and knock a grown man from the banking, even if he was drunk. I remember PC Jackson saying *cute little feller*, and glance towards the kitchen corner where Jasper's bed should be – only to find it missing.

I eye the empty washing machine. Then yank open the front of the drier. There it is, soft and clean. I pull it through the opening and it smells of fabric softener and a little of stale water, as if it's been in there too long. It doesn't smell of Jasper at all; not a single hair clings to it. Ethan must have done this, getting it ready for Jasper coming home, but instead it feels like all traces of him are vanishing too.

And it hits me: Jasper isn't coming back. Maybe Ethan already knew, deep down, even while putting up posters in Sandsend. *The dog*, he'd kept calling him. When did he last even say his name?

I sit on the floor and tears stream down my face. I'm not sure whether I'm crying over the washed dog bed, that my husband is gone, or that his ex-lover might have taken her own life. Unless it's all of it. I want to be us again, like we were. We've come so very far to keep our family together.

'Mum?' A voice calls softly.

Zack is standing in the doorway, looking down at me. His face is pale. I can hear music drifting through the air from the lounge, a tune Libby loves: 'Under the Sea'. Zack goes to check on her before coming back and shutting the door behind him.

'Dad's gone,' he says, and I don't know if it's a question or a statement, so I just nod. I go to tell him it won't be for long, it's all fine, though he can tell from my face that it isn't fine, nothing is. He reaches out, idly touching my phone where it sits on the units, turns it towards him. Sees what I was looking at. Then pushes it aside.

'But it's okay now,' he says. 'It's supposed to be okay.' His voice is tight. He's crying too, his face crumpling in a way it hasn't since he was small, a little boy who'd skinned his knees trying to do a wheelie on his bike, trying to impress his dad.

I scramble to my feet and pull him into my arms. I can't work out what he means but I can feel the tension in him, every muscle a taut wire. And something else, sensed but not seen: that bright thread of guilt. It's there again, buried deep inside him. I sense it even before he says, 'It's my fault.'

'Sh, Zack, of course it's not.' I hush him, desperate to show I don't blame him for any of this. 'None of this is your fault, or Libby's. It's down to *us*. And we'll – sort it.' I find myself echoing Ethan's words. I don't even know how to fix anything any longer, but I determine that I *will*. I'll find a way. The kids shouldn't have been touched by this. But infidelity can't simply be forgotten, can it? It can't be consigned to the past or carried away with the tide. It forms connections. It goes on leaking its toxins, poisoning everything: the words we say, the water we drink, the air we breathe. But I brought my family here and I'll keep us together. The Kellaways, forever.

'Then why's he gone? You *know*, don't you? He told you.' He glances at my phone again. 'But *they* don't even know anything. He said they haven't a clue. He didn't have to tell you a thing. He didn't have to go.'

I can't take in what he's saying. I can't speak.

'I'm sorry, Mum. I'm sorry. I'm sorry.'

His words tumble over me like a river, threatening to pull me under. An ocean of cold water. I hold onto him more tightly than ever. Suddenly I don't want to let go; I'm afraid my son will vanish too.

'What the hell do you mean, Zack?'

I feel him go still. He draws away from me. His face, so close to mine. Distorted. Hardly like the Zack I know at all.

'I thought you knew. I thought he told you everything.'

'*You* tell me, Zack,' I say. 'All of it. Right now.'

And he does.

41

A memory.
 A boy is searching for his dog, though he doesn't truly expect to find him. He doesn't expect to find his dad either; let alone the woman with him, holding onto his dog's lead. But Jasper is there, barking excitedly to see Ethan, up on two legs, the breath rasping in his throat as he strains against his tether. The lead is bright red and ends in a chain, not Jasper's usual collar, and it's pulled tight. It's nothing Zack recognises, but he would know his dog anywhere.

The two of them are standing by the road, on the banking above that weird pool. They just got out of their cars. Zack had heard engines slowing, doors banging, and then, after a scurry, that rasping sound, punctuated by a familiar yip. They haven't noticed Zack. He'd walked there across the moor, is standing by the water. He can't see anything in its surface but clouds.

He can hear their voices, though. This is how he knows there's something between them. Because Dad doesn't say, *Great! You found our dog.* He doesn't even say *Hello*. He just asks, 'What are you doing with him, Sienna?'

His voice is low. There are layers in it. Zack isn't certain what those layers mean, but he can guess. Those car doors, slamming, almost in unison: this meeting wasn't accidental. It was arranged, though Dad hadn't said anything about that, didn't tell them anyone had called, didn't say, *Hey, someone found Jasp! I'm going to pick him up and bring him home.*

It's *her*, he realises. The bitch. The one who'd messed up his family. Made his mum cry. The reason they had to move.

'I found him, Eth,' the woman says, her voice lilting and smooth. 'He came running to me, across the moor. He was so glad to see me again. I gave him some food. He'd missed me. Did you—'

Did you *miss me*. That's what she's going to say, and Zack ducks down below the banking. He doesn't want to be seen, can't bear to look at his dad's face. He doesn't want to hear how he's going to reply. Still, everything inside him is waiting.

'You took him? You came to our *house?*'

'What? No, of course not. I was on the moor, camped out for a night or two. It was nice. Beautiful. It was good just to be near you, Eth. I did message you. It would have been better if you could have got away, you know? Given us a chance to talk. But Jasper came, didn't you? You found me, didn't you boy, hmm? Jasp?' Her tone shifts, soft and babyish, and Zack curls his hands into fists. *He's mine. My* dog.

'Ellie saw you, standing in our *garden*.'

'She can't have. I don't know what she saw, but it wasn't me. I was careful. I told you I'll always be careful, didn't I? If that means we can see each other. I haven't even told my own mother I'm here. You don't have to—'

'Yes. Yes, I do. You should have done exactly what I said.'

There's a long pause. 'Jesus, Eth. Don't you even – didn't you ever—' She's crying, the woman is crying, Zack can hear it in her voice, but it doesn't soften him towards her. She deserves it. She deserves all that's coming. Everything that's happened to his family, to him, is because of *her*.

She hasn't finished. 'I care about you, Ethan. Don't you get that? I know you had to come here for the sake of your kids, I *know* that, but that doesn't mean I can just stop feeling what I'm feeling.' She sniffs. 'I took care of Jasper, just like I took care of Libby that day, when no one else did. And I'd have got him back to you sooner, but I didn't want to come anywhere near the house, and you didn't answer my messages, not until now. You know I'll always take care of anything of yours. Always. I love you.'

Zack waits for his dad to reply. He wonders what tone will be in his voice when he does; if it will be the same voice he uses with his mum. If there will be any trace of love in it. He holds his breath, waiting, but it never comes.

Instead there's a new voice. A man calls out, 'All right there?'

After a pause, Ethan replies, 'We're fine.'

'She doesn't look fine. Are you fine there, love? You don't look fine. Seem upset to me. This man bothering you, is he?'

'Leave us alone.' Ethan's voice is tight, curled around the words. 'This is private.'

'Not that private out here though, is it?' the man chuckles. 'You need any help, my love, just let me know.' He's slurring, as if he's drunk, Zack realises. *Jush let me know.*

There's a snuffling sound from the woman, no words, not now they're needed. Zack can't tell if she's unable to speak or if she won't, but it doesn't matter. He's heard enough. That's *his* dog up there. His legs are already moving, carrying him up and around the banking until he sees them clearly. His dad stands furthest away. Closer are the woman and Jasper – who's no longer straining for Ethan, but for Zack.

Closer still, there's a stranger. The man is a little taller than Zack and softly rounded. His hair is a shade lighter, though similarly long. He's older, but Zack wonders for a moment if his mum nags him to cut it, too.

'Zack?' His dad's voice is sharp, but there's no time to reply because the woman gasps and suddenly, Jasper is loose.

The dog bolts across the grass. Zack has found him, and Jasper has found Zack. Crouching down, Zack holds out both hands, ready for his dog to fly into them, when there's a yelp and Jasper is sprawling on the ground.

The man he doesn't know, the drunken man, has moved faster than anyone could anticipate. He's stamped down on Jasper's lead.

New sounds arise from the dog. Not sounds he's made before. Guttural, choking sounds. The chain has snapped tight around his neck, crushing his windpipe. Jasper's struggling to breathe. He isn't getting up.

Zack runs towards him, shouting his dog's name. He isn't seeing his dad or that woman any longer. He isn't seeing anything except Jasper, lying on the ground. But the man is closer and reaches him first. He stoops, wobbling, rising once more with Jasper balanced across his forearms.

'All right, all right,' he says. 'No harm done, there, see?'

Jasper is still breathing, he must be, because Zack can hear air whistling in and out of him. It isn't a good sound, though, and he stops a couple of strides away.

'Let him go.'

The man wobbles around in a circle, taking in Sienna's teary face. 'Yours, is he? He'll be right, love. Be right, in just a minute. I'm bringing him back to you.'

'Let him *go*,' Zack repeats. He wants to loosen that chain. To see if his dog will still be able to move, stand up, lick his face.

The man stumbles. And Jasper panics – writhing, scrabbling, desperate to escape the person who hurt him. The man leans back, away from Jasper's flying claws, and blood appears on his cheek. He convulses, flinging out his arms, pushing Jasper out and away.

One last scrabble and Jasper is gone.

From somewhere below him, Zack hears another sound: a high, brittle yelp. He blinks, trying to take in what he just saw: Jasper's dark, formless shape flying out over the drop. He's picturing something else too: the fragile bones down the length of Jasper's legs. He's felt them beneath the skin so many times, stroking Jasper, curled up with him on the sofa, playing lie down and paws.

Zack doesn't think. He's running towards the stranger who's just thrown his dog away like a sack of garbage. He doesn't care if the man's face is scratched and bleeding. He hates that face. Hates the man and he pulls back his arm and his fist flies out and the man sees him too; a split second before it lands he's suddenly fast, again, and he tries to dodge the blow and then he too is gone.

Zack blinks at the space where he had been a moment ago. Now there's nothing. Just a wide green expanse, and below, a pool reflecting the clouds. He steps to the edge of the bank, right up to the tufts of grass jutting over the drop. Below him is a shape on the ground. It looks a little like a rumpled coat. One arm is stretched out, as if reaching towards the pool. Perhaps he wanted to see what lay within it before he died.

Then his dad is beside him. Turning Zack away, grabbing his arms, holding him close. Zack looks down, this time at the knuckles of his own right hand.

It seems very important to him to see if there is bruising; to see if there is blood. He tries to gauge if his hand hurts, but he can't. He's numb all the way through.

Did he hit him? Is that why—

He opens his mouth to ask, but his dad's arms around him say it doesn't matter. Dad is speaking, and Zack can't follow the words but he knows they mean he doesn't need to know, doesn't need to ask, doesn't need to think of anything at all.

With those arms around him, he can be a child. Only that.

And he is.

After a while, the world comes back to him. Dad is still talking, he realises. Going on and on.

He says it wasn't his fault. That the man shouldn't have touched the dog.

He's saying the man shouldn't have questioned Dad, should just have done what he was told. He should have left them alone.

He says he was a coward. Spineless. That if he hadn't tried to dodge, if he'd stood and taken what was coming to him like a man, he'd have been fine. It would all have been fine.

Tried to dodge, thinks Zack, or *did* he dodge? There's a difference, and again he wants to ask his dad, to have him explain to him which it was, yet he doesn't speak. If the answer isn't the one he wants to hear, he doesn't know what he'll do. He doesn't know who he'll be any longer.

Zack lifts his eyes to the blue sky, to the clouds, and green; green everywhere. He sees his dad's shoulders, his stubbled cheek. Behind him is a woman. She stands watching them both, and her eyes are full of depths.

After that, it's all a blur. Only flashes stand out: his dad and the woman at the bottom of the banking, crouched over something. Not the fallen man – they already went to him, leaned in close, before stepping away. No: it's Jasper they're looking at.

There are words. Quick, sharp. They're arguing. They don't know what to do. His dad bends low, wrapping his arms around the dog, like he's going to pick him up, but for the longest time he doesn't move.

Then Dad is there, at the top of the banking. The woman is still there too, waiting for him. Always watching. Dad is carrying a weight in his arms. His face is close, lips moving, though the words keep sliding away.

... can't let our dog be found there, with the body ...

... bring them straight to us ...

He says things to Zack. Things about how he'll need to walk back to the house on his own. To wipe that look off his face. To look alive, for God's sake.

Mostly, Zack hears one thing: *The body. The body. The body.*

Dad says it needs to look like Zack has just been out, searching for his dog. All the while, loading his burden into the car.

But I found him, thinks Zack, *I found my dog,* and he starts to cry.

Dad seizes his shoulders. Shakes him till his teeth rattle. When he speaks again, his words are clear. 'Get yourself together, Zack. Right now. *Now*. This is no time for weakness. Do you hear me?' He grabs Zack's face, squeezes, scrunching up his lips, then releases him. 'Don't you dare let me down.'

His dad pushes him away. Not towards the banking; towards the path.

'This is all fine, Zack. Just keep your mouth shut, you hear? That idiot fell. He was pissed. Our dog was never here. *You* were never here. You saw nothing.'

Dimly, Zack realises that his dad is right.

He was never here.

He didn't find his dog. Didn't see Jasper thrown. Didn't run at the man. Didn't clench his fist. He didn't – he *didn't*.

Dad will be silent. So will Zack. They'll never speak of this again. He'll never have to think, see, watch it again, in the darkness of the night, when images press at his eyelids; when they scratch at the door to come in.

He'll never need to hear a voice saying: *Tell me, Zack. Everything. Right now.*

He'll never need to hear that voice as events replay themselves before his eyes, again, again, *again*, telling himself he *didn't*, he *couldn't*, all the things he's tried to believe. To feel hands gripping his arms, digging deep, deeper.

He'll never need to hear that voice ask the question, 'Where is he now, Zack?'

Where the hell is our dog?

42

I'm checking in on Libby. She smells of honey bath foam and her hair is spread around her on her bed like she's a princess. Her room is full of soft toys, cast-off scrunchies, crayons, felt tips, and slim hardback books with bright pictures on the covers. The mermaid doll is nowhere to be seen.

I had thought I'd heard a sound from her room, but perhaps it was me, rather than my daughter, who was in need of comforting. I'd tucked her in hours ago and she's still fast asleep. I'd checked on Zack too, and he hadn't looked like he'd sleep for a long while, but I'd smoothed back his hair and kissed his forehead like I used to, and he hadn't complained. He'd smiled at me and I'd nodded and neither of us said a word because we'd had no need to say them.

Ethan still hasn't come home. I don't know where he's staying tonight. A hotel? A tent, out on the moor? Somewhere else? He hasn't called or texted to say where he is and I won't call him. He was a dream to me once. Now I don't know what I'd even say to him.

He knew that Sienna was here and he tried to make me think I was losing my mind. He'd met her at least once, without telling me. What about all the other times he'd gone off in the car, supposedly searching for Jasper? Pretended to put up posters saying he was missing? Maybe it was Ethan, not the wind, who'd ripped down the one I'd put on our gate. All along he could have been trying to remove all traces of Jasper, in case the police connected us with what happened on the moor. He'd even told PC Jackson our dog had *gone*. Right in front of me, and I hadn't suspected a thing. I suppose it was lucky for Ethan that I'd left Andrew Gregory lying there in the rain, washing evidence away. Or that the police hadn't suspected the dead man could have been holding the dog who scratched him.

It was lucky for *our son*.

Now I see that Ethan's anger, the day I found Gregory's body, was really born of fear. He'd come home after seeing Gregory die and found the police already in our home. He'd protected our son, then found Libby crying, after being *exposed* to *that*. No wonder he snapped. No wonder Zack has been acting odd. Wandering the moors, hardly knowing where he'd ended up. *I was at the pool.*

At least I finally understand what it was he'd found there.

And where is Sienna now?

Where is Ethan?

Libby doesn't stir as I cross to her window. It's the smallest room but it's at the front of the house and I pull the curtains aside, looking out towards the Roaches. I can't see them. Rain is coming down once more, though silently; I hadn't heard its arrival. I can just make out the hills in the distance, lovely, wild, and *ours*, softened by veils of water. The moon has already risen, casting a pale glow, clouds hiding and revealing it by turns.

I shift my gaze to our garden and see a face looking back at me.

It's her. *Sienna.*

I blink the sight away – she can't be here, can't be real. She's only an image in my mind formed of everything I was thinking of, everything that's been troubling me, projected onto the scene below. This time I know that's all she can possibly be, and the reason I know it is that she is truly, finally, a mermaid.

Her hair floats around her head like the tendrils of some underwater creature, not weighted down by the rain but rising around her, lovely and flowing. Even her arms seem to drift on some unseen current, and I catch the metallic glint of something held in her hand – a mirror? A comb? I cannot see, from here, if she has a fishtail, and it doesn't matter. I can tell she's a mermaid, if not by her beauty, then by her skin. She resembles a statue; as polished as marble, as iridescent as fish scales. She is not as pale as marble, though. She is golden, this woman standing in the centre of my garden.

Yet she is still the same woman I had seen sitting beside Ethan on a beach, that same hair wrapping about his arm. The one who had answered his knock at her door and pulled him inside. The one who'd surfaced next to him from the sea.

I wonder what my gran would say. I suppose she'd have some good reason for this, an explanation I could accept, but when I close my eyes it's my mother's face that appears before me, her lips pursed in disapproval.

I blink and all of them are gone.

I lean forward, staring at the droplets coursing down the glass, so close to my face, until they blur together and all I can see is water. Sienna seems to have vanished into it.

I keep staring at the spot where she stood – where she *floated*. Here is the proof, if any more were needed; not that my husband's mistress is here, but that I am going insane. I thought of her then I believed I saw her. I will never be rid of her. It doesn't matter how far we go because her presence is shadows and moonlight and the reflection of my own troubled thoughts. In a way, she *has* followed me here, just as she will follow me everywhere. I might never see her face again, never hear her voice, but she will keep singing her siren song in my ear.

Little wonder if Ethan hears it too. Perhaps he always will, and chasing after it, he will drown.

'Is he coming home?' Libby's voice rises from her bed, heavy with sleep. She's woken after all, though she sounds like she'll drift off again any moment.

'Oh – love, not right now. It's horrid weather, you see. Your dad's just—'

'Not *Daddy*,' she murmurs, her voice muffled. 'The one from here.'

I don't know what she means, and I wonder if she's been dreaming, except that her words chime with something she'd said to me before. It was plural then, though, wasn't it? *The* ones *from here*. That's what she'd said. And I had pictured them: Joshua Linnet. Andrew Gregory. Zack, even.

She says, 'His little girl went in the pool, Mummy. She got sad because her daddy wasn't hers any longer.'

I turn cold. I tell myself I don't know who she means. Linnet's maiden? Bess Bowyer's daughter? Jenny Greenteeth? She's tired, muddling the stories, just as so many of them are already mingled, though what she's saying doesn't quite seem to fit any of them. And it doesn't *feel* like that, not really. Now, with the mist pressing in around us, the moon glowing through it all, with the vision I'd seen so fresh in my mind, it feels more like a premonition.

His little girl went in the pool. She got sad because her daddy wasn't hers any longer.

And then:

I want to swim with the mermaid, Mummy!

In my mind's eye, I picture Libby walking into Blake Mere Pool, eyes blank, mermaid doll clutched to her chest, listening to the voice calling to her from beneath the water: *Lib ... Lib ...*

No. I force myself to speak. 'Who do you mean, sweetie?'

'The one from *here*. She went into the pool, Mummy, but she didn't come out again.'

'Are *you* sad, Libby?' I make sure to speak evenly. I won't let her see my fear.

She sniffs, sounding more annoyed than sad – or am I just telling myself that? If Libby were unhappy, in a way that made her want to go into the pool and never come out again, I'd know, wouldn't I?

And she *isn't*.

'I wish Daddy would come home,' she says. 'He should come home, shouldn't he, Mummy?'

Now she doesn't sound sad at all. If anything she seems impatient, tired of waiting for her dad to walk through the door to give her a hug and a kiss. To put everything back to normal once more. I open my mouth to tell her he'll be here *soon*, then close it again. I can't promise that. I don't know what to tell her so I lean over and kiss her myself. She's half buried in the covers and her skin is warm and I peck the end of her nose, and she giggles – she's *fine*. I arrange the quilt around her, tucking her in tightly, and when I go, I leave the door ajar. It'll give her a little light from the landing, and I'll hear her if she stirs. I'll hear her if she cries.

I tread softly downstairs, avoiding the creaky steps. When I reach the bottom, I go to the twist under them, standing face to face with the mermaid carved into my home.

She stares back, as pagan, barbaric, and unpretty as ever. Nothing but carved lines, hacked, *stabbed* lines, but *there*: face, torso, arms, but no legs, just that curling fishtail. One hand raised to comb her hair. The other held over her heart.

In front of her, seated in rows, are Libby's toys. Teddy bears and beanies and a stuffed elephant. A purple pony and a little brown dog and a fairy. And at the centre of them, dolls, all staring at the mermaid with featureless black eyes.

The one from here, I think, and I shudder.

43

Another day and yet another new start, in a way, though I feel a hundred years older than I did when we moved here. There's an Ethan-shaped space in the bed next to me, a numbness where my feelings should be. It's as if something has been ripped out of me and I haven't yet adjusted to the shock. When I think about Zack, I feel a raw ache, and Libby is a worry too. *Those dolls*, lined up like supplicants at a religious service; like an offering.

I have to fix this, all of it, though it feels like there are too many pieces to put together, nothing but Libby's broken hag stone in my hand, shattered into fragments. But I know where I must begin, even if I scarcely understand how: the only place I can.

The three of us are subdued over breakfast, Zack staring at the table as he scoops cereal into his mouth, even Libby munching her dippy eggs and soldiers in silence. Zack finally asks, 'So where's Dad?' and

Libby pauses with her toast held halfway to her buttery lips.

I don't know how to answer that question. I can't admit I don't know. Not knowing is the worst thing of all, but it's also the truth, and so I decide it's better to lie. At least I've had time to think about this, while I'd lain awake in bed last night. 'He had some things to sort out at his old school.' Once I start, I'm surprised by how easily the words come. 'A bit of paperwork they need for next term. He's popped back over to help them with it. He'll be in touch soon.'

I'm careful not to say, *He'll be* back *soon*. No more promises that I don't know I can keep.

'Actually, Zack, I want to ask you a favour this morning. I need you to watch Libby for a while. Can you do that for me?' I turn to him.

He pulls a face – for a moment, he looks like the old Zack – and opens his mouth, probably to demand to know where I'm running off to, then his expression changes as the clouds descend again. The memories; the guilt; the shame. 'Are you sure you—'

'Of course,' I say, before he can finish asking his question. I want to stride across the room and hug him. I want to tell him he doesn't need to be afraid, doesn't need to wonder if he can even trust himself, but I can't do that because Libby is watching us both. She's perceptive enough to pick up if something is wrong between us. And she knows everything isn't right, of course she does, but she doesn't say a word. I force a light tone and add, 'I'd trust you with my life, love. More importantly, I'd trust you with Libby's.'

I wink at her, trying to make it into a game, but Zack knows I mean it. I won't have him doubting himself for the rest of his life because of a mistake. Because of an *accident*. He'll never have to look at his mother and wonder if there's something hidden there in the layers of her eyes, like I did when I was his age.

I smile and tousle Libby's hair, as if we're joking around, and she goes back to her breakfast. Zack continues looking at me until he nods. 'Course I will,' he says, and I know that I can put my plan into action.

Thorncliffe village is hardly a village at all. It's a cluster of pretty stone buildings huddled into a cleft in the land, sheltered from the vastness of the landscape. No one is about; I can't even see a tractor working the fields or a single car on the road. It is peaceful and silent, save for the hollow wind echoing over the hill. It feels closed off, with no answers in sight, but I have to try. I'll go door to door if I have to. Somebody must know something.

About the mermaid in our home.

About the *ones from here*.

I decide to start at the place where they always know pretty much everything: the village pub. The Reform Inn is ivy-covered and appears as sleepy as the rest of the buildings around here, but I go up to the porch with its neatly painted white windows and try the door. Locked. It's way too early and I realise my mistake. I exhale, impatient at the thought of waiting around for hours, but then, through the glass, someone steps into the porch. She's about my age, wearing an apron and carrying a caddy of cleaning products. She waves, as though expecting me, and unlocks the door. 'Is it the delivery?' She eyes me doubtfully, looks around as if for a van or a truck, then says, 'Sorry, we're not open till midday.'

'It's not actually a drink I'm looking for,' I say. 'Not quite yet, anyway.'

She smiles at my feeble joke and starts to wave goodbye, but I stop her. I tell her that I'm a neighbour and her expression warms. I tell her what it is I'm seeking and it falters once more.

'You've heard something about that, have you?' she asks. 'If you're sure you want to know. It's not such a nice story, I'm afraid.'

I'm reminded of the cyclist we'd met on our first day here, as if things have turned back to the beginning again. *There's a whole other version of the story. Though that one's not so nice ...*

Another mermaid tale. More local lore, but this time – I sense it – it is more recent still.

She sighs. 'I can explain some of it, love,' she says, 'if you really want. Step inside. I'll make us a cup of tea.'

She shows me into a large, spacious room and disappears to boil the kettle. All is calm and quiet and it's strange being in a pub without anyone else. Ancient beams, empty chairs, and light falling across stripped oak floorboards. On the far wall, a huge mural depicts a lion; on another is a framed image of boxing hares. I stare at that for a moment before taking the seat beneath them. *Here*, I think, though I don't know why. I only have an inkling that there is *something* – an odd feeling that seems connected to my grandmother and the scent of freshly baked parkin in her kitchen, the clack of wooden bracelets on her arms.

The woman returns and introduces herself as Lisa. She pours cups of tea from a ceramic pot, passing me a biscuit. She asks me where we're from, what we do, whether we have kids. I like her. She's practical and friendly in a way I've missed since leaving the other mums and Sally in Sandsend. It's easy to chat and laugh and sip tea. For a moment, the past few days feel like nothing more than a bad dream. But Zack and Libby are waiting for me at home, so I get to the point and ask her why we have a mermaid carved into our home.

She sighs and looks uneasy, until she seems to decide I really do want to know. That I *need* to know.

'That stone used to be an old way-marker,' she explains, 'back in the day. It stood at the boundary between the edge of the village and the start of the moor. It was built into the house years back, but there weren't any carvings on it, not then.

'It was Derek Tomlinson and his little girl had the place before you. But he had – problems, I suppose. People keep to themselves around here, sometimes a bit too much. Not enough time in the pub, see? Spending time with their neighbours.'

She smiles and I nod my agreement, as if I'm in on the joke with her.

'He was lonely, by the sounds of it. So he went a little off the rails, I think.'

He's hers, I think. *Like the other one.* Is that what was wrong with him? He'd found something up there on the moor, so close to his home, something he couldn't altogether understand, but its voice had called to him anyway …

'Not sure if it ran in the family or if she was just worked up over her dad, but his daughter was peculiar too. She took to wandering the hills. Locals would see her going here or there, always on her own. They worried about her.'

I sympathised with their concerns. A child, wandering like that.

'She especially liked the pool,' Lisa adds. 'Blake Mere.'

Here it is, the thing I sought; and yet her words come as a relief.

His little girl went in the pool, Mummy. She got sad because her daddy wasn't hers any longer.

Libby never was talking about herself. She was talking about the *ones from here*, the ones she thought I'd glimpsed outside her window. And the reason she'd thought that was that she must have seen them too. I think again of her expressions sometimes. A quirk of her mouth. A pursing of her lips. The reflections and echoes of my grandmother, seen once more in my daughter. I think of candles and incense, a velvet cloth covering a table. I wonder what else of Gran's Libby has inherited. Perhaps it's more than physical traits, and she's also been picking up on *energies*.

'A bit of a strange place,' Lisa is telling me now. 'Tragic, really. There's been a number of drownings there, over the years. Too many.'

I tell Lisa I know of the pool. I don't tell her about the way it seems to have bewitched my family too.

'Sadly, this girl was captivated. She went up there one day and didn't come back. They found her – well. You don't need to know the details. But her father was devastated, as you'd expect. He'd have blamed himself, I suppose. You would, wouldn't you?'

I agree in earnest.

'Anyway, the man got worse after that. He had a brother who came and took him away from here, but before he left, he carved that mermaid into the house. Some say it's supposed to be his daughter, that he was trying to persuade himself that's what she'd become. An attempt to make it less sad, I suppose. To give her a happy ending.'

But Libby hadn't been fooled by it. Little girls know heartbreak when they see it.

'Others – well, around here they've always said there's a mermaid that lives in the pool. It's just an old story, but they reckon her father fixated on the idea that if he carved that mermaid there, and gave her – I don't know, his loyalty, offerings, something – that maybe she'd give his lost daughter back. That he'd see her again.'

'And is he still—'

'Oh he's alive, somewhere, I suppose. The brother organised the house to be sold without him ever coming back here, though. I hope he's doing better, wherever he is.'

'That's so sad,' I murmur.

'There's a picture of them, if you want to see it.' Lisa gestures over to the far corner, which is different from the rest of the pub. Everything else seems newly decorated, airy, light. This one preserved a corner of history, with a grouping of photographs in gold frames. Some of them are in black and white. Some are in sepia. 'This is an old place,' she says. 'Goes way back. We wanted to keep a little bit of the past.'

Most of the old pictures show the pub in various stages of renovation. Others depict long-gone families, friends and neighbours standing outside the door. 'There,' she points out.

This photograph is in colour. It shows a man perhaps in his thirties, wearing a grey jacket and trousers, a hat pulled low over his head. His eyes are in shadow, difficult to make out. And at his side—

'But that can't be right,' I exclaim. 'Are you sure it's the right one?' I scan the others, but I can't see another father and daughter image anywhere. 'I thought he had a little girl.'

'Oh – well, people always call her that. She grew up here from a bairn, you see. And I suppose that's how he spoke of her – people do, don't they? They never believe their kids are all grown up. But she was, or almost, when it happened.' Lisa pauses. 'She's beautiful, isn't she? Such a shame. He's older than he looks, too. Hardly seems old enough to be her dad, does he? But he must have been in his forties at least.'

On closer inspection, the woman *is* beautiful. She's tall and slender and perhaps eighteen years old. She has long, flowing hair, though it is not golden; her hair is dark, blowing in the breeze, wrapping itself about her father's arm. That isn't the strange thing, however. The strangest thing – the one that makes my words dry in my throat – is that I recognise her.

And I have to leave. Now.

I make my apologies to Lisa. I thank her for her story – perhaps the most important of them all, at least to me. I agree not to be a stranger and to call by again before I step out of the inn, turning to face the hills, the moorland and my home. Before I start to walk away I pause, one more question coming into my mind.

'Oh – yes,' she smiles. 'I do know her name. It was Grace.'

Grace. That was the woman I had seen standing outside our window, that very first night we moved here. Staring at our house. Watching my family. Watching me. I had thought it was Sienna, her hair darkened by the moonlight, her features softened by the distance, but it hadn't been Sienna; of course it wasn't. Even if Sienna had followed us, she could hardly have arrived so quickly, could she? She couldn't have raced so fast along the road from Whitby that she could lie in wait for us here, like a – *like a mermaid,* carved into our house.

I had assumed it was Sienna. It made sense that it was her. I'd expected it to be her, and so the young woman I'd seen had become her, forming and re-forming, taking on the shape that was so present to my mind. I had seen something and taken it for something else …

Didn't you *see?*

But I *had* seen. I just hadn't recognised what I was looking at.

I see it again now: a second figure standing outside our house, this one definitely fair-haired, but hadn't that hair appeared a little too pale for Sienna's? And she'd seemed even younger still.

A third sighting and her hair had been full of shadows, dark once more, perhaps even darker than before. She had been beautiful too, but so very solemn – a little like Sienna, certainly, but *not* Sienna. And something had been wrapped around her. I had thought I was seeing things, imagining fishing nets or seaweed, but I don't think I'd been far from the mark.

She had been bound in rope, after all, before she'd been thrown into Blake Mere Pool.

I hadn't been seeing one woman, distorted by moonlight or darkness or rain or anything else. I'd been seeing different women.

Dead women.

Only the last of them had been Sienna. I had seen her plainly then, knowing her to be the woman who'd tried to win my husband, despite the strangeness of that golden skin; despite her floating hair.

And Libby had seen them too. She must have. She'd sensed the instincts of a distraught father, making that carving, presenting his *offering*, and she too had begged the sea witch to return what was lost. She'd turned it into a child's story, but the reality was still there, *beneath*. Libby has my grandmother's blood in her, no matter if it skipped a generation with my mother. My gran, who claimed to have conversations with the dead. To *channel* them. Things I had tried so hard to reject, as if in so doing I hadn't also been rejecting *her*. Everything she was; the special piece of her that was in me too. The part of her that is in my daughter.

I'm sorry.

I hurry back towards my home. When I reach it, and walk through the front door calling for my children, there is no reply.

I check the lounge but Zack isn't watching TV and there's no Libby dancing around the floor in time with a perky song. She isn't lying on the sofa combing out her honey-coloured hair, her legs wrapped in a blanket adorned with fish scales. I run upstairs, checking her bedroom, then Zack's. Both are empty. The whole house is. I can feel it. It's happening again and everything flashes before me: reaching into the water to pull my daughter back, my fingers closing on nothing. Zack, half naked, shivering in a cave, his eyes unfocused and empty. Running along the beach, children everywhere, smiling, laughing, but none of them mine.

Jasper. Ethan. Now Libby and Zack. My whole family is gone.

I tell myself they'll come back at any moment. The door will open and they'll spill inside and everything will be as it should. Things will return to normal. We'll reach out and embrace one another. We'll pull ourselves from the water. The past will be washed away, as if it never even happened. This is our new start, the life we had planned together. It's still here, but only I am left and I cannot breathe.

I close my eyes and try to calm myself. I trusted my son. I *promised* to trust him. With my life; with Libby.

And I know that I can. I *do*. I reach for my phone to text him and find that he has messaged me already.

All fine here. Taking Lib to the pool.

I don't know if that comes as a relief. I don't want them there, but I text him to ask a question and for once, my son is prompt in replying. I smile at his response.

Then my knees give out and I find myself sitting at the top of the stairs. I gaze at the screen, knowing there's someone else I need to contact to answer a final burning question. One detail, seemingly inconsequential yet vital, will help me fit all the pieces together.

I send my message and wait. It isn't long before Sally replies and when she does, I stare down at the answer for what feels like an eternity.

Now I know exactly where my husband went that day in Sandsend.

And I know where I need to go.

Before I do, I send one last message. This time, for my husband.

Those three little words that will bring him back to my side.

44

I run across the moor. Heather claws at my legs, the thin, dark twigs like wires scratching me and trying to slow me down. But I won't be slowed. I don't stop until the path opens into a little shelf of land with what appears to be a hole in the world at its centre. The pool is silent. Reflected clouds mask its depths. The ground welcomes me when I kneel, softening beneath me. Only the water appears to be a hard surface, a mirror offering nothing, not even a glimpse of all that it has taken.

But every woman from every story lies here, as clear to me as if I can see them, as if they are gliding from the water to stand at my side. Sisters, now: Grace Tomlinson, Linnet's maid, Hannah Bowyer. For a moment I see them lined up behind me, reflected in the water, then the breeze disturbs the surface and turns it a dull dead grey revealing nothing.

There *is* nothing. Only the cold and the deep.

Yet that is where I must go.

I slip off my coat and throw it behind me. I kick off my shoes. My top and jeans follow, until I'm shivering in my underwear. I'd had no time to grab anything more practical, not so much as Libby's aquamarine blanket.

Libby. My daughter; my blood. She had once curled inside me like a sea creature, her tiny fingers like fronds, her soft eyes like anemones, her skin so delicate it needed the shell of me to survive. I suppose she was a mermaid then, as we all were, once. Now I know she is safe; she's with her brother. I'd paused to send him a text before I left the house.

I don't want Libby near the water

I knew Zack wouldn't want to be within a mile of this place again, but his sister has a voice and I was concerned she'd persuade him. His reply put my concerns to rest:

Don't worry. I told Libby we're going to Doxey but we won't even get halfway ;-)

I peer out across the moor, but if they're out there, heading towards the Roaches, I can't see them. Libby might already have tired and been persuaded to go home; they could be sitting in the lounge, sneaking biscuits from the snack tin and watching TV. I know that Zack will take good care of his sister.

I step from a tussock of marsh grass onto peat, as sodden with water as a soaked sponge, and from there into water that is muddied with earth. Against my skin, it's the colour of tea, but stone cold. The bottom of the pool is silken, an almost-there sensation of slippery soft silt. I can't see where the next step will take me. The water ahead is as opaque as it always looked from the bank. It might really be bottomless. I might keep swimming forever, down and down …

I remember what the cyclist said. *I try not to stir anything up. It's best just to float.* And so, when the water slides over my knees, then to my thighs, I don't keep moving forwards but allow myself to fall. I break the surface, and then I am swimming. I am *wild* swimming.

This is what I wanted to show you … It's just you and the elements. You and the water, in the moment, and nothing else. It makes you feel what it's like to be completely alone.

But I don't feel completely alone.

I'm soon at the centre of the pool. It isn't far but I'm gasping as if I'd swum for miles, the cold seeping into my muscles. I turn and lie back, floating until I adjust to it, though the water feels like ice against my scalp and I don't like to consider the bottomless depth beneath me. Gradually the sting of the water begins to fade, subsiding to intermittent prickles darting through my hands and feet. I tell myself the thought of diving into this water is worse than actually braving it so in one fluid movement I twist onto my front, tilt my pelvis and swim straight down.

I can taste the peat, the hillside, the minerals and the years of rain. It has a salty tang that surely once came from the sea – unless the water really is full of a mermaid's tears. I open my eyes and they sting with brine. The pool at once expands around my body and pushes me out, guarding its secrets. Suspended in the liquid, a million tiny particles dance, confusing my vision. There almost seem to be shapes within them, forming and re-forming, shifting in the murkiness. I tell myself it's only a reflection of my movement, but I can't find my way through. I can't see and I can't find the bottom, not yet. I keep undulating downward. I refuse to read anything into the forms darting towards me, retreating again. I have to try and truly *see*.

I pass down through layers of cold, but I try to keep my focus until I make out something that doesn't belong: straight, sharp edges that speak of man, catching faint glimmers of light. It appears to be the cyclist's farm machinery, dumped in the water. I swim towards it, but don't seem to draw any closer. This pool feels bigger than it should be, and deeper, as if I've passed through some tunnel and am in the ocean itself, and lost. I glimpse something that shouldn't be there; in the next moment, I can't see anything at all.

Then I'm kicking towards the surface, eyes squeezed closed, my body responding to the need for air before I could make a conscious decision. I burst from the water. There's a rushing in my ears like the sea, roiling shapes that take a moment to resolve into clouds. Clean air fills my lungs. I don't even feel cold, not now I can breathe. It's exhilarating; it's *life*.

This is what Ethan spoke of. The sound grows louder, pressing in against my ears, and I *feel* it: water, droplets in my hair, landing on my face, and everywhere, prickling the surface of the pool. Rain is coming down, hissing like waves on the shore, water above and around and below me.

I take a breath, gasping as much air as I can, because I need to go back once more, to see what the depths hold. I push downward and the water responds, roiling at my intrusion. It resists at first, then welcomes me in, claiming me for its own. Particles shift and simmer, catching at the light, glistening gold before turning dark once more. This time I know where to go. There: I make out metallic struts and spikes and jags, an implement that might once have been attached to a tractor, designed to work solid ground. A suggestion of silver, of crimson paint, of rust. And there, in its claws, drifting like kelp: fronds of golden hair.

A mermaid's underwater garden. At its heart, a statue.

This statue doesn't depict a prince, however. It's a woman. She is trapped in the cage formed by the machinery and only her golden flowing hair floats free. Her skin is golden too, her limbs sheened as if with iridescence or fish scales. And she is pale, but this woman isn't made of marble. The peat has turned her to gold.

I taste her name on my lips. *Sienna*. Here she is: the image I have carried in my mind for so very long, that has followed me and haunted me, always in my thoughts, both dreaming and waking. She is here in the water, her skin gilded and glistening, one hand raised to her lovely hair. The other floats just in front of her heart. She is holding something – a comb? A mirror? It catches the faint light that reaches her.

She has become that thing I could never be: perfect. She is a mermaid. Temptress and siren. Seduction and peril. And yet she is still a woman, someone who deserved to find her prince, to have the perfect family, the perfect life.

A woman, drowned.

I had so badly wanted her to be a monster. But she never was.

I had hated her for so long. Now I see her clearly at last.

Her eyes stare into mine, as sightless and clouded as fish eggs. And I see that her golden skin is tarnished, not smooth and perfect after all. Beneath the glisten lent her by the peat are patches of darkness, discolorations that might be bruises or decay; impossible to tell. Her limbs are misshapen, her body softened and swollen. The metal jaws around her have sliced through her filmy dress and into her body. I see the layers within, liverish hues, pale fat, the rainbow tones of meat gone bad. Even the pale gleam of bone. She no longer possesses beauty; unless it remains in the still-bright gold of her hair.

This is the truth of her.

I focus on her hands, her wrists; on the thing wrapped around the one closest to her heart, and the object she clutches in the other, twined in her fingers, long after it could have been any use.

My hatred for this woman dissolves into the water. There is nothing left. No more answers I need to find. There is only the need for oxygen, a demand I can't ignore, throbbing through my blood and bones, the insistent pulse of life. My lungs burn; my vision blurs. I swim towards the surface. The air floods into me like a gift.

I breathe and the world comes back to me. Through the water, through the rain, I see the figure who stands at the edge of the pool, waiting to see what might surface. He might be Joshua Linnet or Derek Tomlinson or Andrew Gregory, but I know that he is none of them. I am not looking into the past. This is the present, and the story is mine.

My husband raises his head and looks into me with eyes as cold and clear as meltwater.

45

'You lied to me,' Ethan says.

I don't deny it. He looks down at the mobile phone he clutches in his hand. On it, my text: those three little words that had brought him to my side. Not *I love you*, not this time. Instead: *I found her.*

Ethan had seen those words and known exactly where to come.

'You hadn't found her, not then, had you?' he says. 'But now you have.'

I am still half submerged, the cold water pricking my limbs, my hair drenched and dripping. All around me, the rain on the water hisses like snakes. The downpour has stolen the hills, the sky, the view. There is only the pool, all around me and everywhere. It comes to me that I must look like a water spirit: a cursed, misshapen creature rising from its depths. Not a goddess, certainly, but nothing entirely natural. Something as wild as a hare; as bewitched as moonlight.

'I found her here too,' he says. 'She just couldn't get over our break-up. Losing me. She—'

'Don't.'

Ethan meets my eyes for a brief moment, though his expression is unreadable. There is something about the way he stands so still, the way he won't or can't bring himself to look at me. It's as if he's Ethan but not Ethan, as if the man I thought I knew is lost, buried away somewhere deep inside him. Whoever this stranger is, I don't need to hear his words. I already know the story he will tell me. Sienna had been swimming, wild swimming, one last time. She'd done all that she could to win her prince and having failed, she longed only to return to the water. She was a good swimmer, a strong swimmer. Maybe she'd found drowning harder than she imagined. So she'd pulled the mouldering metal down on top of herself, to prevent her body from betraying her, rising again and demanding air. Because she just – couldn't – get over him. And then what? He'd known her so well, he'd guessed where to search for her? Had she left him a note? I shake my head in disbelief, but Ethan tries anyway.

'I love you, Ellie. I always have. You asked me to fix things, and I only did what you wanted. I broke it off with her, but *she*—'

She. The way he says the word makes it seem like Sienna has become nameless to him now. That he is trying to make her something less than human in his mind.

'I know what happened with Zack and Andrew Gregory,' I tell him. 'I know about Jasper. Sienna saw it all. Why don't we start there?'

He flinches, or I think he does. The cold is taking hold of me. My skin is numb all over, like something strange to me, something I might at any moment cast off. I have to get out of the water. I need to clothe myself, warm up, fend off the risk of hypothermic shock. And so I step towards the edge, where Ethan stands. At first he doesn't stir; then he reaches his hand towards me.

'I protected Zack, Ellie,' he says. 'Everything I did – it was for *us*.'

I stare at his outstretched fingers, not knowing if I'm going to take his hand, but after an agonising pause, I do. Ethan, who has always been home to me. Safe. I've never had to touch his skin and sense something terrible waiting there, beneath the surface. I've never had to worry that I was eccentric or mad, that I was anything like my grandmother. All that had stopped when I was with him.

I feel nothing when my numbed skin touches his. There is only the cold: only the grey. I close my eyes and for the first time, I *see* it; like a vast seabed going on forever, featureless and empty. Betraying no secrets. No traces of pain for *her*, no love for *her*. I shake my head as I step from the pool, rain still pouring over me. I retrieve my clothes but they're already soaked so I just pull my coat tightly around my shoulders, feeling its lining cling to my wet skin. I hope Zack is wrapped up warm, wherever he is. I hope he dressed his sister for a storm. I pray my children are indoors once more, safe.

'Why didn't you just tell the police the truth about Andrew Gregory?' I say. 'It was an accident.'

He draws in a long breath. 'I did what I had to, Ellie. I looked after our son. What do you think would have happened if the police spoke to him in that state? I looked after both our kids. What would you have done?'

That, I can't answer. Instead, I say, 'So you decided to cover it up. It was easy, really, wasn't it? Jasper – gone. Zack – keeping everything inside. You – silent. There was only *her*, wasn't there? There was only Sienna left who could spoil everything.'

'What are you saying, Ellie?' An unsettling edge creeps into Ethan's voice. 'How can you even suggest – I'm your *husband*. The same person I've always been. It's like you've been losing it, ever since we got here—'

'Maybe she threatened to tell,' I press on, my voice unwavering, 'or maybe she threatened our family. Maybe even *you*. You'd covered things up – the police would have thought the worst, wouldn't they? So you came back here. You got her to meet you at the pool, early, before anyone would be around, and you killed her. You drowned her, Ethan, because you knew *you'd* keep quiet and you could make sure Zack kept quiet, but you couldn't control her, could you? You hadn't even been able to stop her from following you.'

His jaw is clenched. Droplets of rain are running over his skin, dripping into his eyes. He doesn't wipe them away. 'That's insane, Ellie. You can't think that. It was an accident.'

'Another one?'

He doesn't reply.

'Your watch is in her hand, Ethan.'

The colour drains from his face at this detail, one he'd perhaps overlooked. Then he gathers himself. 'I lost that ages ago, El. I didn't like to tell you. You know how I loved that watch. If she has it on her now, it must be because she found it. Maybe she kept it as a souvenir of me, after I broke things off with her. Something to keep with her when she did that to herself. It's nothing more than that.'

I picture it again, entwined in a dead woman's golden fingers in the depths of the pool. *For the years to come. All my love, Ellie.* The watch I'd chosen so carefully for Ethan so that he could keep it with him everywhere and always. But he hadn't, had he? And why? Because he'd been so afraid that *Daddy's mermaid* would find a voice at last. Now he sounds so reasonable, so calm. So earnest that it is hard not to believe his version. His words pour over me like water, quenching the thirst for answers I've held for weeks.

'You know how unhinged she could be, don't you. The way she took Libby that time, you remember that, don't you?'

Unhinged. The very word I'd used for her. And yet now I can picture Libby too, glancing out of our window in Sandsend and seeing a mermaid, a real live mermaid, coming to visit her. I can see her reaching up to open the door. Skipping outside, taking her by the hand.

I had so wanted Sienna to be a monster that in the moment I'd blamed her for snatching my child. But I see things differently now; she wasn't a monster.

Now she is here, with the others; with her sisters. I know that because I've looked out of a window and

I've seen her too. I've seen all of them. Not one woman, but different women. Dead women, drowned women, stepping out of their stories and walking off the moor, emerging from the pools on moonlit nights. I've witnessed them standing outside and looking in; at life, at the living. *Ghosts.* Spirits of the water. Nothing I could ever believe in, yet have been seeing all along, just as if I were my grandmother seated at her velvet-draped table.

And the reason I've been seeing these women, unsettled, drowned, is that they are not at peace. They cannot ever be, because somebody drowned them on purpose.

I sense it: Sienna was murdered just like Linnet's maid and Hannah Bowyer, her sisters of the pool. Joined by a single fate; united in a shared purpose.

I cannot say these things to Ethan. I can't say them to anyone. Such words belong within the realm of stories, not reality. They are not evidence; they would simply be washed away by the rain.

But I can say something else.

'Just answer me this,' I ask him. 'What did you do with the posters of Jasper you took to Sandsend?'

His eyes look steadily back at me. 'I – I threw them away, Ellie. You know why. There wasn't any need to search for him. I'm sorry—'

'No, there wasn't,' I say. 'So why did you go and visit Sally? And Mel, and the other neighbours? Asking after our lost dog? You didn't need to do that to humour me. You knew I'd already called them.'

'I – I didn't, El. I didn't see them.'

'Ah – well that's the thing, isn't it? Because I know you *did*. You went all over the court. Knocking on doors, being friendly, making enquiries. Showing your face. I asked Sally, you see. She said you'd been everywhere. You must have carried on even after we spoke.'

'I—'

'Showing your face,' I repeat. 'That was the important bit, wasn't it? Because first, you'd met Sienna here. You arranged to see her early, hours before anyone was around, while it was still dark. I suppose you used me as an excuse for that?

'Because you knew that one day she'd be found. But first she'd be in this peat-ridden water for however long, and who knows how exactly that would affect a body? They're not likely to determine an accurate time of death. But if the worst happens and someone manages to pinpoint what day she disappeared, well, you weren't even here, were you? You were in Sandsend. And you made damned sure that everyone saw you there, that you left a trail of posters behind you – because you needed a fucking alibi when the police inevitably showed up and started asking questions.

'And the reason you wanted an alibi is that you knew exactly what you were going to do. You planned it all. So don't try telling me Sienna killed herself. Don't try to claim you argued and things got out of hand and you just couldn't help yourself. Don't lie to me anymore.'

Ethan continues to stare at me with pale eyes. The rain pours all around him, and he doesn't seem to feel it.

'You're right about part of it, El,' he says. 'They will come looking for me. I tried to contact her using message services that don't leave a trace, but there were phone calls too. Texts. They'll get her phone records, and they'll see what date she stopped calling anyone at all. They'll come to me with their questions, but you know what? I *do* have an alibi.' His lips curl into a smile. 'They'll know she must have done something to herself, because I was in Sandsend. All day, El. It took me all day. And everyone we know there will back me up. It's not perfect, but it's close. Maybe they won't even look for her here, after that. They might never find her, El. Not for years. Maybe not ever.'

I am rooted to the ground. It's as if I'm the one who's made of marble. And the rain goes on falling, water covering the ground, filling each fissure and crease, glimmering like eyes opening everywhere I look. Ethan holds out his hands and catches it for a moment before letting it run through his fingers.

'And now let me explain something else, Ellie. Because I did this for *us*.

'I didn't want to hurt her. It was Sienna; she didn't give me any choice. You have to understand that. She saw what happened that day, you're right. And she wanted to use it to break us apart. She *did* use it. She kept insisting I had to see her, meet with her, because of Zack. Because of Jasper. She said she couldn't decide if she should call the police – that depended on *me*. Not her conscience, you understand, not her bloody *emotions,* because she was cut up or upset or whatever, by seeing a man die. *Me.*'

I try to picture it: Ethan heading off as if he was searching for our dog, as if he was in control of the situation, when he was actually compelled to answer to her whim; her siren voice.

'She kept contacting me, saying it would help her clarify things, if she could only see me. If we could talk. If I could just hold her hand for a while. You know? She thought she could use my family, use Zack – for *that*. It was as if she thought she could do whatever she wanted with us, like Zack was *hers* or something, and she got to decide.'

He's hers now, I think, and swallow down the sickness that rises in my throat.

'It was pretty clear that I had a choice, Ellie. I could be with her and save Zack but lose my marriage. Or I could have my family blown apart anyway, see Zack go to prison, see you shattered into tiny little pieces. So tell me, Ellie. What was I supposed to do?'

I can't reply. I don't know if I can trust his words. It's not as if Sienna can speak for herself. I can't ask whether she really was upset and confused after what she'd seen. She's been silenced; her story is as Ethan chooses to tell it.

He stares down into the pool. His next words are so soft, they are almost lost beneath the sound of rain.

'I took her into the water, El.' He's staring down as if he can see into the depths of it, as if he can see her there still, but the surface is grey, the mirror obscured. 'I think, in a way, it's what she wanted. She'd never have been happy without me. I made it look as if she could have done it herself. I suppose she will be found, eventually. But by then, I might already have been disregarded, because of my alibi. And I'll tell them how upset she was. The police won't be searching for a victim. They'll be searching for someone who must have taken off somewhere by herself. Who was upset. Who had a *reason*.'

'You watched her drown?'

Of course, I'd already seen something of the kind; Ethan's arm striking out to push someone beneath the water. But this is different. I see it happen as if it's before me. I picture him deep in the pool, pulling that cold metal down on top of the woman he'd once held so close to his heart. Holding her again, making sure she didn't, couldn't get away, reach the daylight and the air. Looking into her eyes and all the time knowing that she was drowning. Not as I had, unknowing as a child floated on the surface of the sea, his lips now in, now out of the water, but as anyone would expect: with struggling. Flailing. Fighting. Trying to get away; to *live*.

And what had he thought, in those moments? Was there any love left in him?

Was there ever?

But if there was, Ethan doesn't tell. Instead he says, 'We're going to be fine, El, you and me. You're my wife. Ellie Kellaway forever, remember? We made our vows. We swore we'd do whatever we have to, to keep our family together. We meant that, didn't we? You'll come home with me now.' For the second time, he holds out his hand towards me. 'We know what our story is. If it comes to it, if the police turn up, you know how to support me in it. So will the kids.'

I see the glint of his wedding ring as he waits for me to take his hand, as I always have. His eyes are so clear, as lucent as a man just drowned, and I remember all of the wonderful stories he would tell me. The stories that promised the two of us would be happy; better; *best*. And I know we can capture that magic again. We can go on living in our cosy house with our children, always happy, always smiling, a family to be admired, envied, even. Ethan and Ellie, the perfect pairing, the picture he had always painted of us; the loveliest of postcards.

If I remain silent. If I give up my voice. If I choose to be the quiet woman, the subservient woman, the one deserving of the prince's love.

He mouths the words now, *I love you,* as his eyes shine back the cold grey sky. The rain continues to fall but I can no longer hear the sound it makes. Those three little words, magical words, but there is no magic in them, not now. I can only see again what I'd glimpsed the last time I touched his hand: *nothing*. Only a barren seabed; only emptiness where his emotions should be.

I look at Ethan and I have no idea what he's thinking. I don't know if there's a soul looking back at me behind those eyes. I don't even know if love is something he can feel. And I am so very cold; too cold to say the words Ethan wants to hear, or even speak at all.

I can only shake my head. *No.*

'For our *family*, El.'

His voice is insistent, but I'm not listening any longer. I don't believe that Ethan drowned Sienna for Zack's sake, or Libby's, or mine, to save me from being broken into tiny little pieces. I know his actions had protected Zack; but mostly I think Ethan was trying to protect himself.

If in doing so he'd also protected his family, it was by extension. He can't uphold the picture-perfect image without us. The perfect dad needs the perfect children, the perfect wife. It was never about us, not really. We were only a shining pool giving back a reflection; nothing to be seen in its surface but him. We were his pretence of normality. A mirror to hold up to the world, to prevent anyone from seeing the ugly truth.

Even I hadn't seen it. But I do now.

I shake my head. I open my lips to tell Ethan what's going to happen – but I don't need to. There's no need to say anything to him; we've been married too long. He sees everything he needs to know in my eyes.

He smiles at me. It isn't his familiar smile, nor a comforting one. It's as if something has been stripped away, revealing what was beneath the surface all along, under the skin of him. He steps towards me, not to help me this time but to cut me off.

'I told you you'd love wild swimming one day, Ellie.' His lip twitches. 'You'll see. Just try it again. I need you to fetch my watch for me.'

'What? No,' I say. 'It isn't yours, not any longer. Anyway, you said you'd lost it. You said that no one would find her.'

His laughter is harsh. 'Of course I need it. It's on a fucking *dead body*, El.'

A *body*, as if that's all Sienna is to him: not someone he had once touched, kissed, taken to his bed. The lover who must have grasped at his wrists while he drowned her. Who had clung so tightly to the watch she'd found in her hands, as if it was the lifeline she desperately needed.

'We're done here, Ethan. I'm going home. To my kids,' I tell him, but those words ring strangely even as I speak them. It's as if the whole ordinary world I had known, the past memories, are dissolving away. Ethan, telling me I'm the most beautiful girl on campus. Me lowering myself to the ground, clumsy with my bump, asking him to marry me – to marry *us*. All of it, washed away. There is only here. There is only the endless rain.

'Ah – but I don't think you are. You're in the water already, aren't you? You're my wife. You can do that much for me. It's all I'm asking. One little thing.'

He moves closer to me and Ethan starts to sink into the ground, water welling around his trainers. He kicks them off. Takes another step. 'Don't try telling me you're afraid of the water now, El. You just need to dive in. You've done it once. Now do it for me.'

'Ethan.' Only one single word, and yet it is not. In this moment, it is everything: an attempt to reach him, in spite of everything, this man I have loved. This man I thought I had known. My whole body is shivering. His eyes cut into me, colourless now. There is no warmth in them. I'm no longer convinced there ever was. Had it only ever been a reflection of my own feelings? And beneath, going deeper and deeper, these layers of cold ...

He steps towards me again. 'The two of you had a fight,' he says.

'What?'

'You hated Sienna, didn't you? Of course you did. And she followed us here, all the way to the Peaks, because she loved me, Ellie, in ways you never could, that you weren't capable of, and so you were jealous. Spiteful. A woman scorned – so you lured her here to get rid of her.'

I blink. The world blurs around me.

'The kids will back me up. The way you made them move here, leaving everything behind – the way you kept on staring out of the window, saying you'd seen her – you'd lost your mind over her. You were obsessed. It's not like you were subtle about it.'

I shake my head. I want to remind him of everything we've survived, the distance we've travelled, but I don't because I'm not sure how to reach him anymore. I'm not even sure I want to. I don't have to ask him what the story he's fabricating on the spot means. Worse, it sounds understandable: an older, discarded woman who can't accept reality, an *unquiet* woman, had gone mad when her husband preferred someone else. I see again the contempt in PC Jackson's eyes when he'd looked at me. It's a story he'd be happy to believe in. Anyone would.

I step back from Ethan. Beneath my feet is nothing but half earth, half water.

'You drove me away, and that's when you really cracked, isn't it? You couldn't cope without me. You couldn't face life on your own. So you came out here to put an end to it, leaving those poor kids all alone, without a mother.'

Ethan has adopted a new expression, as if he's the grief-stricken victim. Always blameless. I suddenly realise this is the expression he'll wear at my funeral.

Or will it be Sienna's? I'm not sure it matters to him any longer. What he cares about is the way he'll look: the handsome widower, a man who made the mistake of falling in love with someone he shouldn't, but still, the cruel way he *lost* her – he was robbed of her and he's suffering, but oh, so *brave*. And he's still carrying on, being a great, no, *perfect* dad, in spite of everything …

I back away from him. I'm in water over my knees, no kind of footing beneath me. With another stride, Ethan is standing in the pool too. He's smiling. This is his element, after all. He is at home here in the water, where I am not. He is used to the cold; I am not.

It occurs to me that Ethan might not need a story at all. I might never be found. I'll simply remain here, entwined with Sienna. We'll be together always and always, sisters of the pool, until eventually we dissolve into ghosts. We'll be monsters, spoken of only in whispers. We'll be witches, both cursing the same man with our last breath. We'll be mermaids. We'll join with Joshua Linnet's nameless love, with Hannah Bowyer, with Jenny Greenteeth. We'll turn the water to salt with our tears.

There's no relenting in Ethan's expression, no memory of the years we've spent together. He's wrapped in this new story he's told himself: the one where the broken-hearted man's wife vanished without a trace or backward glance. He's burdened with their children, but he's doing his best. He always does that, doesn't he? He deserves admiration. He deserves pity. He needs all of those things, those emotions, for he has none of his own. There is only a reflection; only a surface. The children will cling to him all the same, because they'll have to, and he'll watch over them, a doting father. Nobody will ever think badly of him. And perhaps, one day, there will be someone else: a lovely, modest, *quiet* woman, who will be beautiful and adoring and as voiceless as he could wish for.

With another movement, I'm sinking. Ethan is fast. He lunges for me. He reaches with the same hands that have touched my skin, that have held me close, that have stroked my belly while I carried his babies inside it. Hands that passed me cups of tea. Washed my hair. Raised and fell in frustration when I said something he didn't like. Took a screaming child from me, to give me a little respite. He reaches with the hands that once held mine, our fingers entwined, and promised to love me.

I throw myself back into the centre of the pool. I am in deep water, my head is under and there's a world of noise, bubbling and rushing and a voice I can't make out. Steely fingers sink into my arm and a hand on my chest pushes me down. The water is dark. There are only confused, distorted glimpses: the surface, so far away, surely further than it should be. Nearer still, strange forms, twisted and broken, metal corroded and rough, ready to stab and rend.

I close my eyes and see Zack, adrift in teenhood, not yet sure of the man he will become. Libby, too young to think about anything of the kind, simply holding out her arms and expecting me to be there. I want them both so badly, it's a tight pain in my chest. I hope they're at home now, safe. I hope Libby is watching her film, the one she chose for herself; the one with the happy ending.

I reach out and my fingers close upon metal. Blood spools into the water but the blade doesn't reach my body and I force myself to tighten my grip, to push myself away. But other hands are around me, tighter still. They don't let go.

Through the murk, I see a face. It isn't Ethan. This is a woman's face, and she doesn't blink or look away from me, though her eyes are blind and white.

I am nothing but lungs that crave air and a heartbeat that echoes through the water. I am limbs that struggle and prickle and thrum. I am a tiny point of light. I am an animal, trying to live. But I'm not going to live. I am drowning.

Particles in the water writhe and pulse, then coalesce, turning the edges of my vision to black, a darkness that begins to spread. I battle the urge to open my lips, to let the water in. I flail and fight, but Ethan moves with me. He is drawing me close. He's holding me to his body, as he has so many times, but now his touch on my skin is vile.

All I can see is Sienna. Her skin, gilded and gleaming. I watch her as she watches me drown.

And I think: *Please.*

I was never what you wanted.

I was never what any of them wanted, what the spirit of the pool wanted. Not when I was fourteen years old, sitting on the bank of a pond and waiting for Jenny Greenteeth, and not now. That was not why they had come to me, standing outside my house, looking in. They had come because they knew that one day, I would be here, at this pool that belonged to them. They had come to warn me.

That voice I'd heard, coming to me through the water: not *Lib* ... *Lib* ... as I had thought, as I'd feared, but *Live*.

I am not the prince they had craved. I am not the lover who'd betrayed them. Now I am nothing, not even a voice. I am in Ethan's arms and this is where I will die. He is stronger; all he needs to do is to hold on. And so, instead of fighting, I stop struggling and let myself go.

There is nothing around me but blackness. I can't even see Sienna's face any longer. There is no end to the water. This pool is bottomless; an ocean. It is forever.

And then I am not certain what it is I see.

There's a brief impression of water-sleek skin. A flash of iridescence, of fish scales. A memory of aquamarine and turquoise and periwinkle, all the colours of the sea. There is a sinuous ripple that moves effortlessly through the water, then the muscular flick of a tail, curling upward beside me.

The mermaid is beautiful. Her movement is as silent as the deepest water, but I know that she is singing. If I hear no sound, it is only that her voice is too lovely for my ears; or perhaps because the water is her voice, her voice the water. Perhaps it is because her call is not meant for me.

And here, on my last breath, is a curse. An offering. A bargain to be made. Words, intended not for a mermaid, but a sea witch.

He's yours now. He always was.

I find there is something in my hand. A shard of metal: a blade. A bewitched knife that will allow me to return to my home once more, if only—

—I strike.

The water is enveloping me from all around. I feel its incredible power, stretching beneath the land and the rock and the hills and the peaks. It is connected to everything. I feel the vastness of the sea. It cradles me in its arms. And I am alone, but I feel her still. I sense her movement as she reaches out to claim the man she had loved; the one she had so wished to love her back.

Ethan is strong, but she is stronger still. She always was.

For a moment, everything is suspended. Then I am rushing upward, bubbles streaming from my mouth. I am moving towards the light. I am swimming, wild swimming, just me and the elements. I am completely alone.

I burst from the water like a creature just born. Dragging myself to the edge, I find I can breathe again. I shiver as the cold hits me. I twist and stare as ripples settle on the pool and the surface stills. I wait to see what else might rise to the surface.

I wait for a long time, but nothing does.

46

I stride towards home as quickly as I can make my leaden limbs move, trying to warm my muscles. My hands and feet are numb, but somewhere deep inside me there's a thread of warmth, the promise of life. As it begins to grow, the numbness in my feet gives way to pins and needles so sharp that every step feels like I'm stepping on knives.

I'm already beginning to wonder if I really saw what I thought I had. I think of the way that swirls of peat-laden water, catching glimmers of light, can seem to hold forms within it. Of how old machinery, weakened by years of immersion, could collapse into shards. The effect of the lack of oxygen on the brain, the shock of cold water, of panic. The way our thoughts can be driven by the pagan beneath the skin, stories surfacing, imaginings becoming visible, taking on new form.

I think of a sinuous fishtail, curling beside me. Hers – or my own? I'm no longer sure. I'm not certain it matters. We are sisters now, after all.

As I walk through the heather on shaking legs, two faint smudges appear through the rain. I half expect them to vanish, that they too are only a reflection of my innermost thoughts, but they do not vanish and they do not change. When I draw closer, I recognise them as the ones I have yearned for. My entire world. Then my son and daughter are with me. Libby laughs at how wet I am.

'Have you been swimming, Mummy? I was supposed to swim, but it was *far*.'

She slaps at Zack with the sleeve of her raincoat, and I laugh. We all do, though Zack looks at me strangely when I can't seem to stop.

The knowledge of what is waiting for them, out there on the moor in the glimmering pool, cuts deep; the loss that will be theirs, and I am silent for a moment.

I step towards Zack and wrap my arms around him. 'Thank you,' I murmur into his hair, and he doesn't know where to look, but he nods.

Raindrops run down our faces. I know that soon, they'll turn to tears. There will be days of them; weeks; perhaps years. Enough to turn a whole pool to brine.

I tell myself we will face each day as it comes. I will wipe the tears away. For now, I take Libby's hand and walk with my children across the moor. Soon there will be warmth and comfort. For now, there is the knowledge that we are a family, together.

47

The body is found three days later. Ethan is discovered floating on the surface of the pool, his lungs full of water, a deformed blade buried in his heart. It's a passing cyclist who spots him there, and I often wonder if it's the same one we had met on that first day, the one who'd warned us of mermaids and their sorrows. I do not know the answer, for I never had learned his name.

When they retrieve my husband's body and look into his face, they find it covered in scratches. Like the metal that ended his life, they blame it on the old farm machinery that remains submerged in the water, though they do wonder for a time if it was caused by the same animal that had marked Andrew Gregory.

Some, I imagine, still believe so, despite the lack of evidence. Stories have power after all, and the link must have been irresistible. And so it will be passed on, whispered from ear to ear, the start of a new legend: that of a feral dog stalking the moors, huge and black with burning eyes, ready to bring death to any lone traveller caught unawares. A fit companion, perhaps, for a lonely mermaid.

Whatever people may say, they never will know the true story.

48

A postcard.

There are children on the beach: wind-blown curls, shining eyes, bright laughter. They delve with plastic spades and upend their buckets, with never a care in their hearts for the future. I watch their happiness unfold. I see the wealth they possess: sand on soft skin, the tang of salt on their tongues, the relish of warm, clean air. Their thoughtless, casual beauty. Every boy is a prince, every girl a mermaid.

My own children have lost so many things. Before it even began, I'd even torn them from the sea. The least I could do in the aftermath, amid so much loss, was to give it back to them.

I found us a new house in which to live, but in our old home; we are here, in Sandsend.

I walk along the beach with Libby's hand in mine and feel the ocean pulling at my soul. I gaze across the wide blue freedom that stretches from horizon to horizon. It is a lovely spring morning of a new year, and we are going swimming. *Wild* swimming. Libby skips along, her bare toes sending up little flicks of powdery sand. She's left her mermaid doll at home. She doesn't seem to care for it any longer; it isn't much use, after all, when she's in the water. My daughter is wearing her orange armbands and a huge grin and a swimming costume with a unicorn on the front, her latest obsession. I'm in a one-piece, my hair, longer than it used to be, flowing loose.

On our last night in the *other* house, as we have taken to calling it, I tucked her into bed and her voice came drifting to me from the depths of her quilt. 'When is Daddy coming home?'

The memory of my lie about Jasper waiting for her in the morning struck me again and I'd had to bite back the word, *Soon*. I had already tried to break the news to her. To explain how things would be. And yet in that moment it seemed so entirely possible that he would come walking towards us from over the moor, his skin turned golden by the pool.

In the end, I didn't answer. I kissed her forehead, relieved that she was already half asleep, and whispered, 'Good night, love.' The words were inadequate for everything I wanted to say, but in that moment, they were all I could give.

I left her to her dreams and went downstairs, sitting for a long time in the darkened lounge. Zack was in his room, saying his own goodbyes perhaps, and I was surrounded by stacks of packed boxes. It could almost be that first day again, when the four of us had moved in. A new start, rather than an ending.

The curtains were open. A silvery gleam fell through them, oddly bright. I went to the window. The grass in the field rippled and shifted, restless as a wind-stirred sea.

And I saw I wasn't alone. The hare was sitting in our garden, amid the grass. It was crouched with its head cocked, as if listening for something, looking back at me. Only a wild creature, I told myself; only a hare. It must simply be the moonlight that made its eyes appear such a clear, perfect, holiday-sky blue.

Further down the beach, Zack is surfing. He's out there where his heart is, in the waves. He's with his girlfriend, Megan, who's just moved here with her parents, along with her dog, Dex, who runs back and forth at the edge of the waves, never taking his eyes from her. Zack too. Dex seems to have adopted him, and Zack doesn't object. Dogs always recognise the people who love them.

Scurrying after Dex, content with the chase as always, is Jasper.

He recovered from his ordeal. After what happened to Andrew Gregory, Ethan had refused to tell Zack anything about the dog other than he was all right and being looked after. Zack had hated that, thinking Jasper was with Sienna – but could do nothing, and anyway he'd had other worries, other fears to occupy him. But Ethan hadn't left our dog with Sienna. Anxious to distance the dog that clawed Andrew Gregory's face from us all, Ethan had taken Jasper, driven him twenty miles away and dumped him in kennels. He'd paid cash, didn't even give them our real name: no team Kell-a-way for Jasper, not any longer. Little wonder he was so late home that day, nor that our dog had seemed to vanish so completely. Only when the cash ran out and the kennel couldn't reach Ethan, did they take him to a vet and check his microchip.

Now Jasper is ours again. Cared for. Comforting Zack. I shield my eyes and scan the sea for my son. Zack is out in front of all the other surfers, his arms outspread as he rides a wave towards the shore. I recognise the flash of gold at his wrist.

For the years to come. All my love, Ellie.

I'd given those words to Ethan once, but I had taken them back. Before I walked away from Blake Mere Pool for the last time, I had swum down again into its depths and taken the watch from Sienna. It was never hers. The other thing she held, or rather that was wrapped around her wrist, I left with her: a little plaited friendship bracelet. I knew that must have been given to her by my daughter. And it must have been one of Libby's favourites; surely it was only a coincidence that it appeared to be an exact match for the one she had offered up to the spirit of Doxey Pool.

I gave Zack his father's watch after we'd driven back from the funeral. I found him that evening sitting on his bed. For once, he didn't listen to music, tap on his phone, play computer games, watch TV. He was just sitting, staring into space. I sat down next to him and held out the box.

'This is for you,' I said. 'Your dad was always proud of you. He would have wanted you to have it.'

Zack carefully turned the gift in his hands, as if at any moment it might bite him. He plucked Ethan's watch from the box, allowing it to dangle from his outstretched fingers. For a moment I saw her again: her golden skin gleaming like fish scales, her hair floating like seaweed. Then she was gone.

When I left her, Sienna was no longer alone with only my daughter's friendship for company. Her wish had been granted, for Ethan was with her; suspended in the water, his arms outstretched, as if reaching for her. They were together at last, a mermaid and her prince.

I silently thanked her, as I swam back towards the air and the light and my children and my life. If nothing else, she had showed me the truth.

It was a truth that must stay submerged.

Why hadn't I reported him missing? That's the first question the police had asked me. It was a strange detail in a death that took place under odd circumstances, so naturally, they very much wanted to speak to Ethan's widow. I sat there as they stared at me, their expressions never betraying a hint of sympathy. After all, what kind of a wife doesn't try to get her husband back?

It wasn't difficult to appear numb and blank. I was numb by then, numb from answering the kids' questions about where their dad was, from the effort of maintaining my own opaque surface. I was exhausted by the dreams, by drowning in the dark of an empty bedroom, by the images that came. I avoided looking out of the window at night. My rational mind told me I'd never see her again – and yet, what if she was out there, staring back at me?

I dreamed of Ethan too; the blade going into him as he drowned. But he was already drowning, wasn't he? Drowning in a marriage that wasn't enough, a career that had failed before it began. Drowning in the collapse of his perfect family, his perfect life. In an existence that was never as glossy and bright as he needed it to be: as bright as a postcard.

I explained to the police, in a hoarse whisper, that we'd had a row. I looked down at my hands as if it was all too terrible to speak of. Perhaps it was.

'What about?' they asked, not permitting my silence. Their voices pulled at me like dangerous waters.

'Another woman,' I said.

They sat up straighter and exchanged glances. Of course they knew who I meant. It hadn't taken long, once Ethan's body was discovered, to find Sienna too, though they hadn't mentioned her to me. By then, I supposed the police in Sandsend had checked Sienna's phone records. I was glad to be the one to mention the link first.

I told them about their brief affair, something I'd imagined was long over, I said, something that need never have troubled me again. We'd left it a hundred and forty miles and an ocean behind us, but it wasn't far enough. I told them I suspected Sienna of following us, desperate to resume things with Ethan. Of stalking him, as if she'd lost her mind. As if she'd been driven to despair.

Another exchanged glance told me they'd taken note, so I continued. I told them about our row.

That Ethan had admitted he still had feelings for her. That he'd tried to leave her behind, he really had, because I was his wife, and we had our children to think of. But he resented the way I'd forced him to leave everything he loved behind. Her.

I said he'd told me he'd made a mistake. A terrible, stupid mistake, in coming here with me. In choosing me.

'He said all he wanted was to see her again,' I recounted. 'That she was the only woman he could love. But she'd vanished.'

I was crying by then. Salt tears; it wasn't hard to summon them. One ran down my cheek to my lip and I remembered, with absolute clarity, the taste of brine on my husband's skin after he'd been swimming in the sea. The glow of him.

'I think he would have done anything to find her,' I went on. 'He said he had to tell her how he felt. That the worst part of it was that she didn't know.'

One of them nodded, almost imperceptibly. I knew he believed my version of events. He thought Ethan had been obsessed with Sienna and only her. Why not? She was the youngest, the most beautiful of them all.

My eyes lost focus as I pretended to reach for a memory. 'He said something about her being reported missing. I wasn't sure. I hadn't really been keeping up with the news. But I could tell he was worried.' I let a note of bitterness colour my voice.

'I think he was afraid of what she might have done to herself. So he left. He walked out. He was going to try and find her. When he didn't come back, I assumed he had. I thought he was staying with her, trying to decide what to do. Whether to get a divorce, I suppose. I thought that was why he hadn't contacted me, because – well, he couldn't face telling me. Not yet. I couldn't face it either. I didn't want to know. I didn't want to chase after him, only to hear that he was done with me.'

I answered more of their questions – quietly, but with assurance, without hesitation. And as I did, a great calm came over me. They had pieced together the story I wanted to tell, or enough of it, anyway.

Still, I cried. I cried as I spoke of Ethan, as I convinced them he'd been in love with someone else. I sobbed like an abandoned wife. A discarded woman. And I saw the epic romance weaving itself together in their minds: Sienna and Ethan, just like Romeo and Juliet. Sienna, despairing over the loss of him, had drowned herself in the pool. And Ethan had dived in after her, desperate to find her, only to be impaled on the sharp metal that broke away like a dagger in his chest.

I rather think they'll decide he impaled himself on purpose. That the lovers each took their own life for the sake of the other. Who wouldn't want to believe in a story like that?

By then, they'd found other evidence of Ethan and Sienna's trysts. Records of calls. Texts. Her tent, left on a moorland hillside, not that far from our home after all. Her car, abandoned behind the Mermaid Inn, until concerned guests began asking who it belonged to when no one claimed it.

The only thing left to explain was how Ethan had found her.

'He loved that pool,' I said. 'It seemed to call to him, right from the start. I think it reminded him of her, even then. They first met in the water, you see. I suspect he was seeing her there after we moved here. It's what they did together. They both loved wild swimming.'

Three deaths at one pool. And that pool, renowned for strange deaths ... It was as outlandish as all the old tales of mermaids. *Too* outlandish. Yet there was nothing to connect the three bodies found there. Nothing, unless it was me.

But I was no one of importance. Just an unwanted wife, abandoned – even by a story. When it came to Ethan and Sienna, they must have thought I had the motive but not the means, and there were heavy doubts about the opportunity. And I'd never had any reason to harm Andrew Gregory, who was a stranger to me.

No: two lovers, united in death – that story was the more compelling. Gregory didn't fit into it. He was reduced to a passing sentence in the newspapers when they covered these latest events. And so was I. Who was Ethan's wife in this story, after all? It was the mermaid who deserved the prince. The mermaid people obsessed over. I was mentioned, but only for a line, and never by my name.

When it was over, I had Ethan interred here by the coast, in the same graveyard as Sienna. I suspect he'd have preferred cremation. But in the version of events people believed, he would have chosen to be near her. So I gave him that.

Of course, I feel guilty that her true story will never be known. But Sienna had wanted his love – and now she has it forever, if only in death.

Saint Oswald's church isn't far from here. Just a short drive along the coast road. It nestles amid rolling fields, but the view is of the sea; the whole vast expanse of it, reduced to a perfect line of blue.

I run into the waves with Libby, who squeals as we splash the water around us. Then we're in, gasping with cold, paddling harder, laughing at the sting. Libby's giggles rise like bubbles of joy into the sky. I glance into the clean blue: seagulls wheeling above us, shrieking. Today, the sea is the colour of holidays – though I still feel the power in it, restless in its ceaseless motion.

We turn onto our backs and float side by side, grinning like sharks. Then we begin to swim: *Just like a fish*. The old strength in my arms returns as I remember the strokes, cutting through the waves. I trust them. They pull me into the next moment, and the next. There is nothing else: only now, only this. Just me and the elements, and my daughter.

After all, I've made my deal with the sea witch. I paid her price. I took up the blade she gave me. *He's yours now. He always was.* I offered her my prince, and in return, I was allowed to return to the sea.

Libby ducks beneath the water and emerges with a cry of joy. She's unafraid. Sometimes I think she's the bravest of us all: happy to demand what she wants, never reluctant to jump in, or indeed to use her voice.

Lippy. Flibbertygibbet. Those names are no longer insults. They're blessings.

Down the shoreline, Zack hops neatly from his new surfboard to the shore. He checks his father's watch. It hasn't been easy – learning about Ethan's affair, his death, his abandonment. At times, the grief was a tide so strong I worried it would engulf him. But nothing stays the same and I know that Zack will heal. He still has things to cling to: memories all around him, held in the sea, the shore, the cliffs. He can cherish the ones he has, and imagine the ones he never got to make. He'll never know his father planned Sienna's death. Or that he tried to kill me too.

In a sense, Ethan turned out to embody his words: *Ordinary people can do extraordinary things*. Extraordinary, perhaps, but not always *good*. Not always *right*.

I have told Zack what happened when I was fourteen. How I watched Ben drown. I didn't want my son to feel alone. I wanted him to know I understood, that he could move past it, like I had.

He'd tilted his head and said, *But you didn't know what would happen. You didn't mean for him to die—*

I had waited. Allowed his own words to sink in.

I know he'll be all right. I'm certain because of the things I sensed when he cried over Andrew Gregory as I pulled him into my arms. The pain and guilt I'd intuited in him. He'll be all right because he *felt*.

It had been so different, placing my hand in Ethan's for the last time. That emptiness inside him. The absence where his emotions should have been. All I saw was grey, like a barren seabed stretching on forever. Nothing growing there. No life of its own. Only grasping polyps reaching for the life they sensed in others. A witch's garden, with only a bad deal at its heart. I suppose I must always have sensed it, that *nothing*. But I'd tried so hard to deny what my grandmother taught me – whether it was something uncanny or simply my own intuition – that I blinded myself to it. I mistook it for simplicity. For straightforwardness.

For home.

It has been easier with Libby than with Zack. I can always tell what she's thinking. And I've managed to keep much from her. I told her that her dad had an accident trying to help a lady stuck in the water, and she swallowed it whole. As far as she's concerned, her dad's a hero. He's a prince, and always will be.

So I have been silent about the true story. I gave up my voice, as the little mermaid did, and I would do it again. My silence lets my children move on. It allows Zack to believe his role in a man's death was never intentional, not some dark inheritance in his blood. It enables Libby to smile. To believe her dad was the very best. And it allows Ethan to be what he'd always desired to be: perfect. He is that now – in memory, in death. A beautiful fairy tale I can tell my daughter. He would have liked that.

I returned to Sandsend not as I had left it – half of a lovely, enviable couple – but as a cliché. A tragic wife, abandoned for a younger model. Someone who hadn't even lost her husband when he died, but long before. What kind of woman does that make me? Not the heroine of any story, that's for certain. Many would say it makes me no one at all – but I don't care. Not for a second.

At least Sally has stopped bringing round shepherd's pie with pity in her eyes. Now she shows up with a bottle of plonk and a mischievous grin. Sometimes we meet Kath, who still lives in our old house, or other mums, and we laugh and talk about things I can't even remember afterwards. And we know that we are not alone.

Next week, I will have other visitors. We've been to see Mum and Dad a few times lately. I've laid flowers on Gran's grave: red and white roses, one each for Lancashire and Yorkshire. I like to think she would have enjoyed the joke. My parents have loved spending time with the kids, and Mum and I have begun building bridges. Now they're coming to stay. It seems she's ready. Ready to be by the sea again with her daughter.

I am focused on raising my children. They are all the magic I need. And I know what matters most is the lessons I will teach them. I don't need Zack and Libby to be extraordinary. I don't want them to chase anyone's approval or provoke their envy. I won't teach them that they need to have the best or strive for perfection. I will simply teach them to live … live … *live*.

Libby spins, kicking her legs and splashing salt water. I blink it from my eyes and laugh. If the sea pulls her away, I'll take her hand. I will grasp it in mine and pull her close to ensure she's safe. I am her mother. I will always be enough.

I let her swim ahead and feel my burdens dissolve. The sun warms my forehead and eyelids. I taste brine on my tongue. The water rises and surges, revealing and hiding my daughter by turns. I don't panic when she vanishes. I know I will see her again in a heartbeat, and I do. There is her head, bobbing on the waves.

And someone else is swimming beside her.

His hair is paler, shorter, curling over his forehead, bleached by the sun. A young boy, with his gaze fixed upon me. His lips hover just above the surface. No fear in his eyes, no panic. He isn't drowning anymore. He is only there. Watching.

And someone else floats nearby. They have darker hair and features I know better than my own. I should; I have held that face in my hands. Traced its contours in the night. Kissed those lips.

Plunged a dagger into that heart.

I try to inhale, but salt water rushes in. A wave strikes, and I am under. I hear his voice, muffled by the pounding waves. Not a promise, as I once thought, but a premonition.

I'd do anything – go anywhere – as long as it means my family is together.

The water might be endless. It might be anywhere. A pool on a moorland hillside, quiet and glimmering, keeping its secrets. I might be lost in it, sinking deeper, uncertain whether I will ever feel earth beneath my feet again. Maybe it's bottomless. Or perhaps I will find a hidden tunnel that leads all the way to the sea. Maybe someone else found it too; not a spirit of the water, but a drowned prince.

I surface, shaking droplets from my hair. I search for him again – for both of them. But they're gone.

Ava Morwood

Nothing remains but foam on the ocean.
And there, cresting a wave without a trace of fear, is
Libby, my water-baby, swimming back to me.

Acknowledgements

There is a book in my possession. It is rather old and worn, but still beautiful for all that. It is a copy of Hans Christian Andersen's fairy tales, given to me for Christmas when I was five. My favourite story was 'The Little Mermaid', for all the same reasons as Ellie – so thank you to Andersen, but also to my mother, Ann, for giving it to me, and showing me the power that words can possess.

Skipping forward, I am hugely grateful to my agent, Oli Munson of A.M. Heath, not only for the approach to HarperNorth but for invaluable advice and support during the process of bringing *Until We Drown* to the bookshelf. Thank you, Oli!

A big 'Yay, team!' to the wonderful people at HarperNorth. Special thanks to my fabulous editor, Megan Jones; and to Genevieve Pegg, Alice Murphy-Pyle, Jess Haycox and Taslima Khatun. Also to cover artist, Claire Ward. You are all amazing, and I'm lucky to be working with you. Thanks too to Daisy Watt and copy editor, Morgan Dun-Campbell.

I am grateful to the people of the Peak District. This story was shaped by my experiences exploring its locations, as well as by written folklore. As in the book, it seemed that everyone I met begun recounting a mermaid tale, without my needing to ask; those encounters found their way into these pages in the form of fictionalised conversations and characters.

Blake Mere still glimmers in its shelf on the hillside, though I have taken some small poetic licence with the setting, adding a path to Ellie's home along with a steep drop and some well-placed rocks. The Quiet Woman was closed when I visited, so is in part fictionalised, as is the Reform Inn, which as far as I know doesn't have a lost corner of mysterious photographs – but it does have a rather lovely lion. The Buxton Museum and Art Gallery is similarly closed and now in search of a new home, though I caught up with the Buxton mermaid in a special exhibition in London. She's well worth seeing if you can: just don't make her any rash promises.

I have spent many happy times in Sandsend having a coffee at Tides Café or walking along the beach, though sadly, the little store closed its doors during the production of this novel. Hunting for hag stones is often rewarding; there is one in front of me now as I write.

I have read numerous books on folklore over the years and am grateful for these particularly useful sources of information about locations, lore and indeed wild swimming:

The Penguin Book of Mermaids, edited by Cristina Bacchilega and Marie Alohalani Brown, Penguin Publishing Group, 2019.

Folklore, Myths and Legends of Britain, Russell Ash, Reader's Digest, 1973.

Folk Tales of the Peak District, Mark P. Henderson. Amberley Publishing, 2011.

Leap In: A Woman, Some Waves, and the Will to Swim by Alexandra Heminsley, Cornerstone Digital, 2017.

Waterlog by Roger Deakin, Vintage Digital, 2011.

https://folklorethursday.com, www.icysedgwick.com, https://folkrealmstudies.weebly.com, Wikipedia.com, https://peakdistrictwalks.net, https://roaches.org.uk, https://www.mysteriesofmercia.com, https://outdoorswimmingsociety.com, https://www.wildswimming.co.uk, https://mariovittone.com.

Lectures by The Last Tuesday Society were also of interest, particularly those by mermaid expert, Professor Sarah Peverley.

Thank you to Gary B. Foley, MBA, MRCPod, DPodM, for information on plantar fasciitis.

Thanks too to Tim Lebbon, author of many fine works of dark fiction as well as the addictive memoir, *Run Walk Crawl: Getting Fit In My Forties*, for invaluable advice on triathlons and the evocative term, 'washing machine start'.

Huge appreciation goes to Steve Shaw of indie publisher Black Shuck Books, for lending his expertise in creating a lovely sparkly new website, www.avamorwood.com.

There are many in the writing community who have been generous in offering help, support and friendship over the years. I love you guys: you know who you are. Two of them, Cate Bestwick and Priya Sharma, make a little cameo appearance in this novel.

And of course thank you to my partner, Fergus, for sharing the journey, both literal and metaphorical; also to my dad Trevor and brother Ian. You are the best. Dare I also mention my dogs, Dex and Vesper? I probably should, or I'll never hear the end of it.

Lastly, I would add that the process of producing this novel was a very human endeavour. I visited its locations, talked to people, hiked, went swimming in cold waters, dreamed, wrote, drafted and redrafted and in short, worked very hard over a timescale of years to bring you the best book I possibly could. It was a labour of love, not of machine. I did not use AI in its production and have no plans to use it in the future. Books are a vital part of any society's soul; so thank you to everyone who helps keep them living and breathing, including librarians, teachers, spreaders-of-the-word, reviewers, booksellers, and of course you, most important of all: the Reader.

Harper North

Book Credits

HarperNorth would like to thank the following staff and contributors for their involvement in making this book a reality:

Fionnuala Barrett
Peter Borcsok
Laura Braggs
Sarah Burke
Alan Cracknell
Jonathan de Peyer
Anna Derkacz
Morgan Dun-Campbell
Tom Dunstan
Kate Elton
Sarah Emsley
Simon Gerratt
Imogen Gordon Clark
Lydia Grainge
Monica Green
Natassa Hadjinicolaou
Emma Hatlen
Jess Haycox
Megan Jones

Jean-Marie Kelly
Taslima Khatun
Holly Kyte
Rachel McCarron
Millie Morton
Alice Murphy-Pyle
Adam Murray
Genevieve Pegg
Amanda Percival
Dean Russell
Florence Shepherd
Colleen Simpson
Eleanor Slater
Hilary Stein
Emma Sullivan
Katrina Troy
Claire Ward
Ben Wright

For more unmissable reads,
sign up to the HarperNorth newsletter at
www.harpernorth.co.uk

or find us on socials at
@HarperNorthUK